The Lethal Linguist

the spy who killed with a whisper

Joseph Warner

Cacophony Press

Copyright © 2024 Joseph Warner

All rights reserved

ISBN: 978 1 3999 8820 9

Cover design based on an original painting by Gemma Warner.

The characters and events portrayed in this book are fictitious. Any similarity to real persons, living or dead, is coincidental and not intended by the author.

No part of this book may be reproduced, or stored in a retrieval system, or transmitted in any form or by any means, electronic, mechanical, photocopying, recording, or otherwise, without express written permission of the publisher.

Cacophony Press

For Jan and our family.

Your love and support keep me safe and sane.

"It's quite an undertaking to start loving somebody.
You have to have energy, generosity, blindness.
There is even a moment right at the start where
you have to jump across an abyss: if you think
about it you don't do it."

Jean-Paul Sartre

PRESENT

I'm not quite sure how I got here, wherever here is. This prison, just a concrete box really. I have no idea if there is anyone else, other captives, or even if there are any more cells. Is it just me and my keepers? I don't know what I am supposed to have done or not done and now I'm starting to sound like a petulant teenager.

I remember a man, tall and broad, I had never seen him before, but his scale and shape were familiar to me. It was late, I shouldn't have been in that part of town at night. I'd got too blasé about my ability to talk my way out of danger or better still, fight my way out. The man was wearing large expensive headphones, I knew then that I was in trouble. Suddenly, from behind, close to my ear a breeze lifted the wispy hair on my neck, no not the wind, it was a breath. There were two of them, both with high-tech ear protection, this was well planned. Definitely not the gouttière habituelle that I had been exorcising my demons on lately. Then, rough cloth on my pampered skin, a hood over my head, the sour smell of some narcotic, I could almost taste it. The prick of a needle and the thick liquid warmth turning cold, quicksilver spreading through the corded muscle tissue in my neck.

Then I woke up here, a bare stone-walled room, eight strides by eight, a thick metal door with a wide letterbox shaped opening at the bottom, where they slide food and a carton of juice through twice a day. There is a peephole at head height, which goes dark for a couple of seconds as they check on me before they push the tray through. Large hands with dark wiry hair on the backs, definitely male, no rings or tattoos though. Nails clipped short, not bitten, he looks after his hands and that should scare me. I wonder if it was those fingers that pushed the needle into my neck or the ones that held me still, unflustered by my unvoiced shouts for help, knowing that in that place of thieves and rapists no one would come.

I have always observed things in great detail, actions slowly unfolding, I wondered how they had got behind me. I never noticed until that slight sound, that warm breath, it could have been a whisper, "your dead", or even a kiss. I would not like to kiss a hairy man. No talking my way out this time, not that it mattered. I'd got careless, my anger and grief had made me sloppy, it was as if I was daring someone to harm me, to kill me, whilst all the time pretending to myself that I was the one in control. Suddenly I think of a handsome olive-skinned man and smile, he could have been a friend in different circumstances. He and his family are safe now. I remember him telling me about a Syrian painter, Marwan Kassab-Bachi, it wasn't about his paintings but something he said - "I think utterly existentially… a painting is like a wound." The images I have painted in blood, without the need of weapons, hang forever in my private gallery.

They took my phone and the blade from the inside of my boot but left me with my watch, a gold Rolex, unfortunately not thieves or kidnappers then, at least I knew I had been here for three days and so far, no one had come to see me or even spoken a word. On the bright side, no one had come to kill me either, but perhaps that was the biggest puzzle of all.

In the widest sense I do know how I ended up here if not the specific offence, there are plenty to be taken into consideration after all, or even the particular corpse. It's a history I wouldn't normally linger on, but it doesn't look like I am going anywhere soon. I am sure I could get out if I really wanted to, but for now I'll bide my time and wait for the tell-tale steps on the silken thread of my web.

PAST

My name is Joshua Renoir, I am 24 years old. My maternal grandfather was born in Egypt and speaks Arabic, French, Farsi and English. He met my nanna in Paris, she is fluent in French, English, Greek and Turkish. My paternal grandparents are equally gifted and diverse when it comes to linguistic ability and nationality. My parents met in England, inevitably they were both studying modern languages. As a child I remember we had many extended family gatherings, celebrations and holidays. At these parties it seemed everyone played a game with no real rules, winners or losers, they spoke in different languages, switching frequently from one to another, sometimes in the same sentence and everyone tried to keep up with the conversation. English and French were frowned upon unless you were under sixteen years old, for the adults both languages were used like oil or buffers to get you through sticky patches but would earn you boos and whistles for your lapse. Children were only ever praised in our family, my sister and I could do no wrong, at least not as children. When we were very young we moved around quite regularly, thanks to my father's work as a diplomat, and I grew up without a mother-tongue as such. But from about the age of four I was somehow able to pick up on the sound and meaning of words, then soon after start to form sentences in the many languages that filtered across the dinner table.

My first coherent memories of growing up start around my third birthday, before then there are jigsaw pieces, fragments but no big picture and plenty of blank spaces. My parents liked to fill in the gaps when I would bring up an image or partial event from back then, especially when I was in my early teens, and particularly if it was embarrassing. I was never sure how good their recollections were, but it was clear that they thought I was some sort of child prodigy even then, and it turns out they were right. They still love me, but I'm not so sure they would be quite so proud of what I've become, though I think they would understand what has driven me to this meaningless place deep inside myself.

In the darkness I feel a tear slip down my cheek, I am sorry I'm not the person they nurtured so well and still love so much.

By six I was fluent in French and English, greatly aided by my father's posting to the French Embassy in London a year earlier, and I could count to 100 in half-a-dozen other languages. Both sets of grandparents along with uncles, aunties and cousins had settled in and around London before Charlotte and I were born. We all gathered together at least one weekend every month at our *residence* or at my grandparents' homes, the four of them had somehow managed to buy a pair of derelict semi-detached houses together just outside of west London. The houses were hidden from the main road and well away from all the other properties in the village, down a single track, tree-lined lane. At the rear there was a large garden backing on to a small copse of Birch and Alder trees, with a pond or mud hole as my father called it. They renovated the original houses, keeping them separate but then added a huge extension across the rear of both properties, creating one super-sized kitchen-diner and family space linking both houses together. Outside they built a large pavilion, which acted as office, summerhouse and bunkroom for all the cousins at our weekend gatherings.

In the city we lived in a very large, four-storey Georgian terraced house near Lancaster Gate tube station, an easy walk to the French Embassy on Knightsbridge or through Hyde Park, to either the other Embassy at Kensington Palace Gardens or the French Consulate on the Cromwell Road. The first "incident", as father referred to it, took place in the August I turned nine, after that he began to take me to work with him about once a week. He viewed these little forays as part of my education, he said coming to work with him would open my mind to a bigger world. On the way he would speak to me in other languages, he would set me sums or ask me to name a plant in a different tongue. He liked to play with words and, much to my regret, even then, he had a thing for making puns. I'd heard Charlotte and my mother often groaning and telling him to stop when we were at home and he did try, but on our walks to the embassy it seemed like he was let off the leash and they would flow from him like some weird stream of consciousness.

I loved it when we walked through Hyde Park and across the Serpentine, but then he would sit me down on a sofa at one end of his office with some books and puzzles to keep me occupied, which worked for an hour or so before I became bored and restless. Luckily, my father often held meetings around the table at the other end of his office, which provided some small interest at least. With a large desk occupying the middle of the room and partially blocking me off no one took any notice of me, I think they forgot I was even there. They spoke in French, like my father they all had Parisian accents apart from one lady with a lilting voice who pronounced her words quite differently, she sounded like she was singing and it sent tingles up my back, around my ears and down my arms to the fingertips. Klarra was her name, she had been born in Guadeloupe in the French Antilles and lived there until she was 18 before moving to Paris to study at the Sorbonne. Klarra was tall and her skin was a rich chocolate colour, she was my first crush, even though I wasn't old enough to realise what a crush was.

Feet up on my comfy sofa, I held a pencil in my hand and rested the Sudoku book on my lap, just in case someone looked my way. I would lay there listening to their conversations, I understood the individual words but it was hard to follow what they were talking about. "Trade delegations", "satellite images", "currency rate changes", "cyber-attacks" and many other subjects were thrown into the mix. Sentences and whole topics seemed to be left hanging as they triggered switches to new subjects beyond my ability, at that point, to make the connections and understand the significance of what was being discussed. Despite my lack of understanding I loved to listen, I picked up new words and phrases and if asked, I could repeat most of the conversation word for word. After a while, I realised that this was always my father's intention, something that became very clear when after one particular session he asked me if I understood what the meeting was about. I relayed what I thought they were discussing, to which he said, 'very good Josh, you certainly got the gist of what was going on, can you repeat any of it?' I paused for a few seconds, took a deep breath then spoke clearly but quickly as though I needed to get it out of my head in one go, it was like when one of my tutors asked me to recite a poem from memory. When I had finished my father looked at me, he seemed a little worried, a bit like he had at the party the night the "incident" happened. Then he spoke slowly, I could tell he was choosing his words carefully, I think he was doing his best not to frighten me. I didn't really get scared, it was both a strength and a weakness, something I would only fully realise years later.

'Josh, this is another secret you must keep. Not what you heard, though it's best not to say anything about what you hear in this place or anywhere else when it has to do with my work. What I really want you to keep to yourself is your ability or should I say abilities, your memory and languages. Yes, our friends and the people I work with all know you are good at languages, like the rest of the family, but you are way ahead of where your mum and I, and even your grandparents where at your age. When you combine that knowledge, those skills, with your photographic memory it's a powerful mixture and others will want to make use of it and will not hesitate to do you harm or make you promises to get what they want from you. Do you understand?'

'Yes, it's like Kurt, isn't it?'

'Very similar.'

'What about the ambassador, he was there he knows?'

'The ambassador is a good man, I wouldn't have taken you to him that evening if I'd not been sure of his loyalty, but he's not family and even good people can turn bad, especially in the work I do. Now he owes you a favour and a big one at that, but you can be sure that he always pays his debts, especially a debt of honour.'

'Are you a spy, dad?'

'Well, I'm not James Bond but I do keep secrets and sometimes I discover other people's weaknesses, but I use my brains not my muscles and I don't have a gun.'

Part of my father's work involved hosting parties for important people that the French Government wished to do business with, as well as diplomats from other countries. The receptions, as they were called, were largely the justification for us living in such a grand house. Charlotte and I were encouraged to be present for the first hour of these soirees, when people milled around drinking champagne and eating canapés. My father liked to show us off, I realised years later that he also did it because it relaxed the guests and made them less guarded in what they said and who they mingled with. We were tasked with providing the pre-dinner entertainment, Charlotte would play her violin and then the guests would be persuaded by my father to ask me a question in their native language. Father was careful to pick guests of a kindly disposition and who spoke a language that I had some understanding of and they invariably asked me something simple, like what was my name and how old was I, or the day of the week and the date. To begin with I memorised the questions and answers in a number of different languages, then one Tuesday before the next

Saturday party I noticed my mother going over the list of people invited and realised that it not only had their names, but their nationality listed as well. When she had finished with the list, she left it on the table and I studied it for a few minutes committing the names and countries to memory. I spent the next three days learning the answers to the usual questions in six new languages and then on the Saturday morning I told my father what I had done and asked him if he would pick people I had chosen from the list. It was just a party trick but I repeated it again at the next reception and the reaction was distinctly greater the second time, as people tried to add up the number of languages I'd spoken over the last three parties.

Charlotte and I would finish our little performances after about twenty minutes and were then left to wander around the room until people went into the dining room at eight to eat. Charlotte usually dashed off in search of her favourite cake but I liked to walk about listening in on all the side conversations, it was my favourite part of the evening. People stood in pairs or small groups of three or four, some talked loudly with great animation, arms and hands gesturing wildly. Others spoke quietly and some seemed quite nervous, looking around quickly, scanning the room before speaking. If they noticed me nearby, though often they didn't as I was below their eye line, they would force a smile and then look away dismissively. They did not see a cute little blonde boy as a risk to their secrets and indiscretions. They dismissed the party trick for what it largely was, a child memorising answers to simple questions, they took no account that such a feat should not have been possible for a nine-year old. Most were careerists and were largely childless, with no interest in or any idea about normal child development.

I had started to notice my ability to understand other languages without really trying to learn them a few months after my seventh birthday. If I listened to another language for long enough, regardless of its origins, I somehow started to recognise patterns, repetitions, intonations and then words. By the time I was eight I was getting some idea of the sentences being uttered; I still did not understand them though, not the subject matter or meaning, it was all too old for me. But I loved the sound of the words and the way they seemed to link together or sidle up furtively next to each other in some breathy caress that meant something I could almost grasp but not quite. A year further on and I was really beginning to understand the average conversation though.

When it was time for the guests to go into dinner, Nicola our au pair would magically appear to get us ready for bed. In between the main and dessert course my father would come to kiss us on the cheek and say goodnight and my mother would appear after dessert to read us a story. Charlotte, who was three years older would stay with me until I went off to sleep, then make her way back to her own bed through our shared bathroom.

***

It seemed my cleverness was a bit of a Marmite talent, dividing even some of the guests at my father's soirees. At one party my father decided to indulge in our mutual appreciation of history for a change and at his prompting, I reeled off a string of dates, battles and other historical facts for his guests, resulting in a loud round of applause. Having *earned my supper,* I meandered around the room listening in on the various conversations, just before the au pair came to collect me, I heard one lady say to a tall thin man beside her. 'Oh, don't you think young Joshua is a genius?' The man replied, 'More like a precocious little brat that will burn out by the time he's twelve.'

I had to look precocious up, I already knew what a "brat" was, I had been called that and more a few times at school. Still, it didn't take me long to get my revenge, not that I thought about it in that way back then. It was about six months later at another of father's dinner parties, though this one seemed to have everyone in a tizzy. I overheard my father tell mum in the morning that the ambassador had confirmed he would be attending. By the afternoon the house was in a frenzy and my mother was running between the kitchen and the dining room, checking on the chef and the team of people setting out the tables and decorating the room. Charlotte and I were getting quite giddy with it all, before father spoilt the mood. He came to tell us that we would not be performing that evening to ensure the ambassador had enough time to talk with all the guests before dinner. Then he looked at our faces and saw our smile had gone. 'Don't be so gloomy' he said, 'the ambassador loves children, and he is looking forward to meeting you both.' When our expressions remained downcast, he added, 'I am sure he will bring the two of you a present each.' That did the trick, and we suddenly rediscovered our smiles, unfortunately the joy would be short-lived as this was to be the night of the incident.

So that evening we met the ambassador, he was maybe a little older than our father but seemed very energetic as he jumped from one group of people to another, a few words and some cheek kissing, and he was on the move again. But he did slow-up a bit when he spoke to us, he squatted down to our height and looked us in the eyes as he spoke. Back then I thought he had a kind face, but that might just have been because he did bring us presents, a toy gun for me and a silver wrist bangle for Charlotte. We were usually given *educational* toys by our parents, and we were both pleased to get something different, we both agreed that we liked the ambassador, the two of us were easily bought back then. The ambassador was soon on the move again, going from one little group to another, he never stayed very long with any particular set, though he lingered a bit if the gathering was large.

While I wandered around waiting for Nicola to appear and collect us, I found myself looking at the man who had called me a precocious brat at the last party. I'd discovered that his name was Kurt Stein and he worked in the German embassy in Belgrave Square, he was talking to another man that I didn't recall seeing before. Kurt was tall but thin, he had a little goatee beard and black, slightly oily, shoulder length hair that he combed back from his forehead. Strange, I took all this in while I watched him talking to the other person, who was shorter and had to tilt his bald head up to keep eye contact with Kurt who seemed to enjoy his advantage. They talked quietly, almost whispering, but somehow even with the hubbub in the room I could hear them clearly. They were speaking in German, and I watched as Kurt looked around checking out the other people in the room but he didn't see me, I was too short and well below his sight line. Kurt took the other man's shoulder and moved them both toward the windows and a little further away from the other guests who hovered in the centre of the room, as close to the ambassador as possible and where the waiters circulated with trays of canapés and champagne. Almost without realising it I also took a few steps toward the windows and closer to the two of them. Kurt lowered his voice even further, he was whispering now, but somehow I could still hear them. The short one said almost nothing, his back to the window he raised himself on his toes to peek over Kurt's shoulder, surveying the room, but I remained well below the horizon.

Kurt was still speaking in German, I was sure of this when he said the number 27, siebenundzwanzig, and then having seized on that, I realised I could understand every word he said. After a minute or so I began to feel a little uneasy at my eavesdropping, I did not want to get caught and embarrass my parents. I thought about moving away, finding my sister and saving the au pair the job of rounding us up for bed. But then I heard Kurt say 'Ambassador Dubois', I froze, not sure why but definitely not liking Kurt speaking about my father's boss for some reason, the nice man that had given me a gun. I listened more carefully, it was like Kurt was whispering in my ear as he spoke to the other man.

'Dietrich it's set, siebenundzwanzig Gore Street at nine o'clock tomorrow, the ambassador will be with Julia. You have the bomb?'

'Yes, but what about Julia?'

'She thinks it's a honey trap to blackmail him, but it's too late for that, Dubois is on to us. Don't let the glad-handing and smiles fool you, he has us clearly in his sights, in two or three days he'll have us all. Julia needs to die with him, she thinks she has been playing him, *his beautiful young mistress*, but he's been leading her on. I have watched them the last three nights, when she leaves their little love nest Dubois' bodyguard follows her, he tracked her back to the embassy and last night back to your flat. If she goes up with him it will throw them off the scent long enough for us to finish what we started and get out of here.'

'What about the bodyguard?'

'Pierre sits downstairs until she goes, so we get him as well, no loose ends.'

Minutes later I was surprisingly calm when I edged alongside my father, he was speaking to the ambassador's wife when I tugged on his sleeve. He looked down, I thought he might be annoyed that I had interrupted him, but he gave me a broad smile and introduced me to Madam Dubois who seemed delighted at my sudden appearance. I pulled on father's sleeve again and he got the message and squatted down next to me. I told him I needed to speak to him in private, that I was sorry, but it could not wait. I thought he would be angry or at least irritated, tell me I was tired and send me off to bed. Instead, he studied me for a few seconds then took hold of my hand, he excused himself to Madam

Dubois and gently lead me out the room and down the corridor to a small salon. He closed the door, picked me up and hugged me, it felt so reassuring, and I knew everything would be okay, then he sat me on table in the middle of the room and waited. After a few seconds I repeated carefully what I had heard Kurt and the other man say. My father asked me to describe the man whose name I didn't know and when I did, he just nodded his head and reached inside his jacket, taking out his phone he sent a very short text message. While we waited, he sat down and pulled me onto his knee before speaking.

'You are a very clever child and a most wonderful son, I am so proud of you. The ambassador will be joining us soon and you will need to tell him exactly what you told me. Is that okay?'

'Yes father. Will he be angry?

'Yes, but not with you and he will want to make sure you heard things right.'

A minute later the ambassador walked in with another man trailing a few steps behind him. I had seen this man earlier, always close to the ambassador, it was hard to miss him, he was taller than my father who I knew to be 1.86 metres, and as wide as the door across the shoulders. He wore a plain black suit and a white shirt with an open collar, in contrast to the DJs and bow ties that filled the reception room. My father, rather bravely I thought, put a hand on the man's shoulder and whispered something in his ear. The man looked a little surprised, he looked over at me, but said nothing, instead he patted his side just below his armpit and then put his finger to his ear and tapped it twice. When I looked at where he had touched I could see he had some sort of earpiece, it was flesh coloured and barely visible, he moved away from my father toward the door where he silently remained. All the while scanning the room, the window in particular he glared at as though it had personally offended him. I noticed he had unbuttoned his jacket and I could just see the butt of a gun poking out, I knew this one was real, unlike the plastic gift from the ambassador.

The ambassador looked around the room and then spoke to my father, 'Paul, what is this all about, why is Joshua here?'

At last, my father spoke. 'Please bear with me Philippe, you need to hear what Joshua has to say, he overheard a conversation between Kurt Stein and Dietrich Gutmann earlier. Joshua, please tell the ambassador exactly what you heard.'

I repeated, word for word, what I had told my father to the ambassador, who listened to me without interruption. When I'd finished the ambassador began to pace around the room, he seemed to be getting more agitated and the beast of a man at the door was flexing up and down on the balls of his feet waiting to spring into action. I could see the Ambassador was in turmoil, uncertain of how to deal with something so important with just the word of a young boy to rely on. I took a deep breath and stepped forward then spoke clearly and calmly, much to my own surprise. 'Sir…, ambassador. Grown-ups, some at least, don't seem to notice children especially when they have important things to talk about. Mr Stein and his friend were speaking very quietly, well away from everyone else and I was looking out the window, too short to catch their eye and too quiet to be noticed.'

'Josh, I know you are smart way beyond your years, but this is very serious, are you sure that's what they said? I didn't even know you spoke German.'

'It is a new language for me, but I am sure I understood them, do you speak German sir?'

'Fluently.'

'My father thinks I have a photographic memory, would it help if I repeated what I heard in German, ambassador?' The ambassador just nodded his head, and I reeled off exactly what I had heard, the whole conversation, word for word. The ambassador was looking at me, his face had gone a bit pink and he seemed nervous. 'Josh, can you keep a secret?'

'Seulement si mon père dit que ça va.' The Ambassador looked over to my father, who came over and squatted down at eye-level with me and put his hand gently on my shoulder, squeezing it lightly. He spoke in a whisper that somehow seemed loud and very clear inside my head. 'Josh, it is so important that you keep this secret. To keep yourself and our entire family safe you must never speak of it to anyone else, not even Charlotte or your mother. Can you do that Josh? I am sorry I have to ask you to do this, but can you keep this secret for the rest of your life?'

'Yes father.' I had no idea then how difficult that would be or the personal costs of all the secrets that would accumulate over the years.

'Good, very good Josh. If you need to talk about this again, at any time, just come and see me in my study. The ambassador will see that Kurt and his friend behave themselves, you won't be seeing them at the house again.'

***

After that day things quietened down, at least it did for Charlotte and I, my father thought it wise that we were released from our entertaining duties at his soirées. Mother did not question his decision, indeed she seemed pleased, and Charlotte was relieved as she was not keen on "performing" as she put it. I was a little disappointed being something of a show-off at heart but was also glad, given what had happened.

The second incident took place two years later, at the start of my first year at the International School. Students attended from many different countries including quite a number of children from the various diplomatic families based in London. I am sure Kurt would have called it the academy for spoilt brats and he would have had a point. It wasn't cheap to attend and most of the kids thought they were a cut above everyone who went to the state schools. Status was a big thing in the playground and the kids were quick to try and rank you according to what your parents did and how much money they had. I was not one of the popular kids, but no one ever tried to bully me, well not after the first week of term.

I had made it through to Friday without any problems and I was looking forward to the weekend, but at first break that was well and truly blown out the water.

Boris Wilson was fourteen, three years older and considerably bigger than me in any direction you cared to measure. Boris had only just started at the school though, his father was also a diplomat and they had been stationed overseas until recently. I was talking to another boy called Clive in the playground, he lived on the same road as us and though he was fourteen he was quite small for his age. I was already an inch or two taller than him. I noticed that Clive's face had started to turn red, and his hands were trembling, he was looking over my shoulder into the distance, so I turned to see what had caught his attention. Boris was striding toward us, glaring at Clive who was clearly terrified, as Boris closed in on us, he pointed his finger at Clive and called him a little shit. I could see that Boris had curled his other hand into a tight fist, it looked like he could hammer nails in with it. As Boris got within a few metres I stepped between him and Clive, and he slowed at my foolish and unexpected action. Without thinking, I stared him in the eyes as he came a stride closer. I said one word to him, 'STOP!' I didn't think I had shouted but it seemed everyone, from one end of the playground to the other, heard me and for a few seconds all movement and sound ceased. A rumour circulated later that even the birds in the nearby trees had stopped singing.

Having clearly got Boris' attention I quietly, but in a very low pitch that seemed quite different to my usual voice, told him he would leave Clive alone, now and in the future, that he would not bully anyone else and to turn around and go away. Boris tried to say something but then started to stutter badly before going silent and then, much to my surprise, he simply turned around and walked across the playground until he was out of sight somewhere on the other side of the gym. Boris didn't turn up for school on the Monday or the rest of the week. The following week a rumour started to go around that his father had sent him to a boarding school almost a hundred miles away.

Despite defending Clive, I seldom spoke to him after that day. I think he was a little embarrassed at being rescued by a first year and did his best to avoid me. Thankfully my father did not get to know about this incident, I did not want him to worry about me and Charlotte agreed that it was best to say nothing. The rumours about Boris died down after a month or two, though most of my fellow students still tended to keep a safe distance from me.

By the time I was nearing the end of my third year the year nines and tens still did their best to ignore me but some of the older kids said hello and sometimes chatted a bit. It was starting to bug me and so I decided to ask Charlotte, who always seemed to know all the school gossip, if she thought the other children at school were a bit odd? It was a good job our parents were out at the time, as my sister just started to laugh louder and louder until she was virtually howling, clutching her sides as she rolled around the bed, tears streaming down her cheeks. When she finally calmed down, she smiled at me and flung her arms around my shoulders crushing me to her chest and kissing the top of my head over and over again.

'Josh, I'm sorry, it's not them that's odd it's you. I mean you're amazing, super computer for a brain, handsome as fuck and all my friends fancy you, even the guys. But you're scary, in a good way, but still scary. You're only fourteen and just look at you, you're already six feet tall, you don't play in any of the school teams or work-out in the gym. The only exercise you do is a three K jog every morning, you don't even run fast enough to get out of breath or sweaty, but you have a six-pack and muscles rippling everywhere I look. You know my best friend, Tracey?'

'I've seen the two of you together, she is very pretty?'

'Oh my god, she would faint if she heard you say that. Apparently, you took your blazer off on the quad during break last week.'

'It was hot.'

'Well, you certainly got Tracey hot, she said you were sweating, and your shirt was clinging to you like a second skin and as you walked toward her she could see your chest muscles rippling and the outline of your pecs. Then as she watched you walk past her the muscles at the top of your shoulders and back were undulating under your white shirt.'

'Is that bad?'

'It's definitely bad but in a very good way. It's just that all the other boys in your class, and probably almost every other fourteen-year-old on the planet, are either short and fat or tall and skinny, not to mention full of spots. Oh, and there is the small matter of you not only standing up to Boris, who was three years older and four inches taller than you at the time, but effectively seeing him off the premises. You're not bad Josh, you're just too good to be real, and everyone your own age is either jealous or scared of you. Most of the year 12s and 13s are good with you though, they know me which helps, but they are just more confident and comfortable in their own skins and don't see you as some kind of weird super-hero. It helps that you have such an awesome sister.'

'You are awesome sis and thanks, I was beginning to doubt my own sanity. By the way, I run 5K every morning and workout at the outdoor gym at Holland Park or go for a swim in the Serpentine, they think I'm 18.'

'Well, when you are 18 or at least 17, if you want Tracey or any of my other friends to take your virginity just ask.'

I don't think I had ever gone so red before or since then, and I had never been stunned into silence before, never.

***

As it turned out I accepted a better offer. After finishing school my parents organised a party for my eighteenth birthday a couple of weeks before I was due to set out on my year of "travel and adventure" as my mother described it. Apart from family about half a dozen of Charlotte's friends, all back from university, turned up for the free booze. They included Tracey, who made sure she kissed me full on the lips and pinched my butt as soon as she walked in the room. I guess the offer was still on the table and I am sure I would have taken her up on it but for some reason, best known to my father, some of the people from the embassy, regulars from the meetings I used to eavesdrop on as a child, were also at the party. Klarra Klein the women from Guadalupe whose voice still did strange things to me was one of them. When she wished me happy birthday she pulled me in close to her, kissed me on the cheek then whispered in my ear. 'I know you will remember this', then she reeled off her phone number. 'Call me later, I have a special present for you.' For the two weeks before I left for France, I spent every night at Klarra's place, we made love and then she would tell me about her home on the butterfly shaped island between the Caribbean Sea and the Atlantic Ocean. Klarra's home was on Basse-Terre, the west "wing" of the island, in Bouillante not far from the still active volcano La Grande Soufrière. It seemed an idyllic life, but it wasn't enough for Klarra, she needed the buzz of the city and the high-octane environment of the embassy to "juice her up" as she put it.

No one asked where I went or what I was doing, which I thought was a bit strange for my parents, who usually insisted on knowing my whereabouts at all times, but I didn't care, and I had better things to occupy my mind and body with.

When I flew out of Heathrow for Nice I rather superciliously felt my education, or at least what really mattered was complete when it had barely begun. As well as paying my airfare my parents had given me a credit card with a very generous limit, apparently my grandparents and the ambassador, or uncle Philippe as he insisted I call him, had all chipped in to cover the cost. If I was careful I knew I could last the year without having to work, I planned to stay in hostels and travel as cheaply as possible. After I landed I took the tram to Massena Square and then walked the short distance to Villa Saint Exupery, it wasn't the cheapest hostel in Nice but it was close to the shops and the beach, plus it had a bar, if nothing else on this trip I knew I needed to relax and be with people my own age and at least try and make some friends.

I needn't have worried about getting on with others, fluent in French, German, Italian and English I was in demand as the resident translator. Suddenly I was popular, my "gifts" and intelligence no longer seemed a problem. People of my own age as well as older adults seemed comfortable around me, talking freely and listening to what I had to say, even happy to follow my suggestions on places to visit and things to do. I hung out at the beach with a group that varied in size from eight to twelve, some new faces replacing those that moved on or returned home. A couple of times we all hired a boat to go along the coast for the day, they were all my age and seemed content to get drunk and jump in the water. I drank very little but I loved to swim away from the crowds and visit some of the secluded coves. My real obsession was to visit the galleries, which I did alone, especially the Musée Matisse. After about three weeks though, I started getting restless and I decided I needed to move on, to explore the Cote d'Azur and beyond.

Charlotte often said that I had weird taste when it came to movies, I watched old films rather than the latest releases, it was probably the influence of my grandparents. Being three years younger than her I loved to sit and watch TV with them when she had her friends over, our favourites were the Bogart and Bacall movies, especially The Big Sleep. I was also obsessed by Casablanca, and I definitely had a crush on Ingrid Bergman. Charlotte said you couldn't crush on someone who died in the 80s but it didn't stop me getting goose bumps when I heard her first speak to Sam in

Rick's Café. Whatever the reason, I had Casablanca down on my bucket list of places to visit.

My plan was to follow the coast through Cannes, St Tropez and on to Marseille. I thought about getting a ferry from there to Algiers then through Oran and across the rim of Africa to Casablanca just like the route the voice-over describes at the beginning of the film, but I didn't like the idea of being cooped up on a ferry for almost twenty-four hours. The mediterranean coast seemed to call to me, so I decided to carry on by road to Spain, almost as far as Portugal, to Algeciras where I could cross continents in less than a couple of hours. I could have got the train but that took over twenty-eight hours, it wasn't the time it took really, unless I flew it was going to be a long journey either way, but the thought of being stuck on the train was even less appealing than the ferry from Marseille. I wanted to be close to the sea, to travel the coastline that had become almost a fantasy for me ever since our first family holiday in Villefranche-Sur-Mer. I wanted to stay by the sea, tick off all the famous resorts and explore the small coves and fishing villages my father went on about rather than telling us a bedtime story as mother had told him to.

The first day went smoothly, a middle-aged gay couple took me as far as Cannes and even bought me lunch on the way. I booked into the Chanteclair hostel close to the Floreville food market and just half a kilometre from La Croisette. After a few days of taking in the sights, I particularly enjoyed the quirky Movie Car Museum – Les Murs Peints, I decided to move on. It took a bit longer to hitch a lift this time but after about an hour stood at the roadside with my thumb out, a bright yellow Renault Mégane with a few patches rusty orange pulled over and the passenger window creaked down. I squatted level with the window, inside were two women in their mid-twenties, at a guess. I greeted them in French and told them I was heading toward St Tropez but anywhere along the way would be good, they said they could take me as far as St Raphael. I could tell they were not French, but they had enough of the language to hold a conversation with me. From their accents I thought they were probably German, and I was about to ask them where they came from, partly to make conversation and also to get a chance to speak a different language, when they began talking to each other in German. Pleased with my initial guess I quickly became concerned, it seemed they had a plan to take me to a bar at St Raphael and spike my drink before luring me to their apartment with the promise of a threesome but on the way, they would rob me. They had a friend, a man used to violence, who would take care of me if necessary. It seemed this was something they did regularly.

At first I was scared, and felt myself getting nauseous and my pulse rising, in the rear-view mirror I could see I had gone quite pale but still had a sheen of sweat across my face and forehead. I realised I could use this to my advantage and asked them in French if we could pull over at an Aires de service, they took one look at me and said they would stop at the next one, which was just a few kilometres ahead and asked if I could I hold on until then? I just nodded my head. When we pulled over I dashed into the bathroom and immediately splashed my face with cold water, soaking my shirt in the process. I had thought I would sneak out the back and wait for them to go but as I looked in the mirror the fear started to quickly fade and I began to feel angry instead, I realised that I needed to stand up for myself and teach the two of them a lesson, but I knew it would be easy for them to turn this on me. I was a foot taller than either of them, it would be easy to deny what I heard and play the victim. I felt my anger starting to subside to be replaced by something else I wasn't sure of and then realised this was the same way I felt when I confronted Boris or when I was eavesdropping on Kurt. I stood up straight took another look in the mirror and headed back to the small café, the two women sat, side-by-side, at a table in the back corner. I took one of the chairs opposite them, my back to the other tables. The driver, I think she said her name was Sylvia, but I doubt that was her real name, asked me if I was feeling better? I spoke to them in German, the surprise on their faces was almost comical, but unfortunately for them I wasn't amused. I began speaking in that same strange voice I used with Boris but this time I made sure to keep the volume down, almost whispering.

'So, you thought you would rob me?' They both answered, speaking in unison.

'Yes, you looked an easy mark we thought your dick would do all your thinking.'

'Give me your car keys.' Sylvia passed over her keys, her arm moved slowly but without any sign of hesitation. 'If anyone asks, you leant me your car. You will wait here for twenty minutes then you can hitch your way back to St Raphael. Is that understood?'

'Yes.'

I left them there and drove off, I went beyond St Raphael, in case anyone recognised the car, to Sainte Maxime and I left it parked outside the police station with the keys in. I thought it best to spend the night somewhere a little more secure than a hostel, now the adrenaline had subsided I was a little anxious again. I checked into the Hotel Les Palmiers in the centre of town, less than a hundred meters from the ferry port where I could cross the bay to St Tropez in the morning. I ended up staying four days in Sainte Maxime, it was the understated little sister of St Tropez. Much quieter but very charming, the hotel had a restaurant with a terrace overlooking the marina, I eat there every evening feasting on whatever the fishing boats had brought in that day. You could see the masts of the yachts bobbing gently on the water and hear the rigging tinkling in the breeze. Just behind the marina was the pedestrian only Promenade Aymeric Simon-Lorière, cool beneath pine trees and palms it took me to the beach which was a mixture of sand and gravel. There were boules courts and a hut where you could hire a set of the heavy metallic balls. A group of old men chain smoked and drank absinthe mixed with water while they played, somehow, I ended up joining in their game that first morning and the next three, before I got restless again and felt the need to move on. The old men, their heckling and jibing at each other, even the smell of aniseed seemed to combine to take my mind off the way I had controlled the two women. I knew it had to be faced though, even if I couldn't explain it I needed to understand it, I needed to confront it somehow. I seemed more in control of it the second time, with Boris it was just pure instinct and I think I may well have done him some harm, mentally.

In 1915 absinthe was banned in France until 2011, the wormwood used to make it was alleged to cause hallucinations and madness, I thought the old men were a little saner than I was right then, but I knew I was not hallucinating, I just didn't understand my own reality.

When I eventually crossed the bay, the more mundane reality of an overcrowded and very expensive St Tropez repulsed me, and the idyllic dream I had of the white sand of Pampelonne beach and laidback youths was shattered, I took to the road again after just a day. I managed to hitch a ride to Toulon with a sweet older couple in their seventies who insisted I came to their house and have supper. Despite or perhaps because of my previous experience I was not afraid to accept their offer and after too much red wine, and at their insistence, I ended up staying the night in their spare room. I was a little scared that I somehow, accidentally, might do them some harm, but realised I now had some control over whatever this gift or power was, and I was fully responsible for my actions, good or bad, and this in itself made me a little more anxious.

When I woke, any trace of nerves disappeared immediately at the smell of freshly baked croissants and hot strong coffee. My elderly hosts offered to put me up for a few more nights, they said I reminded them of their grandson who they had seen little of since he moved to Paris. I felt the need to keep moving and did not take them up on their kind offer. They seemed anxious about their grandson and for some unexplained reason I offered to look him up when I visited Paris. This seemed to make them a little brighter and they rather casually gave me his address, his name was Tomas, he was twenty-one years old and living in the 11th arrondissement. I am not sure why they seemed so reassured by my offer, I was three years younger than Tomas and could hardly be expected to be able to offer him much support or guidance. They may have thought he needed a friend and for some reason people always seemed to think of me as being older and wiser than I was, they mistook intelligence for wisdom but there is a vast difference between the two.

After Toulon, time seemed to slow down as I made my way around the coast, with brief stops at Bandol, La Cioat and Cassis, before I landed in Les Goudes a small fishing village, too perfect to be real but it was. I managed to hire a moped and travelled the short distance to the restaurant at Cap Croisette, the sea a two-tone green and blue with hardly a ripple to disturb it. For some reason I felt the need to stay longer maybe forever. By chance the dive school needed someone to clean kit and help at the restaurant or anything else that came up. I stayed at Les Goudes for a month before I felt that urge to move on again, it seemed that even paradise was not enough to satisfy me. Between the *voice* and the restlessness, I was beginning to think I had some sort of neurological disorder, it was probably only a matter of time before I started hearing and seeing things as well. I headed off to Marseille, hoping the city would quell my itchy feet but I never got the chance to test that theory out. Marseille turned out to be as close as I would get to Casablanca that year. I arrived in the middle of the afternoon and booked myself into the Meininger hotel, just North of the Old Port in La Joliette district. I only planned to stay a couple of days, I'd spent more than one night under the stars on some deserted beach over the past few months and wanted to recharge my batteries, my own physical one and my iPhone which had been flat for the last three days. So, I ate, showered and then I slept twelve hours straight through, until seven the next morning. I reluctantly got out of bed, as my stomach was growling, and headed downstairs in search of breakfast. The young woman on reception called me as I walked toward the exit, 'Monsieur Renoir', I turned to see her waving a white envelope in her right hand as I walked toward her. She wore a tight-fitting navy blazer, a French tricolour scarf and a name badge. 'Ca va Justine?'

'Ca va bien, Monsieur Renoir. I have a letter for you, it was left at five this morning.'

Justine raised her eyebrows as she said five and was clearly curious, it seemed not many people got hand delivered notes at dawn. I took the envelope from her and noticed she deliberately made contact with the back of my hand as she passed it over then looked away busying herself with something behind the desk. As well as the envelope I realised she had also given me a folded slip of paper from the hotel stationary supply, I unfolded the note first, it was Justine's phone number and the time she finished work. Before my imagination got carried away, I opened the letter, which was in fact a first-class TGV ticket for the Paris train at 2pm. The note was from *uncle Philippe*, telling me not to worry everyone was well, but if possible he needed to talk to me privately that evening at the Foreign Ministry on the Quai d'Orsay. It seemed Justine would be disappointed, there was no number to call to confirm or refuse my attendance. Given that the ambassador was able to locate me and have a letter delivered in less than 24 hours of my arrival in Marseille he would probably also know the minute I got on the train. Whatever was going on, I was too intrigued to miss out on it and ended up at the station half-an-hour early. I was surprised, though not much, when a few minutes after the train rolled out the station; Pierre, uncle Philippe's trusted bodyguard, sat down in the seat opposite me.

'Bonjour Pierre, was it you who delivered the ambassador's communiqué?'

'Oui, I was also asked to ensure you arrived safely should you choose to meet with the ambassador. I hope you don't mind some company.'

'You're not a talker are you Pierre, more a man of action?'

'I'm not a diplomat, I prefer to communicate directly.'

'In that case we should get along well, I will snooze my way to Paris, and you will be spared the ordeal of chatting to a spoilt brat.'

Pierre just smiled and almost unconsciously tapped the gun beneath his jacket. Pierre was not hairy, a bit of a brute but I would not have minded kissing him, back then.

***

The ambassador adeptly sidestepped the questions about how he knew where I was and why he even wanted to know in the first place, someone must have been tracking me for him. I smiled at Pierre, the gun was blunt but true depending on your aim, words were devilish things, and the ambassador was well trained. Uncle Philippe got to his point directly though.

'Joshua, I have a favour to ask of you, I should tell you first though that your father does not know and would not approve of me asking. I would prefer it if he remained blissfully unaware, but you are free to talk to him nonetheless, I would never force you to keep secrets from Paul.'

'Tell me what you need me to do, then I will decide if I need to talk to my father.'

'That's fair. To business then, there will be some delicate trade talks going on over the next three days, representatives from a number of countries will be in attendance. Some of our guests are, shall we say, less interested in the negotiations and are looking for opportunities to cause a little mischief, maybe even recruit a government official or two to their cause.'

'And what would you like me to do?'

'The official gatherings and talks will take place in the ministry, there are cameras and microphones everywhere, so no one is going to utter a word out of place inside the building. Not far from here is a brasserie, plenty of cosy secluded booths with high backs to sit in, music playing low enough to allow quiet conversations but loud enough to frustrate any bugging device. It's the place the delegates drop in to when they want a private chat, mostly it's innocent enough but we also believe that some conversations are happening that shouldn't be. To be blunt, we think one of our own is passing on information, we are not sure if it just relates to the trade discussions, or it extends to some of our recent military acquisitions. I am asking if you would be willing to hang out at the brasserie on the off chance you might hear something, rather like you did that night at the party?'

'Will any of the people who came to my parents' parties be there? If they recognise me the game will be up straight away.'

'Unlikely, these meetings are mainly for the technical experts to sort out the details and red lines before the senior diplomats, like those that went to your house, get into the wrangling and horse trading. Klarra did do a cross check on those attending the London parties and those invited to these talks, and it all looked good.' I smiled at just the mention of Klarra's name, the ambassador noticed, I would need to get better at this spying game. 'Ok I'm in.'

'And your father?'

'I never tell him about my drinking habits or friends.' The ambassador was sharp enough to know that I expected him to keep my interest in Klarra to himself. This time we just smiled at each other and nodded.

'Très bien! I have arranged for you to have the use of one of our apartments, nothing special I'm afraid, but it's opposite the brasserie and there is a good view of the front door from the bedroom window. You're not expected to watch the comings and goings, but if you are curious make sure you are not noticed, Pierre will give you a few tips when he drops you off. Tomorrow there is a formal lunch before the talks begin, Pierre will collect you in the morning about

11am. There is a security room with the feeds from all the cameras, you will be able to see the delegates arriving and having lunch. Does your formidable memory extend to faces as well as languages and conversations?'

'Yes, how many people will there be?'

'Twelve countries with five delegates each, so 60 in total, is that too many?'

'Sixty is good, if there is a list of their names, nationalities and a few details about their particular interest or expertise I could memorise the lot by the time they have finished eating. Knowing something about them actually makes it easier to put the faces and names together.' I thought Pierre's eyeballs were going to pop out of his head, he saw me looking and wound his neck back in.

'Bon, très bien. From our observations in the past, between mid-day and eight is the time when people meet up, try and spend as much time as you can there but if you think someone is on to you, go back to the apartment. Do you have a hat or a scarf?' It seemed an odd question, but I answered anyway. 'It's August! But yes, I have a red baseball cap.'

'Bon, if you think someone has spotted you put the hat on and leave, go straight back to the apartment. We will have someone in the brasserie, they will make sure you're safe and will contact Pierre.'

I looked at Pierre, 'I suppose you would be a bit noticeable in the restaurant' Pierre smiled as he spoke.

'Yes, I stand out like, how do you say, yes like a "sore thumb", everyone knows I am the ambassador's personal bodyguard.'

'Not to mention that you would barely fit through the door.'

The apartment was comfortable with a huge bed, a modern kitchen and a sitting room, the shower had more nozzles and jets than a Jacuzzi. There was a glazed door leading on to a narrow balcony just big enough for a small bistro table and two chairs. Pierre told me to keep the lace curtain drawn across the door and to stay a few feet back with the lights off, he said it would be better that I never switched the lights on at all, day or night, while I was there so the window just blended into the background. He placed a bar stool where he knew it could not be seen and then handed me a pair of powerful binoculars, he explained that the lenses were coated to stop any reflected light alerting someone below. Finally, he pointed outside to the far corner of the balcony, where a thick rope, like the ones in my old school gym, was tied at one end to the metal railing and the rest coiled around on the floor like some kind of circular rug. 'Josh do not go out onto the balcony unless there is no other option, the rope is your emergency exit. I hope you are not scared of heights, we are thirty feet up and the pavement is unforgiving.'

'I noticed the door was heavy, how long will it hold for?'

'It's got seven levered bolts, the frame and door are reinforced with steel, it would take too long and be too noisy for anyone to break through. If you lock it your safe, outside you are vulnerable but we've got your back.'

'Merci, Pierre.' After that he left, I locked the door and went to bed, I needed to be refreshed and ready for my new job.

***

By one o'clock I had committed all but one of the delegates to memory, Gjon Murati from Albania had been taken ill that morning and someone else would replace him tomorrow, but no one knew the name of the replacement yet.

By one-thirty I was sitting in the brasserie with a large bowl of moules and frites, from where I sat, I could see the door and most of the booths lining the rear and one sidewall. I had already made friends with the owner and one of the waitresses who happened to be his daughter. I was struck by two things at the same time, how attractive she was and how useful she could be, and wondered if one negated the other or was it ok to mix business and pleasure in this little game. The restaurant was busy, mostly regulars by the sound of the greetings and conversations. By four o'clock the place was starting to empty, outside I could see predominantly male office workers walking home with a baguette under one arm chewing on the end of the bread they had torn off. I had been lingering over my coffee for far too long and thought I should probably leave and come back in a couple of hours when the door opened and in walked two of the delegates from the Italian group. If I could hear them, I would at least be able to understand what they said, though I did not think they would have much to say of interest to me. Rightly or wrongly, I reasoned that any one up to no good would come alone and meet up with another loner from a different country. I decided to stay anyway and ordered a beer. Michelle, the patron's daughter, took my order smiling widely at me and I smiled back, then I saw her father looking over, but he didn't seem put out by my obvious attraction. I decided Michelle was to be my reason for spending so much time in the brasserie.

But for now, I turned my attention back to the two Italians, Antonio and Giovanni the head of the delegation. I heard them greet the owner in French and he replied in Italian before showing them to one of the more secluded booths. I was wondering how I could get closer to them so I could hear what they were saying. I thought of asking Michelle if she could show me to one of the booths, making the excuse that I would prefer to eat dinner away from the more noisy open area. But before I got the chance I heard a few words in Italian, then a whole sentence and then a reply, I looked toward the booth, I could barely see them from where I sat but I could hear them clearly. It wasn't like hearing a conversation, it seemed like I was in their heads, no not both of them, it was just Giovanni, he had spoken first, and I had sort of latched on to him.

After some small talk about their families' health and the children's schools I could tell that they had lowered their voices, but it made no difference I could hear them as well as they could hear each other. It appeared they suspected one of their own group was selling industrial secrets to another country. Unfortunately, they didn't say the person's name or which country they thought was paying him. Still, that narrowed the suspects, or at least one of them, down to one of the other three Italians.

No one else on the delegate list came in that night, at seven I ordered the salad Nicoise and Michelle brought it to my table and we started to chat, after a couple of minutes I asked her if she was free to join me. She looked over to her father without speaking, he nodded, and she sat next to me. A few minutes later her father sent over a bottle of wine and two glasses. By then it was eight-thirty and the place was almost empty. I found out that Michelle was twenty-two, an artist who helped her father out to pay her bills and keep her in canvas and acrylics. At nine I decided it was time to leave, the bottle was still half-full and Michelle put the cork back in.

'Pour demain, oui?'

'Oui demain c'est bien, on se voit à l'heure du déjeuner.'

'Bon nuit, Josh.' We politely kissed on the cheek and I left. I hadn't told Michelle where I was staying, I would need to talk to Pierre about how to manage things first, so I turned right and after thirty metres I crossed over and headed back toward the apartment. There was an alley that went around the back of the building, it was much darker than I expected, and I could feel myself getting anxious. My hearing seemed to be dialled up to radar capacity and I thought I could actually hear rats scurrying along the back wall. I leapt up the two steps to the rear door and quickly used my key to unlock it and scrambled in. Once in my apartment I made sure the door was properly locked, I left the light off and sat on the stool looking across the road, losing track of time. I watched Michelle's father show out the last customer, an elderly man who I had seen earlier sipping at the same small glass of maison rouge for a very long time, he locked the door after him and shortly afterwards the lights went off inside. By that point my breathing was back under control and I phoned Pierre as instructed, I told him what I had heard, he was very pleased. Less so when I told him about Michelle.

'The good news is that we have already checked out Michelle and her family as well as the staff that work there and they are all clean. The bad news is you have complicated things, you now have to manage a relationship with Michelle while spying in her father's restaurant, oh and she can't know who you really are. Simple!'

'I understand your concerns, but this is all new to me and it will make hanging around in there a lot easier.'

'And you're happy to use her like that?'

'Que feriez-vous?' With Pierre and others, I'd noticed I tended to slip between English and French especially when I was stressed, French was better for stress and for anger, more passion.

'Ok, let's calm down, let's think it through.'

Eventually we agreed that Michelle was more of a positive than a negative. Pierre was adamant that I was never to use the back entrance again, it was too risky, which meant that Michelle would need to know that I was staying for a short while and where I was living. Hopefully that would also deter her from getting too attached, Pierre did not think I would have a problem remaining detached, which I resented but had to acknowledge that he was probably right.

I popped into the restaurant at nine for some breakfast, I was desperate for some coffee and knew I would have to do some food shopping that morning. Michelle was not working, her father was behind the counter, and I got the impression that he rarely left his post. He greeted me by my first name and I suppressed a wince, wondering what Pierre would say about that. I didn't linger, determined to make good use of my free time and squeeze in a new exhibition at the Pompidou as well as get some shopping to keep me going for the next three days.

I got too absorbed in the paintings and sculpture, only arriving at the brasserie at one o'clock and no groceries to show for my efforts, or rather lack of effort. Michelle's broad smile as she came to greet me put a stop to any further self-recrimination. By some unspoken agreement we kissed on the lips, as though my return had somehow sealed the deal. She asked me where I would like to sit and I pointed to one of the booths, which seemed to please her. The booth was the first one in the line against the back wall, I could see the front door, the tables in the centre and anyone going to one of the more out-of-sight tables would have to pass by me. It seemed that trade talks were best done in the morning, by one-thirty there was a steady influx of faces I recognised. There was no sign of the two Italian delegates from yesterday but about three-thirty Gino Bonetti, another member of their delegation, walked in. He did not wait to be directed to a table but went straight past me to the last booth in the row. I had already watched Luljeta Mehmeti enter that booth fifteen minutes earlier. Luljeta, was the Albanian replacement for Gjon Murati who had been taken ill, allegedly. Her details and a picture had been posted under my door some time before I woke up that morning. Murati specialised in grain imports, wheat, barley, that sort of thing. Mehmeti's expertise was weapons, tanks, helicopters and recently drones, which it seems were the future of modern warfare according to Pierre. Her first name Luljeta meant, rather ironically, flower of life. She seemed an odd replacement for a delegate who specialised in cereals, I could feel the excitement and nervousness building inside me.

Gino sat down in the booth and there was a pause before either spoke, then Luljeta greeted Gino in Russian. I knew enough to recognise the language, though I was concerned that I wouldn't be able to understand what they were saying, then I relaxed, I could just memorise the conversation and the ambassador would get someone else to translate it. I needn't have worried though, like before I could hear every word they spoke as though I was there inside their heads. Well, Luljeta's head, it seemed that whoever spoke first that's who I latched onto, they became my host. Unlike yesterday, when I understood the language being spoken, this time it was like I was listening to a translation on one of those sets of headphones politicians wear at the European Commission in Brussels.

It appeared that Gino was acting as broker for some arms shipments that were against the trade sanctions on Russia following their annexation of Crimea. The shipment was to go via Albania and Luljeta was to ensure safe passage, the two of them would make a lot of money from the deal. Luljeta left just before four and Gino waited ten minutes before he broke cover from the booth and headed out the door. I waited until four-thirty, I told Michelle I would be back at seven and our kiss lasted a little bit longer than the previous one. When I checked in with Pierre the Ambassador joined the call as I gave my update. They were both very pleased and I think a little relieved that no French delegates appeared to be involved.

'I will wait a couple of days before I pass on the information to the Italians, just in case anyone else is up to no good, we don't want to scare any other prospects off.'

'What about the Albanians?'

'Gino's detention will be enough to scupper the deal, they don't need to know who he was talking to, and the Albanian Government is mixed up in Luljeta's dealings with the Russians and will cover for her. No, we will keep a close watch on her and see if we can catch her red handed on French soil, then we can interrogate her properly while her government witters about diplomatic immunity. Josh, the talks end in two days, are you happy to continue?'

'That's good for me. I am sure Pierre has told you about my attraction to Michelle Ribbon, I would also like to stay on at the apartment for a while, at least to the end of the month, is that possible?'

'Let's call it a bonus for the good work you've already done. Yes, Pierre did mention Michelle, he was surprised and impressed at how cold and calculating you can be. I was not surprised, but then I've watched you grow up, always exceeding even the greatest expectations. I take it you're not in love?'

'Just lust.'

'Good, two days of work and then the apartment is yours to do as you wish, with whom you wish.'

It was just before seven in the evening when I entered the brasserie, Michelle was busy setting down plates of food at one of the tables and didn't see me come in. Her father spotted me straight away and called me over to the bar and I sat on a high stool, he put a glass in front of me and uncorked the bottle left from yesterday and poured me out a large glass of maison rouge and I asked him to join me. We chatted for a few minutes about football, I wasn't really interested in professional sport but I made a point of following it, and football in particular, in the news as it always seemed a good conversation opener and had helped me to get along with other people on my travels, otherwise I had, still have, a tendency to be a bit awkward in company. I wasn't shy or lacking in confidence, it was just that most people didn't interest me enough to want to talk to them. The precocious child had turned into the arrogant adolescent, what would Kurt have said? We were just talking about the merits of PSG's latest signing when I felt a pair of arms slip around my waist, when I turned my head Michelle kissed me full on the lips and when I turned back her father had retreated to the other end of the bar. Michelle showed me to the same booth I sat in before, there was a couple in the one next to it, the table after that was empty, but I couldn't see into the last three booths. Now was the time to make use of my relationship, I reached a hand out and guided Michelle into the seat opposite me. I made a point of looking around, then looking behind us, I smiled at her and did my best to suggestively ask her, 'are we alone?' she smiled and reached across for my hand 'Just Maurice, the old man in the corner, and the lovers behind us but they only have eyes for each other.' I leaned across the table and curled my hand around her head to draw her face toward mine, we kissed, I slid my tongue inside her mouth, and she pushed back and into mine. There would be no work tonight.

With the place virtually deserted we sat together talking while I slowly sipped my wine. I told her where I was staying and that I would be leaving at the end of the month to continue my travels around Europe. I did not want her to get too attached, I was not looking to hook up with anyone on anything more than a *friends with benefits* basis. At first she looked disappointed but then she shrugged her shoulders, smiled and kissed me more passionately than before. I left an hour before closing time, Maurice was still there sipping his everlasting glass of wine just like the night before. I waited impatiently, looking out the window and ignoring Pierre's advice to stand well back, I watched as Michelle's father showed Maurice out. About twenty minutes later Michelle came out the front door and locked it before crossing over the road.

Despite a number of offers I had not got involved with anyone, beyond a brief fling, during my travels along the Cote de Azure. I was certainly very wary after the episode with the two German girls, but also, I hadn't quite got over Klarra. She had made it clear from that first night that she wanted sex, not love, and anything between us would be short but sweet. She even offered to set me up with her sister, who was twenty-one and would be coming to London to study in October, as a more age-appropriate partner. I wasn't quite as cold and calculating as Pierre thought, not back then anyway. I think working for the ambassador, which though it had only been a few days was a serious responsibility, and the time away from Klarra had helped me mature a little. Love was off the menu, I thought, but sex was definitely in season.

In the morning Michelle left for work at ten and I walked over to the brasserie at one. I was a little apprehensive about her father's reaction, but he smiled widely and called me over to the bar again, this time he shook my hand before he poured me another glass of maison rouge. He was clearly jumping to conclusions, I looked over to Michelle and she just shrugged and smiled. As long as Michelle was cool with our friendship, I wasn't going to worry about what her father was thinking. I sat in the same booth as the night before, the restaurant was getting very busy, and Michelle had no time to chat with me. I recognised eight delegates, five of them sat at a large table in front of the windows talking loudly, they were the Swedish representatives and clearly not concerned about secrets. Still the sing-song resonance of their voices was quite musical and very distracting. I almost missed the conversation in the end booth, I'd seen one of the Turkish diplomats go to that table a few minutes before, but I hadn't realised there was someone else in there as well. I picked up on the Turkish voice first, he greeted the other person in passable French but when the other person replied I knew at once he was a native Parisian, it seemed the Ambassador would be disappointed after all. This conversation was not about trade though, legal or illegal, it was about assassination and retribution. There was a day, a time and a place – Place de la Concorde, Saturday, 1500 hours. Then my blood felt like it was curdling, the Turk spoke quietly but fervently, 'Pour Kurt et Dietrich!', I took several deep breaths and resisted the urge to leave as I gripped the tabletop with one hand and used the other to take a shaky gulp of wine followed by a few sips. The Turk left first, I looked down at the table as he passed by, then after ten minutes the head of the French delegation walked by my table. I took a good look at him, there could be no mistakes with this, they had not named anyone, but I assumed the ambassador was their target. A few minutes later Michelle came to my table to see if I wanted another drink. It was still busy, but I persuaded her to sit with me for a minute or two, I slid across the bench toward the wall and pulled her in beside me. I explained that I needed to make a private call about some family business and asked if there was anywhere I could use. She took me through a door behind the bar to a large storeroom, kissed me and left me to make my call, it went straight through to Pierre's messaging service, and I just said it was urgent, that he needed to call me back. I waited in the storeroom for twenty minutes by the time he called I was so strung out I actually jumped a few inches in the air. It only took me thirty seconds to tell him what I had heard, but I was still breathing heavily. Pierre told me to wait in the café for an hour and then go back to the apartment and wait for him to call.

***

As I left the restaurant, I looked across the road and up to the window of my flat, the curtain was drawn just as I had left it, but as I shifted my focus to the ground floor I noticed a man hanging around by the front door of the building. He was tall, broad in the shoulders and wearing a suit that he didn't look comfortable in, and it definitely wasn't Armani. This was a tuneless variation on Pierre, he lacked his good looks and style but made up for it in sheer brawn. As someone left the building, I saw him slip inside, I thought of heading for the ministry but was scared there might be others and went back into the brasserie, I smiled at Michelle and said loudly that I'd forgot my hat. They had never seen me with a hat so looked rather bemused, and then standing in the middle of the restaurant I patted my pockets like some strange mime before fishing out the red baseball cap and putting it on my head. I said goodbye again to Michelle and her father and went back out the door, I stayed on the lower step, hoping the ambassador was serious about my mysterious back-up. A few seconds later, a tall woman that I somehow managed not to notice before, in an expensive trouser suit and a beige trench coat over her arm followed me out the door. She looked all around and then spoke.

'Bonjour Josh, my name is Yve, and I am here to keep you safe. Is there a problem?'

'Bonjour Yve, I think so.' I explained about the man at the apartment entrance.

'Bon. Let's move away from the restaurant toward the ministry.'

'What if there are others?' Eve discretely lifted the trench coat hanging over her right arm with her left hand, in her right hand was a rather large gun, it was much bulkier than the one Pierre carried and had a long magazine hanging down just in front of the trigger guard.

'I've called it in so we will have some company soon, but there is a stone porch at the front of the building twenty metres down, it will give us some cover just in case. I can protect you from there no matter how many of them there are but I doubt they have the resources to support a full scale operation, I suspect the guy at your door is going solo and he's not so bright going through the front door and getting himself boxed up inside.'

Two minutes later a large Range Rover with blacked out windows pulled up and the rear door opened wide. Yve smiled at me and spoke, 'This is for us, you go first I'll be right behind you.' Inside the four-by-four were two men and one woman, plus two more men in a third row of seats facing backwards, I sat in the middle seat and Yve got in beside me. Apart from the driver everyone else was nursing a large automatic weapon on their laps and wore Kevlar vests. Definitely not your average Uber. Ten minutes later I was back at the ministry in a large library with the Ambassador, drinking coffee laced with brandy.

'Uncle Philippe, forgive me for asking but you don't seem very popular. If you can't tell me that's ok, but if you're free to be truthful I would like to know why?'

'Josh, you deserve to know, and I trust you enough to tell you. I am not the usual career diplomat - rich parents, privately educated and three years at the Sorbonne to round me off. Yes, all that is true too, but I rebelled or broke the familiar mould at least. I joined the Marine Parachute

Regiment and after a couple of years led an elite unit, parachuting into places no sane person would consider going to, at some point a very young Pierre became my lieutenant. Back then our friend Kurt ran a group of so called freedom fighters, just terrorist really but they did the bombing and shooting while Kurt and Dietrich made money. We took out a lot of the fanatics, but we couldn't prove either of them were involved, and they hid behind their diplomatic immunity. That worked well for them until Pierre and I, unearthed a few links in a very long chain back to the slippery bastards, we were closing in on them. Unfortunately, I hadn't been discrete enough in my investigations, or careful enough with my relationships, as you well know. That conversation you heard saved Pierre's life and mine, but remnants of the group still exist and want revenge for the loss of their glorious leaders.'

'What happened to the both of them?'

'When Julia realised that she was expendable she gave me enough information for the Germans to disown the two of them. I did a deal with the Russians, we got back one of our own and they got Kurt and Dietrich who had foolishly been behind a few bombings in St Petersburg a decade earlier.'

'Are they still alive.'

'Unlikely, does that bother you?'

'Less than them being alive would, it seems I now have some enemies of my own, so two less is ok with me. What I really need to know ambassador, is how they found out about me?'

'It seems that Francois, who you overheard in the café, recognised you from some pictures on social media posts of your family and me. We picked him up within an hour of your message, but he had already called a *friend*. Luckily, he did not manage to contact the Turkish delegate and we should be able to close the net on a few more of Kurt's little army.'

'What about the man at the apartment?'

'Pierre has dealt with him.'

'Killed him, he's dead?'

'Qui.'

'Bon.'

'You seem remarkably sanguine about all this, if I might say a little blasé about death in general.'

'Only when it is someone out to do me harm, one less assassin with me in their sights is a win as far as I am concerned.' The ambassador was right though, I was changing and even then, I didn't think it was necessarily for the better. I realised that my shaking in the storeroom wasn't fear, it was excitement, and I was getting a buzz out of all this. It was so crazy, but I still wondered if I could have stopped that man at the apartment block by speaking to him like I had done with Boris and the two women. It wasn't anything I was going to try out soon, especially on someone with a loaded gun, but the way things were going it might just come to that.

'What about the apartment?'

'You can't go back there until we are sure no one else knows about you. I have booked you a suite at the Hôtel d'Orsay, Michelle can join you there if that suits you, tell her there is a burst pipe in the apartment. Josh, get her to make her own way there, Pierre will make sure she is safe and that she's not followed. Tomorrow, stay away from the Café, take her to the Musée d'Orsay or the Louvre. Enjoy yourselves.'

'What about her work?'

'It's her day off.' He said it with a smug little smile on his face, that little thrill of knowing something I didn't. I understood it, I felt it, I was hooked – secrets and lies!

'But first Josh, a more difficult issue, your father, I take it you haven't spoken to him since you left Marseille?'

'I wasn't really sure what to tell him, but if I don't call soon he will get worried and call me. What do you suggest?'

'Call him, tell him the truth or at least some of it. That you took a diversion to Paris at my request, he won't like it, tell him about the eavesdropping at the Café. He will likely use some very offensive words about me, but when he calms down tell him it's all finished and you are spending a few weeks in Paris taking in the galleries, that sort of thing. Don't tell him about anything you heard, he won't expect or ask you to, he's played the game long enough to know that if you can tell him anything it won't be over the phone. Never speak to him about the man at the apartment or he might kill me himself and he certainly won't let you out of his sight for a very long time.'

The call went exactly as uncle Philippe suggested, I also told him about Michelle, which he seemed unusually pleased about. Sadly, I was being devious again, if I needed an excuse for staying in Paris longer, then Michelle would provide the perfect reason, one that didn't involve the ambassador.

The suite at the hotel was very fancy and Michelle was impressed, we ordered room service as neither of us wanted to leave our cosy oasis let alone go outside. We spent most of the night in bed but slept very little. When we were eating breakfast at the small table in the lounge, I looked at Michelle who was staring through the window in a world of her own, still naked, and realised I was becoming attached, that I'd been kidding myself all along, and that I would be staying in Paris for as long as this lasted. My deviousness had backfired, I was hooked.

It took five days before uncle Philippe called me to say it was safe to return to the apartment and that it was mine for as long as I wanted it. They had picked up another five of Kurt's exiles and the Turkish delegate had followed his leader over the Russian border, headed for Siberia if he was unlucky enough to live that long.

A week after that Michelle had virtually moved in with me. I realised I couldn't just spend my days hanging around the Café, as tempting as it was, so I asked my uncle if he had anything I could help him with. The way he smiled, I knew straight away that he had just been waiting for me to ask. Two days later I found myself in the back of a van parked outside some very swanky looking houses. There were two benches running the length of the van facing each other, next to me was one of the guys from the back of the Range Rover nursing his deadly machine gun, he told me it was a Heckler Koch 416, opposite him was a tall blonde man, that I had not seen before, he also caressed his HK416.

I had no gun, just a set of headphones, I was listening in to conversations alternating between French, Spanish and occasionally German. I was simultaneously translating and relaying what I heard into a microphone, I had no idea who was listening at the other end, and I did not care, apart from making love to Michelle it was the most exhilarated I had ever felt. On top of all of that, the French Government was paying me stupid amounts of money, I hadn't realised until then how lucrative my skills could be. But in the evenings, Michelle and I cuddled and made love and the buzz of the day became a distant sound, a fading memory until the morning.

When the surveillance ended, I was disappointed and then bored. Pierre sensed my restlessness and suggested we do some training together, he taught me how to fight, how to use a knife and how to fire a gun. But I kept thinking, what's the point when, maybe, I could just talk someone to death. The guns were the worst, they were so loud, but to keep Pierre happy I managed to fire three shots into a dummy's chest and one in the head, just to be certain. I learnt how to block a punch and break someone's nose. I preferred the knife, it was silent, and slipped between their ribs and straight into their heart, but at what cost? "Put out the light, and then put out the light." It was easy to be brave in your head and when you know your opponent won't harm you other than a stinging slap to highlight your error or to get you back on track. Pierre was a good teacher, but I was lazy and easily distracted, he was patient and determined and after a week or so I started to take it more seriously, but I avoided the guns. I could see he was as pleased with himself, as much as he was with my progress. I'd have to give him that one in this little battle of wills that we indulged in most days.

It was half-way through September when I got to test my theory about talking someone to death or at least out of doing me some serious harm. I was walking back to the apartment, I'd stayed late to translate some documents, it was boring but I was being well paid, so nothing to gripe about really. About one hundred metres from the building a man stepped out of an alley waving a knife in my face and demanding my phone and credit cards. I probably should have just handed them over but instead I felt myself getting angry and then it happened, the voice, I could hear it in my head I could almost see it rushing from my mouth to his ears. I could see his head jerk back as it took hold of him. 'No! Stay where you are, do not move!' He completely froze on the spot. 'Hand me the knife!' I watched as he turned the blade around to point toward himself then proffered the handle to me. I took it off him and held the blade to his throat, if I am honest with myself, I was tempted to slash open the vein that was now pulsing before me. Instead, I pulled it way and thrust it into a gap in the mortar of the alley wall and snapped it at the hilt. 'Aller au commissariat confess all your crimes and take your punishment.' I'd no sooner spoken the words than he walked off, presumably to the nearest police station. I neither knew nor cared at that point, I was too fascinated by the fact that I had controlled a thief, intent on stabbing me if necessary, to hand over his weapon and then turn himself in.

When I got into the apartment, Michelle had fallen asleep on the sofa in her Disney Princess PJs. I felt the tears trickle down my cheeks, she was so sweet but so vulnerable, I started to feel angry again at the thought that it might have been her having to face the man in the alley. I heard what sounded like a low rumble, then I felt a faint tremble and I just knew I was the cause. I took deep breaths and slowly knelt next to Michelle and stroked her cheek gently with the back of my hand. My anger started to fade, the vibrations stopped, I kissed her lightly on the nose. I knew she would not wake, she was a very heavy sleeper, and it would have taken a real earthquake to disturb her slumbers. I stood and then scooped her up in my arms before carrying her to bed, stripping off my own clothes I spooned in behind her and went straight to sleep. The fear and the rage gone, at least for a while. When I woke up, I was still cuddled up to Michelle, but she had turned to face me and as I put my arms around her back to draw her even closer before kissing her, I realised she was now naked. It seemed my Princess wanted to play.

I was an hour late for work, but no one said anything, everyone logged into the building and logged out and I knew the ambassador would have checked the late hour at which I left and made allowances. I also knew he wasn't clock watching, he felt responsible for my safety and that's why he was keeping an eye on me. If I told him what happened last night with the thief, I knew Yve or one of the others would be put on baby-sitting duty. So, I said nothing, besides how could I explain what I'd done and how would they treat me if I did? I wasn't ready to be a freak in uncle Philippe's circus or anyone else's pampered pet, apart from Michelle's.

I needn't have worried about the ambassador, when I got in the office my father, a far more formidable foe, was waiting for me. He had told me, or should I say warned me, that he would visit as soon as he could get away from London. I suspected that uncle Philippe had tried to keep him busy for as long as possible while I bedded-in, as he described it. He, rather too innocently, asked me about my work. I told him about the document translations I was doing the previous night, not the content just that it was boring. Before he started to probe too deeply, I decided to go on the offensive with my secret weapon – Michelle, and I asked him if he would like to have lunch with the two of us. He was delighted at the idea, up until then I think he thought she might have been some ruse invented by my uncle. Of course, my father took over then, and booked a table at CINQ-MARS for the three of us and I noticed that he did not mention inviting the ambassador.

Well, I have to say that my strategy worked a treat. Michelle arrived at the restaurant by Uber, the two of us were waiting outside for her and I think we both got a surprise when she stepped out on to the pavement. I had seen Michelle in her work clothes, and she looked fantastic, I'd seen her naked and she was breathtakingly beautiful. This was something else. Firstly, the taxi driver actually opened the door for her, something I had never seen before. Then a pair of heels high enough to cause vertigo clicked onto the pavement and as she stepped out I caught sight of the most amazing pearlescent-green dress as it slipped down from where it had rested on her thighs whilst seated in the cab, I followed it down like the curtain call at the theatre, I just about stopped myself applauding. It settled just above her ankles and then I was drawn back up by a split that tracked almost up to her hip, making her legs seem endless. Her waist was cinched in by a thin belt in the same colour, the neckline was a little low but nothing too revealing. She must have been to the hairdresser as well, her long blonde hair lay across her shoulders in loose curls, she wore hardly any make-up, she didn't really need to, just a little green eye shadow that sparkled and matched the colour of her dress and eyes. My father was the first to recover his voice.

'I should have booked a fancier restaurant! Forgive me for staring Michelle, my son did not tell me how beautiful you are, now I see why he refuses to leave Paris.'

When we went into the restaurant all heads turned and as we ate lunch Michelle utterly charmed my father, my secret weapon certainly worked her own magic on him. There was no more talk of work or my uncle, mon père said he had to get back to London that night but invited Michelle and I to come and stay with the family, insisting that she must meet ma maman, and Charlotte if she was home. That reminded me that it would only be a month before Charlotte moved to Paris to attend the Sorbonne. It was after three by the time we finished lunch, well we had finished eating at two, but the conversation continued over the last of the wine and then coffee. My father said he had some things to take care of before he went back, I wondered if he was going to speak to the ambassador or my uncle but decided not to be around either way and took Michelle back to the flat to see what she was hiding under that amazing dress.

About eight that evening I was standing by the window looking down at the street when Michelle took my hand and led me to the sofa, I sensed she had something serious to say.

'What were you thinking about over there, you looked a little lost?'

'About my sister, she starts at the Sorbonne in October. She's three years older than me, I was wondering if we would see much of her. I think the two of us have grown apart a little over the last few months, she hardly ever calls.'

'And do you call her?' I smiled, we both knew that we hardly spoke to anyone but each other. 'Josh, how long do you plan to stay? I haven't forgot what you said when we first met, friends with benefits, I'll still take that but I wondered if there was more, I hope there is more?'

'How trite that seems now. Michelle, Je t'aime.'

'Je t'aime aussi.'

And with those three words I had sealed both our fates. Our plan was simple, I would stay in Paris, at least until I went to university the following year. Then I would either go to London as planned and Michelle would come with me, or I'd switch to the Sorbonne.

I talked to my uncle the next day, he was pleased at the news and said he could keep me gainfully employed for the next year if I was interested. The money I had for travelling would not last long in Paris so I needed a job, but I didn't want to spend my days translating documents or sat in the back of a van like some multi-lingual dictionary.

'There is more interesting work I could employ you on, but it is also more dangerous. Do you think you can handle that? You won't be able to tell your father or Michelle about it.'

'I can handle that, I think.'

'Good, first thing you need to do is get your father off my back. He keeps asking me why you don't visit, I tell him you are in love, but he tells me that you must bring Michelle too. And so it goes on, he calls me about work then he's back to this. Why doesn't he call you?'

'He does but I leave my phone on *do not disturb*, then phone him back when I know he is in a meeting.'

'How do you know when he is in a meeting?'

'I am friends with his assistant Charles, I call him and chat, then I wheedle out of him papa's diary for the week on the pretence that I need a long chat with him about something or other.' For some weeks I'd actually been suspicious that the compulsion I used so forcefully on Boris and the others, was having a subtle effect on Charles, even over the phone, either that or he was having a sly tipple at work. He seemed to be tripping over himself to be helpful and, as requested, never mentioned it to my father.

'Well, this is the deal. Take Michelle to your parent's home for the weekend, I understand that Charlotte is also planning to visit. That should get me some respite from the whole family. When you come back take Michelle on holiday to Corsica for a few weeks, I need you to keep your ears open.'

'I never agreed to get Michelle involved!'

'She won't be, I want you to sit on the beach, swim in the pool and drink cocktails at sunset. If you hear anything interesting then memorise it and tell me when you get back, don't call or text me, you're on holiday. If you don't hear anything I will have something else for you to do when you get back. Yve and Pierre are prepping a job, I think they may need your gifts to carry it through though.'

We travelled by Eurostar to St Pancras and then took a black cab to Lancaster gate. Michelle had a huge case, which would have made the Tube difficult, but the car also made me feel safer. When we arrived at the house both sets of grandparents were there as well as Charlotte. Mum and dad kissed Michelle on both cheeks and smiled so wide they were in danger of splitting in two, the grandparents took possession of her then, while my mum gave me a huge hug. By this point she was already in tears and even dad looked emotional as he took his turn to crush me. As far as he was concerned, I was safe, and I wasn't sure if he would let me go back to Paris. As he released me, I saw Charlotte zero in on Michelle and take hold of both her hands, she leaned forward, and I heard her whisper to Michelle. 'You're beautiful, I hope he knows how lucky he is?' Then, before Michelle could answer, Charlotte kissed her full on the lips, Michelle blushed but she didn't seem to mind. Mum had put us in one of the grandest guest rooms, with a full bathroom, a walk-in wardrobe and a little seating area next to a window, with a chair and a chaise longue. At least Michelle would have space for all the clothes she'd packed, the contents of my backpack would fit in one of the drawers.

Dinner was sort of formal in that everyone dressed up for the occasion, I was relegated back to my old room while Charlotte conspired with Michelle about what to wear and who knows what else. Luckily, I'd left my best clothes at home when I had set off on my travels and I managed to sort myself out a decent shirt and trousers, remembering Michelle's devastating appearance at CINQ-MARS I even found a tailored jacket at the back of the wardrobe. My parents and grandparents had all gathered in the large dining room, my thoughts drifted back to that night with Kurt, not the one when I had overheard his plotting but the time before when he had called me precocious, though it was true as a finding of fact it was the tone of his voice and the linking it to brat that still offended me years later. I felt he was criticising my parents, suggesting that they had spoilt me and encouraged my precociousness. In all honesty I have been spoilt all my life, not with gifts or by over indulgence but with love from my whole family. My parents believed in experiences, not transient objects to hoard, it provided a rich backdrop to my childhood and adolescence.

My reverie was broken by the large double doors opening quickly, as though someone had given them a good shove, by the smile on her face I knew Charlotte had wantonly deployed her size eights. To be fair they really deserved to have two footmen open the doors for them, with an accompanying fanfare of trumpets. The chatter in the room ceased and we all stared open-mouthed at the two of them. They wore matching dresses, except for the colour, with more than a little irony Charlotte wore white and Michelle's dress was black. The necklines plunged in a vee almost to their navels, they must have been wearing at least four-inch heels given how tall they were, but their shoes were hidden beneath the long train of their dresses which spread out like fish-tales behind them. To add to the effect the dresses were backless, held up by little more than thin lace across the back of their necks. Their hair was piled up in curls on top of their heads showing off their long slender necks. Michelle wore a necklace of green emeralds and matching drop earrings that, despite their lustre, could not outshine her jade green eyes. Charlotte dazzled in matching diamond earrings and necklace and when the doors swung back the two of them stood there before their admirers. We all stood with mouths open until my father began to clap his hands and we all joined in. I couldn't resist, I stepped forward and took Michelle's hand raising it to my lips I kissed it gently before lowering it and taking her in my arms, kissing her deeply on the lips I held her tight to my body and then there was suddenly music, a waltz of all things, and the two of us danced to more applause. Formal dancing was one of the skills required of diplomats and their brats, Michelle was a natural and just followed my lead.

    Over the weekend it became clear that Michelle was a hit with all the family, the jewellery she had worn was, I later learned, my mothers who had been in cahoots with Charlotte in organising the whole spectacle that evening. Charlotte and Michelle hit it off particularly well, sending me out the room several times so they could "girl talk." When we left to go back to Paris, Charlotte drove us to St Pancras and when she dropped us off, she kissed me lightly on the cheeks but virtually snogged Michelle on the lips who turned bright red when she came up for air. Then Charlotte was back in the car shouting through the open window that she would see us in Paris very soon.

We had just entered the tunnel when I had to satisfy my curiosity. 'You and Charlotte seemed to get on really well?' Michelle went bright red and squeezed my hand so tightly, like she thought I might run off.

'You noticed then?'

'It would have been hard not to, my sister seemed to want to broadcast it to the whole family.'

'Do you mind?'

'Do I mind what exactly?'

'That she kissed me like that, like a lover and I did nothing to stop her.'

'Did you enjoy kissing her?'

'Oui.'

'Then I don't mind, is that all she did?' I was really enjoying watching Michelle blush, but it was getting me far more aroused than I thought it should.

'She, no I mean we put our tongues together.'

'Well, you are French and Charlotte is Gallic to the core, despite her dual citizenship. Did you want to do more?'

'Oui, am I terrible?'

'No, you are beautiful, and my sister is an irresistible force. If you feel the same when she comes to Paris, I am willing to share.' I wasn't sure why I went along with this so easily, it just felt right, I didn't want to constrain Michelle, to make her conform to some stereotypical idea of relationships. It sounded very hippy, more my grandparents' era than mine, but I wanted her to be free to live however she wanted too. As long as that included me and excluded any other males. Not so liberated after all!

***

In Corsica we had been booked into a suite at the Casa Paradisu, the pool was beautiful and Caruchettu Beach was only a kilometre away. Working for the government definitely had its perks. According to my uncle, someone they had under surveillance for the past year had stayed at the hotel six times, but only for a few days on each occasion. The man was currently in Tunisia, but the ambassador was convinced there was something going on at the Hotel or at least nearby.

Michelle and I had a lovely time at the ambassador's expense, in the morning we walked along the beach before it got too hot and, in the afternoon, we lay on the sun beds under parasols by the pool, which never had more than a dozen people in and around it. I swam endless laps while Michelle read her book. All the time I listened, but apart from an odd conversation in Danish about hidden rubies that didn't seem to make any sense, between two very pale men, there was nothing of consequence, if you could even call it that. A few days before we left, I saw the two Danish guys at the bar, the taller one called the other man Axel, but I didn't get the lanky guy's name. We were eating dinner in the restaurant, and after five minutes the two men were seated by the waiter a few tables away from us. They seemed rather over dressed in navy blazers, cream chinos and brown leather brogues. I was half watching them when one got up and walked over to another table where two women in their forties sat, he said in rather poor Italian, 'Welcome to paradise, rubies are my favourite stone.' The two women said nothing they just nodded their heads and smiled, and he turned to go back to his table. It was then that I noticed he had a small ruby lapel stud in the shape of a fleur-de-lis on his blazer collar. Instinctively I looked back at the two women, now properly taking in what I had given little consideration to before. Both wore identical silver chains with ruby stones, enclosed in silver or white gold, in the shape of a fleur-de-lis. I did not want to give them even the merest suspicion that I had noticed anything unusual, I could not risk putting Michelle in the slightest danger, so I resisted the urge to look at the two men or even to listen to their conversation. I chatted to Michelle, and we ordered another bottle of wine, I drank slowly and half of it remained when the two men got up to leave. It was then I noticed that the man who had remained seated also wore the same ruby lapel stud as his friend.

In the remaining two days of our holiday, I saw a couple in their early thirties who seemed to be trying to convince everyone they were in love, but it all felt false. The women had the same ruby necklace on as the two women from dinner the previous night. The man wore a button-down shirt with the collar buttons unfastened and a lapel stud in one of them. I really wasn't sure if I had stumbled on some nefarious conspiracy or the island's swingers club. In Paris, I reported back to my uncle, he was intrigued but not at all enthusiastic and clearly did not know what to make of it but said he would have someone look into it, just in case.

**

When we returned to Paris my uncle kept his promise and teamed me up with Yve and Pierre, they were heading up one of a number of units watching a group of seven people they suspected of being a terrorist cell and in the process of organising an attack on a target yet to be identified, by means yet to be uncovered. In other words, they knew next to nothing. Part of the problem was that the group seemed to suspect they were being watched or were just extremely paranoid, the other issue was that the members were from four different nationalities and they all spoke another language apart from their native tongue and French. Yve and Pierre only spoke French and English, there were some Arabic speakers in the other two teams, but they were all struggling to understand what was being said when members of the group were in public spaces. Given the group's paranoia or awareness, they could not get close enough to bug and record their meetings, which took place in a small warehouse in a ghetto in the 19th arrondissement.

I was not about to go anywhere near the 19th, I would stick out like a sore thumb and likely as not get all my digits and a few other bits cut off if I found myself more than ten metres from Pierre and Yve. In fact, any new face in that area would be noticed immediately and inevitably result in some kind of hostile confrontation. I thought I had a solution, I was wary it would expose my *special gift,* but I just couldn't see any other option.

'Pierre, do any of them drink or eat alone outside of the 19th?'

'The man we think is the leader's lieutenant has a girlfriend in the 11th he often has coffee or lunch at a restaurant near the hairdressers where she works before he picks her up. What are you thinking Josh? You have that odd look that tells me that whatever it is I am not going to like it.'

'Can you get a bugging device with a decent range, a kilometre at least, that he could easily hide in a pocket?'

'No, but he has a small rucksack he carries everywhere, we have something that would fit in that easily and has a range of about a kilometre or further if it's connected to the Wi-Fi.'

'What about a small tracking device, like an AirTag, so we know where he is without having to get too close to him?'

'Oui, that's easy and we can do a little better than Apple on that one.'

'Okay, you get me the gear and talk me through how it works, then get us to the café the next time he shows up. Can you do that?'

'Sure, but how are you going to sneak the device into his bag? Even if you managed it he would notice the weight, it's over half a kilo?'

'Let me worry about that.'

'It's crazy!'

'Have you got a better idea?'

'I don't even know what your idea is, apart from getting yourself killed! We told you that they all carry weapons and, forgive me Josh, but you don't have what it takes to deal with these guys.'

'I have other skills and you're just going to have to trust me.' I put a little bit of influence in my voice, just enough to make him less stubborn.'

'Okay, I will be inside and Yve will be outside in the car.'

'You can't be inside, he will spot you a mile away.'

'But he has never seen me before?'

'Pierre, you scream secret service. If this guy is their second-in-command his hackles will rise as soon as he spots you and he will be out the door.'

'Ok, Yve can go inside, I will stay in the car.'

'Sorry but no, you can both stay in the car. I will take one of those personal alarms, if I feel any threat at all I will set it off.' Again, I used a little bit of influence to make him more receptive.

'I don't like it but you're right I don't have anything else to offer, do you still have the knife I gave you?'

'Yes, it's in my boot.'

Pierre reached into his pocket and pulled out another knife, the blade was longer than the one I had but the handle was just a flat bar going across to make the shape of a letter T, it was held in a thin sheath with a few straps attached to it. The contraption was secured with Velcro to my forearm and was easily hidden under my jacket sleeve, which was linen and quite baggy. It would take barely a second to drag it out and plunge it into soft, yielding flesh. I was getting seriously worried about some of the intrusive thoughts I was having lately but had no time for an inquest on my morals or apparent lack of conscience.

Two days later we parked the car about fifty metres down the road from the café at noon, thirty minutes later we watched our target, Henri, enter the café. He seemed very relaxed and did not even bother to check the road before he went inside. The girlfriend worked only until one-thirty on a Wednesday, I waited ten minutes then got out the car, reaching back in to grab an exact copy of Henri's rucksack, Pierre reached over and held my hand gently.

'Josh, are you sure about this?'

'Oui.' And then I was on my way before I changed my mind. Inside the café Henri sat at a small table by the window, the single chair opposite him empty. There were just two other customers sat talking quietly on the other side of the room. They seemed to be doing their best not to look in Henri's direction. I sat down at the table next to him, he looked me over suspiciously as I picked up the menu, then the waitress appeared and nervously took my order. There really was something about this man that spooked people, but despite him being quite a bit older than me, I thought of him as a child, and I was hopefully about to make him as helpless and compliant as only a small boy can be.

As planned, I'd left my watch in the car, but now was the time. I turned to Henri, and leaned over realising I was literally putting my neck on the line.

'Excusez-moi, quelle heure est-il s'il vous plaît?' At first, he seemed stunned that I had dared to speak to him, I then saw him sliding his right hand inside his jacket. He didn't take the gun out, but I knew he was nursing it, watching me, deciding whether I was a threat, whether he needed to take me out. He didn't answer me, he just stared, and I knew he was waiting for me to back off or make a move. Instead, I lowered my voice, I felt something change, I could see his eyes start to glaze over and his shoulders slouch. It was working, I glanced around the room but no one else seemed to notice or if they did, they were staying out of it.

'Henri', he trembled slightly as I said his name. 'There is something you must do for me, do you understand?'

'What do you want me to do?'

'What do you have in your bag?'

'A book and an extra gun.'

'Henri, I want you to take my bag and put your book in it but leave the gun and your bag behind.' Slowly, I explained about the device in my bag and how he was to conceal it in the room where their meetings took place and connect it to the Wi-Fi in the building. I handed over the small disc that Pierre had given me and told him to keep the tracker on him but hidden at all times, then I got him to text his girlfriend and tell her he couldn't make it after all before sending him on his way back to the nineteenth. I watched him leave the café and then walk past the window I was facing, heading toward the Metro.

Back in the car Yve and Pierre just looked at me. I was about to tell them that Henri had *agreed* to plant the device when I started to feel sick, I flung the door open and threw up in the road. Immediately feeling better, I closed the door before the smell set me off again. Yve handed me a bottle of water and I rinsed my mouth before spitting it out the window. Surprisingly they both waited silently.

'Please drive, I'll tell you as we go.' The thing was that I didn't really know what to tell them, I didn't want to tell them anything. I waited silently, breathing slowly, trying to stop my hands shaking. Then finally, I handed Yve Henri's bag, I am sure they both thought it was mine and that I had failed. Yve looked inside anyway, and I saw her go pale then smile broadly when she saw the gun. Then she leaned over the front seat and kissed me on both cheeks and then on my lips, which was a bit embarrassing after just puking. She turned back to Pierre, 'Il l'a fait, putain il l'a fait.' Then she looked at me, I could see her surprise I could also see lust. 'Josh, if you weren't so in love I'd suck your cock right this minute.' We all went quiet for three or four seconds, I wasn't sure she meant to say that out loud but it certainly broke the tension. Pierre started to laugh, Yve began to giggle and suddenly we were all in hysterics.

Eventually, I told them a censored version of what happened, explaining to them that I had sort of hypnotised Henri, and that they shouldn't get their hopes up, that he might forget the whole thing by the time he gets back.

The ambassador was in London, but Pierre brought him up to speed over a secure video link while Yve and I sat behind him. I was determined to avoid eye contact with uncle Philippe, if at all possible. I could still see he was sceptical about my *explanation* and though he tried not to show it, he was angry with Pierre for allowing me to get so involved. But as the conversation drew to an end I realised why, given our success, he was still so concerned. He looked over Pierre's shoulder at me, his eyes penetrating even through the video link. I was about to try and slide down my chair out of sight, when he turned his gaze back to Pierre.

'Pierre, if this fails, we can't have Henri looking for Josh. I am sorry but you will have to take care of him, possibly all of them.'

'Oui ambassador, I knew the risks and I have options ready should they be needed.'

'Thank you, Pierre. Josh, a word please.' I reluctantly swopped places with Pierre, who to my surprise stood behind me with a hand on my right shoulder, his grip was quite reassuring as I looked the ambassador in the eye.

'Josh, it is too dangerous for you or Michelle to stay at the apartment until this is all sorted. We have a safe house a few minutes from the ministry, it is bug, bullet and bomb proof, Pierre or Yve will protect you, no one else is to enter not even if you recognise them as one of our own. Is that clear?' I just nodded my agreement. 'Unfortunately that means you will have to tell Michelle at least some of the truth about what you do, I don't think a burst pipe will cut it this time.'

I had expected a *telling-off,* so I was quite relieved, more so because for some time now I knew I had to tell Michelle what I was really doing. She needed to know the risks when she could so easily get caught up in my little game of spies. An hour later, I was sat next to Michelle in the safe house explaining what I did. Out of the four of us I was the only one that had any doubts that Michelle would buy into all this, but of course she did, we were in love. Though the bit about being able to hypnotise people freaked her out a little, especially when I told her about the man in the alley who tried to rob me.

'Josh, are you saying you can make anyone do anything you want?'

'I am not sure what the limits are, but it definitely doesn't work on everyone. When I was twelve and Charlotte was fifteen we were play fighting, she was taller and stronger than me then and she managed to pin me face down on the floor with her knee in my back and her hands pressing on the nape of my neck. I was struggling to breathe, and she was just laughing her head off. I started to get angry, and I ordered her to stop and get off me, it didn't work not even for a second she just laughed some more and said, "your Boris voice doesn't work on me, little brother" thankfully she realised then, that she was hurting me and she let go. Also, when I was fourteen or fifteen, I used to have regular strops and shout at my parents over some minor restriction they placed on me, sometimes that escalated into *the voice*, but it never worked on them. I don't think it would work on my grandparents either, though I haven't tried it, and I don't think I could hypnotise you, I don't think it works on the people I truly love.'

'Josh, you mesmerised me that very first day in the café.'

We made love, having decided it was our solemn duty to test out the new bed. At eight we got dressed and waited for Pierre and Yve to return as planned. We were both sitting silently on the sofa holding hands, watching the computer screen that monitored the external and internal security door when Michelle started to giggle. I had no idea what had set her off and it took a full minute before she was able to speak.

'Did Yve really say she'd suck your cock?'

Before I could answer she started to giggle again, but that stopped abruptly when the buzzer on the solid steel outer door sounded. We looked at the screen, Yve and Pierre were on the doorstep looking up at the camera, behind them was a standard ministry black surveillance van. As instructed, I panned the camera from left to right to make sure no one else was there, before releasing the door. Once inside Pierre and Yve closed the door, the multiple bolts and locks audibly clicking into place, they stayed at the bottom of the stairs for a few seconds and then each put their right hand on top of their head. This was the signal that all was well, that security was not compromised in anyway. When they got to the top of the stairs, I checked back down to the outer door again before releasing the inner one.

This was the first time the four of us had met since the big reveal about what I was actually doing for uncle Philippe and surprisingly Michelle made the first move. Stepping toward Pierre she stood up on her toes and kissed him on either cheek before giving him a huge hug, then she stood in front of Yve and from the side I could see her smiling widely, 'You' Michelle said, 'are naughty, I like that.' Then she kissed and hugged Yve. 'Keep him safe, promise?' Pierre just nodded, Yve still seemed a little stunned or puzzled at being called naughty but eventually managed to answer Michelle, if rather melodramatically. 'I would take a bullet for him.' Michelle gave her that wide smile again before whispering to Yve, Pierre couldn't hear her, but I could. 'In that case, when this is all over, I might just let you suck his cock as long as I can watch.' Yve went absolutely beetroot but somehow managed to smile back and whisper to Michelle, 'I will hold you to that.'

In the van Yve looked at me before shaking her head and turning away, but I saw the smile lingering on her face. Already in position on the hard metal benches of the vehicle were five heavily armed and armoured men, they were our back up. Even though this was purely a bugging operation and well away from any danger, my uncle had insisted on the extra protection. They made me put on body armour and a Kevlar helmet before the van started off. This was it, I was nervous but also excited, I wanted to see if my crazy idea would work, if I could really pull this off. Henri had told me the meeting would start at nine, that their leader whose name was a secret even from Henri would be there tonight to tell them the plan. Just before nine we heard a door opening and the sound of people shuffling in and chairs scraping across the floor. We were recording, but I still memorised everything that was said, the leader spoke in Spanish, I could tell it was not his first language, but it seemed the common currency for the group. There was to be five coordinated explosions on Metro stations and trains at 08.00 the following Wednesday. It seemed there were four other cells around the city, the leader gave no clue as to the identity or location of the other groups and I was beginning to worry we would not be able to stop them. But our luck was in, the devices would be moved from Lille to a warehouse in the 11th in two days time, each of the lieutenants would collect their bomb at a set time over the weekend to avoid any contact with each other. That would give them three days to get ready, if they were discovered they were to set the explosives off and kill themselves and as many others as possible. They would also be given VX gas, which Pierre told me was a deadly nerve agent that would ensure many more people would die, hundreds, perhaps thousands.

When the leader finished, I realised I had been translating this out loud in the van and the marines now looked pale despite the camouflage paint they had smeared across their faces, Yve and Pierre in contrast looked bizarrely pleased. This of course was their chance, to not only stop a deadly attack that would close the whole of Paris down, putting nine-eleven in the shade, but also round up a whole terrorist network. The next day Pierre set up observation on the warehouse in the eleventh but he had something of a dilemma, to locate the terrorist cells he would have to track the leaders back from the warehouse but that would mean they would have both bombs and gas in their possession whilst traveling across Paris.

Pierre and the ambassador agreed that this was too big a risk, that they needed men inside the warehouse to capture each cell lieutenant as he arrived. On Friday morning the operation widened when Henri's tracker showed him heading out of the 19th and then turning up at the Gare Du Nord before heading north at high speed for three miles until he was out of range. It was clear that he had got the 7.46 TGV direct to Lille, CCTV picked him up buying his ticket and again on the platform as he entered the carriage, Henri must have been chosen to bring the explosives and gas in to Paris. It looked like the girlfriend had been more of a cover than a lover for Henri's visits to the warehouse to set it up as the groups' rendezvous. Pierre was beside himself with joy at the golden opportunity that had just landed in our laps. He contacted agents in Lille and sent them a photo of Henri, by the time the train arrived an hour or so later they were waiting for him, they had the frequency of the tracker and followed him at a discrete distance to the Parc du Lion, an industrial estate north of Lille next to the A22 motorway to Ghent. Outside a small warehouse he was met by a man, described as being somewhere between thirty and fifty, very helpful indeed, but they did get photographs. The two men went through a steel door next to a roller style garage shutter, tall enough to get a big HGV through. An hour later the shutter raised noisily, and Henri drove out in a white Citroen van followed by the other man in a large black Mercedes saloon. Henri took the A1 toward Paris, while the Mercedes headed along the A22 toward Belgium. The Lille agents split up and one car followed the mystery man toward the border and the other one tailed Henri as he headed back to us, two of Pierre's men took over when he got to the city limits. At the warehouse in the 11th, Pierre, Yve and a team of six marines in full HAZMAT suits waited. I'd suggested I should be there to *talk* to Henri, to make sure he didn't try and set off any of the devices. Pierre said NON! While my uncle wanted us to go to London and as far away from any danger as he could get us, he was getting as protective as mon père. Michelle and I compromised and agreed to stay at the safe house. I knew I could help with questioning the leaders of the terrorist cells once they were captured, and any delay would likely result in the groups taking flight.

Surrounded by automatic weapons, Henri went quietly, and a team of specialist came in to dismantle the bombs and take away the VX gas. By lunchtime Saturday Pierre had two out of the four lieutenants locked up, but they were not talking, and no one had even managed to trace where they lived. We were also holding Henri's girlfriend and while she told us everything she knew it was, as we suspected, just a cover story spun to her by Henri.

It reminded me of my own dishonourable intentions when I first met Michelle and, not for the first or last time, I questioned the selfless and selfish ambivalence of love and my own morality.

I telephoned my uncle, he was still in London, but he took my call, I pleaded with him to let me help interrogate the prisoners before the others fled. He said he would discuss it with Pierre. Twenty minutes later Pierre collected me from the flat, apparently, they had captured the other two as well, but it was obvious that they were not going to say anything either. Pierre led me into a dark room barely illuminated by the lights coming through from the two-way mirror that showed a man sat in just his pants, his mouth bloody and his right eye swollen and closed. His wrists were handcuffed and chained to the desk, which was bolted to the floor, he also had manacles around his ankles that had been locked to the ground. It seemed we were taking no chances, not that I was complaining.

'Do we know his name?'

'Nothing at all. He swears a lot and screams very loudly when we hit him.'

'You're not going to like this Pierre, but I need ten minutes with the recorders off, sound and video, and this room empty.'

I was right, he didn't like it and neither did Yve, but in the end they agreed, because they had to. They had nothing else left to try and time was most definitely running out. It took just five minutes with the first one to get the names and addresses of the members of the group, as well as where they met, and the places they hid their money and guns. I had not seen the picture of the man at Lille, but I asked some questions, as expected, they had no idea who he was, but they all gave me similar descriptions. In less than half an hour we had everything we needed and by midnight we had them all safely locked up.

I should have been ecstatic, but the descriptions given by the men of their leader sounded a little familiar, I found Pierre and asked him about the picture.

'I've not had a chance to download it from the secure server yet. Why?'

'I've got a bad feeling, I think we need to see what this guy looks like as soon as.'

The picture confirmed what I feared, the mystery thirty to fifty tear-old man was actually nearer sixty, it was Kurt Stein. It only got worse after that, with our agents reduced to one car, Kurt had spotted them and given them the slip in traffic going through Ghent.

That night I held Michelle tightly in bed, not letting go until the sun started to rise, I had not slept but I wasn't tired. There was something about Kurt, that really got under my skin to a degree that no one else had ever done. In his own way he had more control over people than I ever could. He persuaded them to believe, to be willing to die for an idea he didn't even believe in himself, he was content to make a profit from the misery and destruction he inspired. He was a puppet master, pulling the strings of fanaticism to get what he wanted.

My uncle was less concerned by Kurt's reappearance and wrote it off as just one more example of Russian incompetence. The ambassador, as I was beginning to realise, had a lot of balls he juggled with on a day-to-day basis and right now a whole load of them were up in the air and likely to come down with a crash. He relied on Pierre to watch his back and on my father to take care of the front-of-house details. One day he explained to me that my father was the real ambassador, the true diplomat who could deal with the delegations and the detail of agreeing and maintaining treaties, while he played soldiers. Uncle Philippe explained that my father could have taken the top spot at a host of embassies around the world over the last decade and had declined a number of direct propositions. He said, he had even offered to step down himself if my father wanted to stay in London. But it seemed my father preferred the details and intricacies, rather than the pomp and ceremony, and was happy to sit in my uncle's shadow.

After a few weeks, when Pierre was sure they had got everyone, and Kurt was out the picture for a while at least, we moved back into the apartment. With the excitement over, Pierre and Yve were restless, and I was back doing document translations but secretly quite grateful for the boredom for a short while at least. It was mid-October when

Charlotte rang our bell, she was lucky we had the camera installed or I would not have even considered opening the door. There was still a noticeable frisson between Michelle and Charlotte, but neither of them seemed quite ready to act on it. I decided to leave them to work it out themselves, I had given them the green light, but I wasn't about to start directing the traffic.

The next day at work the ambassador called me to his office, inside Pierre and Yve were already sat on one of the two plush red velvet sofas that always seemed quite out of place to me, but I sat on the other one anyway and turned toward the ambassador who remained at his desk one eye on his laptop.

'Josh, do you remember that little break you took in Corsica in August?'

'The ruby club?' The ambassador chuckled which surprised me, I hadn't realised he deigned to indulge in such banal forms of expression. Yve and Pierre were as clearly perplexed by the ambassador's sudden amusement as by the mention of the ruby club. The three of us waited while he deliberately drew out a long pause and tapped the fingers of one hand against those of the other hand.

'I'd heard one or two rumours of something brewing in Corsica and I asked Josh to do a bit of eavesdropping whilst enjoying a little holiday in the sun. Josh didn't hear anything of real concern, but he did notice several guests, two in particular, who behaved a little oddly and who despite at first glance having nothing in common with some fellow guests rather went out of their way to introduce themselves. Josh, I've got that right haven't I, it was not a casual hello but more like something from the 18th century, a formal introduction to someone of a similar rank in society?'

'Yes, that's a very good way of describing it. It was almost Austenesque, if it wasn't for the ruby fleur-de-lis jewellery I think I would have just ignored it.'

'Fleur-de-lis?' Questioned Yve.

'Yes, when Josh told me I had a few things on my mind and I almost ignored it altogether, but I trust Josh's instinct even though he is *full-young*.'

I could see the ambassador was enjoying this, I picked up on the Pride and Prejudice quote straight away and smiled, but the other two were lost. The ambassador took pity on them and cast aside any further literary references.

'Anyway, I asked one of the geeks to spend some time on it. She tracked down the CCTV footage for the two weeks Josh was there, and quickly spotted the lapel pins on the men and the necklaces or broaches on the women. Having identified them she started to track them around Europe, Asia and South America, mainly. These people, eleven in total, kept turning up at the same hotels within a day or two of each other. On the surface they all seemed to be investing in property, all of it off plan, much of it not even under construction. The type of property varied depending on the country, from beachfront condos in the Caribbean to student apartment blocks in the north of England. It's obviously a front for laundering money, probably drugs, possibly weapons. Normally I would hand this over to Interpol or local law enforcement, but there is one peculiarity I want to check on first. You see, we tried bugging them but nothing worked, they are clearly using something to block even our most advanced tech, which is a concern in itself and way beyond your average drug runner and money launderer's capability.'

When the ambassador paused Pierre asked the obvious question. 'But what do you want us to do?' Yve could not resist a quick jibe at Pierre's expense, 'You mean there is no one you can shoot?' I smiled but forced down the laugh, the ambassador was clearly no longer in the mood for humour. I could see his foot flexing up and down against the wooden floor, I'd watched him do this many times before when something was niggling him. He paused for a few seconds, staring at each of us in turn to ensure we knew this was not the time for jokes.

'You three have been sailing too close to the wind of late.' I noticed his gaze lingering on me in particular, before he continued, and wondered if my father had been talking to him again. 'There's to be no engagement or contact of any kind this time. You will be working with Rachel Kent, who has been tracking them and knows the detail of every stop they've made and every Euro they've invested or for that matter what they ordered from room service, what it cost and how they paid.'

'Are they in France now?' I asked.

'Rachel, has confirmed that some of the characters you spotted in Corsica are currently scheduled to arrive in Paris tomorrow and the day after. They are all booked into the Four Seasons on avenue George V for five nights.'

Yve was impressed by the hotel, 'Très chic!' I was more in awe of Rachel's IT skills and glad Michelle, and I didn't go overboard on room service while we were in Corsica.

'There is a suite booked to act as your operational base, Rachel is already installing her gear in the room so she can follow their electronic transactions in case that gives us any leads. Josh, you need to arm yourself with a few books and spend as much time as you can in the public areas, close but not too close. Yve, you watch Josh's back, Pierre, park yourself in a café in sight of the exit, follow anyone of them that leaves the hotel, pick a strong team to make sure you can track them all, if you need to. Rachel will also be watching them on the hotel and city CCTV wherever she can. Josh, an earpiece will be too obvious, Rachel will text you anything useful, but the phones may be compromised given their technical expertise, so she has improvised a simple code. The three of you are to go to the hotel when we finish here, Rachel will explain the code and you can introduce yourselves.'

Pierre was grumpy about the prospect of working with someone new and worst still a nerd, as he called her. Yve enjoyed winding him up en-route and I kept quiet in the back of the car. In the hotel room though, I nearly lost it and almost erupted into laughter at the sight of Pierre's face. He was clearly expecting some short, skinny, mousy be-speckled girl or whatever his "geek" stereotype prejudice conjured up. When we entered the room, Rachel stood up from her laptop and I saw Pierre's jaw drop, she was dressed in buttock hugging spandex shorts and a sports bra, her hair was short, very short and her legs were long, very long. It was obvious she worked out a lot and between her bra and shorts, was the hardest six-pack I had ever seen, apart from Pierre's. I could see Yve was also impressed, but she just burst out laughing and it took her a few seconds before she could speak.

'Excuse moi je suis désolé, Rachel. Pierre, has been moaning since we left the ministry that we would have to look after someone else, no offence Josh. Pierre was definitely not expecting a beautiful Amazonian goddess who could probably kick his ass as well as outsmart him.'

Pierre went bright red, and Rachel smiled at him, clearly not offended. She shook his hand and kissed him on both cheeks and then did the same to me, but Yve she enveloped in her arms squeezing her tight before releasing her and kissing her loudly on each cheek. It was part joke and part dare, I was content to let the three of them work it out. It was six o'clock and I was missing Michelle like I hadn't seen her in a month. Luckily it didn't take long for Rachel to get us up to speed on the latest info she had on their movements, apparently, they were still booked on their flights and their rooms were paid for. There was something that had been puzzling me since the meeting with the ambassador though and I thought Rachel would know the answer.

'I understand that there are eleven of them in total?'

'Oui. Is there something wrong?'

'Non… well I'm not really sure. They seem to travel in pairs, but there is an odd one. I assume they always travel in the same pairs?'

'Always the same. Shared hotel suites, same limousine from the airport and adjoining seats on the plane, first class of course.'

'And the odd man out?'

'Woman actually.'

'Pardon.'

'She has a different pattern. Doesn't travel first class, gets a taxi from the airport and arrives at least a day later than anyone else. Doesn't always stay in the same hotel either.'

'Any ideas why not?'

'I was actually thinking about that before you arrived and decided to review the data. I'm not sure, but I think she stays in the same hotel if it's a large one in a major city. In Corsica and some other places, the hotels have been more resorts, largely self-contained, people stay for longer, they're on holiday they say hello, you get noticed. In Corsica, she stayed in a place used by businessmen, down the coast and a little inland from where Josh stayed. She has just booked in to one of the smaller rooms here, arriving the day after tomorrow.'

'You say "she" do we have a name?'

'Three so far! A different pattern again, the others keep the same identity, hiding in plain sight as it were. Not sure what it tells us.'

Pierre knew where I was going with this and spoke before I could. 'It means she's the boss, at least as far as this little team is concerned. We need to pay her extra attention, but she will be the most wary so it may be difficult. I don't get it, why do the others travel together? It's sloppy.'

Rachel put a hand on Pierre's lower arm. He had been pacing up and down for a few minutes and getting increasingly agitated, I watched as she tugged on his sleeve and the big guy sat down next to her as she spoke.

'I have a theory about them "twinning". You know we haven't been able to bug them, it's obvious they have some personal blocking device, even our directional long-distance mics can't pick up their conversations, all we have so far is what you heard in Corsica. Whatever they are using, has to be a prototype, which means they haven't miniaturised it yet, like anything electronic it starts big then gets smaller and smaller. I think the men are wearing something under their jackets, none of the pictures I have show them without their vestes on, and their sleeves are too long.'

Pierre was struggling, if a suspect took this long to tell him what he wanted to know he'd have shot him in the knee and stood on it until he got an answer. Rachel just put her hand back on his arm and waited as he calmed, and she let him ask the question she knew he needed to ask, no matter how simple it was.

'Their sleeves are too long, I don't understand?'

'Their jackets are expensive, individually tailored but at least a size too big, they are hiding something underneath.'

'What about the women?'

'They all carry the same large tote bags regardless of whether it goes with their outfits.'

Pierre was still baffled. 'Why don't the men carry briefcases?' Yve was desperate to move things on and jumped in. 'Ever see a woman without her handbag on her lap or at least by her feet. Men put their cases or bags in the overhead locker and annoy everyone by getting up and down when they want something. But how do they get through airport security?'

'I haven't figured that out, it's just an idea at this stage.'

At last Pierre seemed satisfied and Rachel could finish relaying her theory. 'I think the device, whatever it is, requires a positive and a negative, just like a battery and the needs to be some distance between the two to create a kind of electronic bubble and each pair then effectively sits inside it, protected from any kind of surveillance equipment we have. Except of course for Josh's big ears.'

We all laughed at that, which brought the tension in the room down a notch or two, just as well as Rachel was now going to explain how the code we would use worked.

'It's simple, we take the words of two pop songs so they're easy to remember but if you're struggling download the lyrics on your phone. I will text you short messages consisting of numbers only, the numbers will correspond with a letter in the song. So, number one might be letter J in the first song and letter D in the second song. The first number of any message will start with either a 1 for the first song or a 2 for the second, followed by the message.'

I thought Pierre was going to have a melt down and Yve looked like she might weep, I decided to take pity on them and make it a bit easier for them to get their heads around.

'Rachel, can I borrow your laptop please?'
'Sure Josh.'

She handed over the machine and I quickly used a blank table to create a grid with the letters from the songs and the numbers underneath before sending it to them. Suddenly it was as simple as Karaoke to the two of them and I could hear them humming the tune under their breath.

***

The next morning I arrived at the hotel at 10 to check in with Rachel and Yve, who had stayed in the suite overnight. They were still in their PJs finishing off breakfast, I managed to squeeze a coffee out of the pot and snagged the last croissant much to Yve's disgust. 'Any updates or changes?'

'Angela Coleman and Maria Townsend, the two from Corsica, are due to land from the States any time now and should be here about lunch time. The two Danes, Otto Anders and Axel Bille are due at the hotel about four today. The odd couple you also spotted in Corsica, Johan Desmet and Marlene Mertens are Belgium, they are booked on a train from Barcelona arriving at the Gare de Lyon at 21.18. I still have nothing on the two Basques, Akil Martinez and Jean Garat, or the Italians, Mancini and Morelli.'

'That's good, more people means more chat, I'll go down and find a nice spot to set up camp for the day. Let me know if any of the other four ping on your radar please.' As I went to stand Yve put her hand on my shoulder and pushed me back down on the sofa. 'I don't think so', she said, 'my job is to watch your beautiful tight ass and that starts now, just give me fifteen minutes to shower and then we can go down together. Well, I will obviously have to hang back a bit, don't want anyone to think we're actually together.' I noticed Yve's cheeks redden the second she said the word "together", Rachel had clearly spotted it too and was smiling, obviously enjoying herself.

'I noticed you didn't download the song lyrics or send yourself the table you created for Yve and Pierre, do you have an eidetic memory?'

'Photographic would be a better description, though I remember text and numbers better than images. I don't actually have to read or see them, in fact I am better when I hear them, is audio-graphic a word? Anyway, I had already heard both songs a few days ago in the car so I was almost there already. The fact there was a melody as well made it quite easy to recall.'

'Wow, that's amazing!'

'I thought the same when I saw the information you managed to gather on our lame jury.'

'Lame jury, pardon?'

'Eleven instead of twelve.' I could see she didn't really get it, the French system is a little different than the English though, but there was something else I wanted to understand. 'Given you can't listen in or track them electronically how have you managed to get so much information on them?'

'Follow the money, follow the money! You gave me a starting point, from the hotel I could get passport and credit card details, luckily the CCTV in hotels tends to be dated, electromechanical rather than electronic so they are unaffected by whatever their using to stop us listening in. It will be interesting to see what happens at this hotel as their cameras are cloud based.'

Yve appeared just then, and we went down the stairs rather than use the lift, as promised she stayed a few metres behind me loudly licking her lips as we descended. But when we went through the door into the reception area it was all business and Yve seemed to just fade into the background. I set myself up in a high winged back chair, which I moved so a large stone column was behind me, just as Yve had instructed me to do on the way down. Apparently watching my back as opposed to my ass meant she sat about ten meters in front of me just off to the left, another column guarded her back and from where she sat, she could see over my shoulder and behind me, as well as the entrance and reception and with a little glance to the left she could also do a quick sweep of the bar. There was a large man sat at the bar nursing a very small coffee, I would have been concerned but I recognised him as one of the marines from the back of the Range Rover when Yve first came to my rescue. I'd bought a French and a German newspaper on the way to the hotel, I'd only heard them speak in Italian so far and thought the German paper might make them more at ease, if they assumed I couldn't understand them. If it proved really dull the French newspaper would help pass the time, I also had a copy of Sartre's Being and Nothingness, it was my favourite book and I hoped that if anyone noticed it they would think I was a student meeting with his rich father for lunch. It was a scenario I was familiar with at least and it gave me a little boost of confidence.

The two women checked in at 12.30, I couldn't see them, but I recognised their voices and poor accents, they were speaking in stilted Italian. They decided to take coffee in the lounge rather than go straight to their suite. They turned down the proffered table in the centre of the room and went to the opposite side to me and as far away from anyone else as possible. Just as they sat down I received a coded message from Rachel, as she suspected the cameras went down as soon as they got within a metre of them, but she'd picked them up on one of the CCTVs outside and their card details swiped by the hotel, to cover any expenses they ran up during their stay, confirmed their arrival. Familiar with their voices I latched onto their conversation immediately, unfortunately they said little of consequence apart from confirming that they knew number eleven or as they called her Signora Bianchi, which was one of the three names Rachel had already identified. There was deference and more than a little fear in their voices when they mentioned her name, it seemed our theory that Bianchi was pulling the strings was holding up. I texted an update to the other three, when Yve finally worked out what the message said she looked up at me, she was clearly surprised and puzzled. I realised I'd let something else slip, this was the first time she had made eye contact with me since we took our positions. Yve could see the distance between the two women and me, she knew it wasn't humanly possible for me to hear them talking. Yve looked away to the bar and our friend, still with the same espresso, and then did a visual sweep of the room, she had her back to the two women, and I realised the guy at the bar was actually there to keep her safe, not me. I was definitely warming toward Pierre, I liked the way he made sure we were all protected.

    Maria, who looked the slightly older of the two women, asked a passing waiter to bring them a menu to look at before they went into dine. After a few minutes studying what was on offer, the other woman, Angela, ordered a bottle of Pinot Grigio to be opened at the table, then they both started to get their things together. Again, I thought it best to get there first and was already seated and hidden behind the menu by the time the waiter showed them to a table. They declined his offer of one near the window, which was where I sat, and asked for a table at the opposite end, in the shadows. The waiter smiled widely but I could see he was not happy, the tables at the back had not been set and he had to lay one especially for them, before pouring their wine. They gave him their order and then waited for him to leave, when he went through the door to the kitchen, they looked at each other and nodded. They had chosen a table with four chairs and rested their bags on the spare seats, they opened them shielding whatever was inside with their bodies, after a few seconds they turned back to each other and Maria uttered a single word, 'sicuro?' and Angela's reply was almost as brief, 'si sicura.' Presumably they were checking that the anti-surveillance equipment was working, Maria used the male version of "safe" while Angela used the female form. Perhaps it was just the way they thought about the devices they carried everywhere, or it might support Rachel's theory about their being a circuit, positive and negative, female and male.

Maria looked around her, the restaurant was not busy, and she carefully perused the occupants of every table, before she spoke. I might have been a tad paranoid, but I thought she watched me for a little longer than anyone else. Seemingly satisfied that no one was close enough to hear them, she turned to Angela and spoke in a whisper. The poor Italian accent had gone, the two women were American, nothing fake about their accents now, they were pure New Yorkers, the pair of them. I was on the other side of the room, but I could hear them as if I was sitting at their table. Angela asked Maria a question.

'I presume Johan and Marlene are bringing the rest of the password so we can transfer the Crypto?'

'We have half of it. They have only a quarter and are traveling on the TGV from Barcelona, it seems they had a little trouble in Bruges and have had to change their domestic arrangements. They're arriving tonight, they should be here by ten depending on the traffic. Otto and Axel have the other quarter, their flight lands in a couple of hours, so they should get here about four.'

'What are the real Italians doing then?'

'Mancini and Morelli are not invited, it seems.'

'They won't like that, even if they are just a couple of Mafiosi hit men, and Bianchi has the account numbers and secure laptop?'

'Yeah, she aint goin to let us get our hands on that?'

'Will there be enough guap?'

'With the Crypto and the cash reserves we can start a run on the dollar, Akil and Jean are off somewhere trying to make it look like the French and Spanish are working together against the States.'

'Is that necessary?'

'Not really, but they're Basques, if they can't bomb their way to independence, they can at least have some fun with the French and Spanish governments while they get rich.'

It wasn't original, destabilise a currency, wait for the big drop then cash in. I knew there had to be more to it, there had to be something else, a political upheaval, a natural disaster or a man made one like nine-eleven given that the forces of nature were beyond us all, thankfully. It was obvious that little detail was above the *twins* pay grade, I doubt even Signora Bianchi knew everything, in fact I was sure she didn't, someone was giving her orders just as she was controlling her little group of ten. That was another puzzle, we had nine in play, if you include Akil and Jean's little aside, so what were the other two up to, or were they just sitting this one out? I didn't really buy the idea of the two Basques making a bit of mischief to entertain themselves either, bullets and bombs were the only technology they knew.

Bianchi's job was to coordinate the group and pull the trigger when the time was right but something else, a cartel or hostile government was pulling all the strings. I shivered as I realised someone else had to be watching or monitoring our little group of miscreants. I hoped the gizmos they carried everywhere also kept tabs on them. But as the nausea started to swell up from my stomach, my instincts told me they were under surveillance by their own side, which meant that I could have been compromised as well. I knew nothing would happen to me in the restaurant or probably in the hotel either, but outside was another matter. I'd had enough close shaves over the last three months and thought it was time to press the panic button. There was no code required for that, I texted two smiley faces to the other three. We had agreed that this would be the signal for us all to get back to the room urgently but no imminent threat, at least that's what I hoped.

I left the table and headed for the lifts, despite my simmering panic I noticed Marie track my progress to the restaurant doors. She was either looking for a toy boy or she was onto me, not sure which one frightened me the most. The elevator doors opened and I stepped inside, I could see two droplets of sweat sliding down the sides of my face in the mirrored wall but I made no move to wipe them away, I just watched as they meandered down to my chin where they collected, then elongated before eventually falling. Yve followed me into the lift, I could see the back of her head in the mirror as she turned and faced out toward any potential threat, too late I realised what an idiot I was to turn away from an open door. I could see she had her trench coat over her arm once again, it was 20 degrees outside so I knew there was only one reason she had the coat. I didn't even know she was carrying a weapon, she was like a magician who could pull a gun from a hat or mac as required. When the elevator doors closed, we remained fixed in the same position, but I could sense myself starting to tremble and I knew Yve would be able to feel it. We were close enough that her hair brushed the back of my bare neck and I felt her as much as heard her let out a long breath. Then without a word she reached back with her left hand and gripped my ass in her fist. I just had to laugh, it was so inappropriate that it was hilarious, and then the shaking and the nausea just stopped, it was clearly what she intended but I noticed she left her hand there until we reached our floor.

'Josh, elevator stopping, turn around but keep behind me. If I fire, hit the floor and stay there.'

The doors slid smoothly to either side, the corridor was empty but then we heard a squeal from the hinges on the fire escape door. I felt Yve tense and saw her left hand move toward the coat and the gun beneath it. The door opened and Pierre stood tall, daring anyone to challenge him, Yve lowered her left arm and pointed her weapon toward the floor in deference to our alpha-male. I felt the tension drain out of her, feeling somewhat safer myself I went to walk around Yve toward the room, but she stopped me. 'Non attends, envoie un message à Rachel et dis-lui que nous arrivons.' I quickly texted Rachel that we were about to join her, by which time Pierre was next to the lift, then with me in the middle of my protectors we casually walked to our suite. Yve used her key card to let us in, Rachel stood twenty feet away by the open bathroom door, the HK416 in her right hand with the stock collapsed and tossing a stun grenade up and down in her left.

'Trouble?' Rachel asked.

'Not sure, but my gut says yes and soon.' I told them what I heard, what I had realised about being watched and that there had to be something else apart from running the dollar down or shorting stocks. 'That kind of thing has been done before, the effect doesn't last, it's short term. Sure, some rich people get richer faster, but they usually ride on the wake of some catastrophe, natural or contrived. Why have Akil and Jean been given leave to pin this on the French government, if that's what they're really up to? Whoever or whatever is underwriting this whole thing is spending a fortune, therefore they are expecting a substantial and lasting return on their investment, they are not going to let two idealists jeopardise the operation.'

Pierre interrupted my ramblings. 'Josh let's just say we know you can do things we can't, that you can sense things that pass the rest of us by. What, I am trying to say is, that I trust your instincts just like the ambassador does. So don't hold back, give us your wildest conspiracy theory, tell us what spooked you?'

'Firstly, Marie has noticed me, not sure how but she is on to me.' Yve grinned as she interrupted. 'Josh, lots of people notice you!'

'This is different, but the real question is how? I have never been close to either Marie or Angela, I've hardly looked at them. They don't know I can hear them, or they wouldn't have said anything important let alone incriminating. I don't think she spotted me in Corsica, I was tucked out of sight watching the two Danes, Axel and Otto. Maria and Angela were gone by the next morning. I think Maria is expecting someone to be watching her, and she's ok with that, you can see she is relaxed not tense, it's like she thinks she's being assessed and is about to get a gold star. But I think Maria and the others, especially our two Basque friends, are being set up to take the fall while someone else takes the prize.'

Yve was starting to get my drift as she hurriedly tried to put the pieces together before the picture faded. 'So, you think the two Basques have a second assignment, that will amplify and prolong the currency con into a sonic boom and they will be the fall guys when it all unravels.'

Pierre was more realistic, 'I doubt they will live that long!'

It was then I remembered what I'd wanted to ask our pretty and it seemed deadly geek. 'Rachel, where are the other four?'

'As of noon yesterday, they stopped spending, all four were traveling together, something they have never done before. They stopped in a car at Ventimiglia, bought diesel and groceries, a lot of groceries, before crossing over to Menton. The garage CCTV picked them up, they were driving a full-fat Range Rover, I've got the license number, but they have not shown up on any other cameras so far.'

'That's odd, Angela and Maria think that Morreli and Mancini are not involved in this particular venture.' Pierre stopped pacing and looked around at us, his back against the external wall, he always kept clear of windows.

He slumped slightly. 'I don't like the sound of that, it looks like they are going to ground, which can only mean one thing. They're planning to kill someone or more likely many people, the vehicle is big enough to carry heavy weapons and lots of explosives.'

I had been stood near Yve and Rachel, who sat together on the sofa when I suddenly started to feel dizzy, I reached out a hand to steady myself and Yve caught hold of it. Thinking I was about to faint, Rachel stood quickly and took my other arm, resting it over her shoulder. She knew I would be heavy, but I was dead weight and her knees buckled a bit, Yve got up quickly and took my other arm and they managed to lower me on to the sofa.

Pierre stood in front of me calling my name and asking if I was all right, I could hear him but I couldn't answer him. Rachel shook her head to get him to stop talking, she was frightened it would do more harm than good to bring me around before I was ready. I heard her speaking quietly to the other two.

'He's in some kind of trance, we need to just quietly wait a few minutes, he will probably come out of it soon, it looks like some sort of fugue. Pierre, get some cool water for him, I think he is going to need it. It reminds me of my uncle he had a sort of epilepsy, he didn't have grand mal seizures, he just went blank and when he "woke" he didn't know it had happened but then he would usually be sick, better get a bucket as well Pierre.'

Pierre, put the unopened champagne into the fridge and got out a bottle of water, he emptied the melted ice down the sink before kneeling in front of me. I could tell he didn't want to ask, but he knew he had to. 'What happens if he doesn't come around soon?'

Yve, didn't need Rachel's expertise to know the answer to that, her anxiety made her blurt it out a little too loudly though. 'We get him to hospital, I don't give a fuck about the mission.' Much to her surprise Rachel and even Pierre nodded their agreement. Then they all turned to me as

I took a loud gasping breath, it was only then that they realised I had actually stopped breathing during the entire period, almost six minutes.

Yve started to panic. 'We need to get him checked out, you can't go that long without breathing and not do yourself some harm.' Rachel held Yve's arm until she calmed down a little and she could listen to her. 'Yve he is going to be ok, the world record free dive is nearly twenty-five minutes, Josh would have gone blue and collapsed if he hadn't been able to handle it.'

It was only when I spoke that the three of them started to really calm down, in my trance I could hear them in the background whilst still focusing on some kind of vision or hallucination happening in front of my eyes. What I had seen suddenly started to scare me a little or maybe a lot. 'Shit! Shit, shit and more shit!'

It was Pierre who spoke first. 'Are you ok? What happened?'

'I'm fine, but before I say anything I need you all to promise that what just happened stays in this room and what I'm about to tell you will remain a secret. We are going to have tell others what I know, but not how I came to know, we will have to come up with a good story instead.' I waited for them all to nod their agreement, I knew this was a great deal to ask of three members of the French security service, to effectively keep a secret from their superiors. Yve and Rachel nodded without hesitation, Pierre paused and then asked a question.

'What about the ambassador?'

'I will tell my *uncle*, he will find a way to share the information without telling them how he came by it.'

Pierre nodded, I was ready to tell them what happened. 'I had some kind of premonition, or it might have been an hallucination for all I know, but let's go with premonition for now. When Pierre said they were going to kill someone or probably lots of people, it seemed to trigger something in me, some kind of realisation, entelechy as the ancient Greeks would say. Then I was seeing things, like I was in the cinema watching a movie, though it was slightly out of focus, and everything was shades of grey. I realised I was in my old bedroom in London, it was still decorated the same as when I was nine or ten. There was someone else in the room, they looked like a sand sculpture their features smooth, not clearly defined. The figure held a large book on their up lifted forearms, there was no title or writing on the front cover or the spine from what I could see. It reminded me a little of one of Magritte's surrealist paintings, minus the bowler hat. I reached out to the figure, but it started to recede back into the wall, and I realised the wall had changed too, it was a mountain and there were faces carved into it and the figure from the room began to merge with the rock until only his face was left proud of the surface and then the image resolved, and I recognised him. It was the current American president, and the rock was Mount Rushmore. They are going to kill the president on French soil, putting in jeopardy relations between the States and the whole of Western Europe, destroying the NATO alliance overnight. That's what this is really all about, the money is just a sideshow.'

Rachel seemed less stunned than the other two and spoke first. 'But there are no state visits planned until April next year, I know because all leave has been cancelled for that whole month.'

I smiled as I spoke, 'Good! That means I'm just going crazy and the US president is not going to be assassinated on French soil or…'

'Or what?' The three of them spoke at the same time, almost shouting, I was liking the new worried Pierre, it was giving me hope that he wasn't perfect after all.

'Or he is coming to France secretly and I am not mad, better still it's something we can confirm or not, as the case may be.' I could see the look on Rachel's face, she was clearly sceptical but then she hadn't known me very long.

'How do we do that?'

'Easy, we contact the ambassador and ask him, we might not know but he will.' Pierre, was the first to speak, 'He won't tell you anything on an unsecured line, we will have to go back to the ministry.'

'I don't think we can. If none of you three know anything about a possible visit and I am not mad then someone here or in the States, with top-secret clearance, is a traitor. If we dash to the ministry asking to use one of the secure lines, at the very least, they will have to be told who we are calling. That could be enough to alert whoever it is, and then all we will have, is a bunch of suspects in a currency scam, if we're lucky.' I think Rachel was struggling with the idea that one of our own was a traitor, although she was seven years older than me she was still idealistic. I had already seen too much and was aging fast, almost as fast as my cynicism was growing. 'It could be someone in America or at their embassy here' she protested but with little conviction.

Pierre was a realist, and even more cynical than me, after years of fighting the bad guys. 'More likely to be one of ours, the American ambassador will have been liaising with the top French officials, but his job will be to see the President gets from the airfield to the Embassy, or wherever he is staying, safely. Wherever the meeting is held the Americans will look after the inner ring guarding him, and the French will secure the outer perimeter. Given he will be traveling in his own bullet and bomb proof vehicle, flanked by US marines and his personal secret service team, there is no real opportunity to get to him. The only plausible weakness is the outer circle, troops will be on standby now with no idea why, their commanders will have been told they are to guard a foreign dignitary, but not who or even given a false name to satisfy their curiosity. The officers will already have the details of where to station their men and will just be waiting for the final orders to move into position. So, if they already know where the French commandos will be positioned and where the surveillance cameras are, they will also be able to figure out how to get between the French and American rings. We must assume that from there, they will be able to establish a position for a sniper to take a shot.'

Rachel slumped on the sofa, looking defeated and Yve was pacing, careless of the windows. Pierre noticed, and gently re-routed her to the far end of the room, out of sight, sniper sight that is, before he turned back to me. 'So, how do we contact him?'

'Rachel, does the ambassador know our code?'

'Oui. He insisted I show him how it would work, he even downloaded the song lyrics and tested it out on me.'

'You're going to use that code to talk to the ambassador?' Yve asked.

'It's the only way. Pierre, you understand the risk of telling him?' Yve cut Rachel off as she spoke over her, though no doubt they were going to ask the same thing. 'What are you going on about, what risk?'

Pierre answered her. 'Normally the London ambassador would not need to know about a secret visit to Paris, so he could neither confirm or deny Josh's suspicions, but as we know the ambassador operates outside the usual diplomatic demarcation lines. Given his background, and that he personally knows the US president, even if he doesn't like him, he was probably an advisor on the French security arrangements. Clearly, Josh is developing all the instincts of a good spy. It is possible that the ambassador is behind the whole thing and has passed on the security details himself. In the end it makes no difference.'

'What do you mean, it makes no difference' Rachel's voice had gone up an octave, it was almost a squeak. Yve sat back down on the sofa and put an arm around her shoulder to calm her down, it seemed to work.

'I'm a soldier not a spy, I trust Philippe the man, he has saved my life many times and I do not believe he would betray us. But that's just the sentimental crap they say in action movies before they die. If the ambassador is involved, he has known since before Josh's trip to Corsica, but the question is why would he send him? If he knows what's going on why would he ask Rachel to track the ruby gang, why would he send us to stake them out? It makes no sense unless…'

I couldn't resist jumping in, knowing Pierre and I were most definitely on the same page. 'Unless this is just a distraction, keeping us focussed on the money to give the other four space to operate and still make him look like he was doing his job to the max.' Pierre picked up the explanation seamlessly. 'I have seven of my best commandos on stake out duty, when the other four arrive, I will have to double that number. Remember it was the ambassador who told me to make sure I had a big enough team to keep track of them all, twenty-four-seven.

I needed to bring the discussion to an end and now! We were running out of time. 'The ambassador is the only one that has the clout and credibility to change the security arrangements or to even get the visit called off. If he's involved, then he already has a plan to take care of the loose ends. We have no choice! Now I just need to get his attention.' I said the last sentence more to myself than anyone else. I thought carefully for a few seconds before I started to type, I didn't want to give too much away, code or no code. "Uncle, are you coming over for the golf tournament, I heard the club President is joining the game, could be interesting?"

Pierre paced, he needed to be doing something even if it was just planning what we were going to do. He turned to me. 'Assuming the ambassador is on our side, what are your thoughts, Josh?'

'Firstly, it doesn't take four people to pull a trigger?' I looked at Pierre waiting for confirmation.

'Obviously one is enough, but two is optimum. A spotter with binoculars and a wind gauge to support the sniper and watch their backs, they won't get a second shot and more people would just make them easier to detect. What are the spares for, any ideas Josh?'

'Just one. I think Akil and Jean are the ones designated to kill the president, they are the fanatics ready to die for the cause. The other two, Mancini and Morelli, are headed this way, I think their job is to tidy up our little arbitrage group. I don't know how they are going to take them out but it won't be a fire fight in the hotel lobby, my guess would be that they will be taken care of on their way back to the airport or station. Whoever is organising all this won't want them picked up and questioned, whichever terminal they're heading for it will be exactly that – terminal. I think we let the DST take care of them, we are not interested in the money, and they know nothing about anything else.'

Just then my phone dinged, I had a text. 'It's from the ambassador' I read the numbers, decoding it out loud for the others as I went - "I'll definitely be there for that game, if I drop by tonight, we could get a practice round in early tomorrow morning." I texted back, "Perfect, I'll revise my plans now things have changed."

***

Philippe arrived at the hotel at ten that evening, Pierre managed to open the emergency exit to the service area without triggering the fire alarm and brought him to our room, where he got straight down to business.

'The problem we have is twofold, firstly the US president is mid-Atlantic so the trip has to go ahead, besides it's our only chance of unblocking some trade issues and avoiding a tariff war we can't win. Secondly, I agree with Josh and Pierre that we have a traitor at the highest level, and we need to draw him or her out, but we can't afford to scare them off.'

Pierre was up for this, I could tell by his rapid-fire response. 'What do you need us to do Philippe?'

'General Moreau is in overall charge of security, I have always trusted him, but I've had him watched for the last month just in case, the same for Major Reins who is in command of the outer ring as well as additional security inside the chateau. Pierre, you know both of them well I think?' Pierre just nodded and the ambassador continued. 'I have managed to have a secure call with them, and they have agreed for you and a squad of your men to pass through the outer cordon and intercept the two assassins.'

Pierre looked worried. 'Ambassador, I know the grounds of the chateau and that track of land between the two rings is almost a hundred metres wide for the most part and over a kilometre around the house, that's a lot of land, with plenty of hiding places to cover with just fourteen men?'

The general will brief the president's security team when he arrives, claiming they have only just found out about the threat and the safest option is to remain in the chateau until the assassins are dealt with. The president's quarters are on the second floor overlooking the lake, on the ground floor is the state dining room and great hall where the talks will take place. American marines will be patrolling the space between the house and the water, there are only two places to get a shot at him, his rooms and the windows to the ground floor, which means that any sniper will have to be somewhere on the other side of that lake with a clear view of the ground and second floor. How does that sound Pierre?'

'Much better, but I am still concerned. If Akil and Jean are experienced they will be camouflaged and well bedded in, which will make them very difficult to spot before they actually fire and give their position away.'

'That's true but we will ensure the shutters are closed on the second floor, unfortunately there are none on the ground floor and the windows are one hundred years old, so definitely not bullet proof. But, forewarned is forearmed, the president will sit at the head of the table and two of his agents will be stood in such a way as to block any direct shot. Coincidently someone declared the curtains a fire risk last week and they have been removed and while that makes it more difficult for us to protect the president, it does give me a lead on who our traitor might be.'

I looked the ambassador in the eye, so far, he had not spoken directly to me. 'What about us three?'

'Josh, I believe you think one of the women is on to you?'

'Yes, she knows I'm watching her, but I'd say that she thinks I'm on the same side.'

'That may well be, but I think you should stay at the apartment, Yve and Rachel can monitor the hotel passively and we can turn them all over to the DST.'

'I know you're not going to like this sir, but I think I should go with Pierre.'

'Mon dieu, tu es fou!'

I could see the others were vying to be the first to agree with my uncle, I raised my hand, palm out toward them in an effort to stop them interrupting me. All three seemed to freeze on the spot for a second before sitting back down. I looked at my uncle then back at them. The ambassador looked at them and then turned back to stare at me while he listened to what I had to say, I definitely had his full attention now.

'I know it sounds crazy, the idea of me going on a mission with a crack troop of commandos, and I may well be going a bit mad, but things have moved on a little in the last week or so. My language abilities are actually increasing but there is something else, my hearing is suddenly supersonic, and I can hear the faintest sounds up to a hundred metres away. I…' The ambassador interrupted me.

'I had my suspicions, your hearing has always been acute but lately your reports have tested even my credulity. But leave that aside for the moment, what I really want, no what I must know is how you discovered the US president is on his way here?'

I realised that just as I had been suspicious of the ambassador, he in turn was wary of me and my unexplained knowledge of what should have been a very secret visit. I could hardly blame him, so reluctantly I told Philippe about my vision as the other three came *back to life* to confirm my account, the ambassador seemed equal parts amazed and terrified. Bizarrely, I think he believed me but I could tell that any further discussion on this development would be between just the two of us, and when this was all over. The ambassador rubbed his face with both hands before focussing back on me. 'Okay Josh, I hear what you're saying, but tell me why you need to be in no-man's land in the middle of the night, looking for two suicidal terrorists hiding between heavily armed French soldiers on one side and fifty trigger happy US marines on the other?'

'When you put it like that it does sound a little crazy but if Pierre goes without me his only option is to kill them both. I would bet that Akil and Jean know more than any of the others, given their role in this whole plot. This is not just a few fanatics, this is an organised and well-funded network, there will be more plots, and some are bound to succeed, we need them alive.'

'So, what is your plan? Are you going to talk them into giving themselves up? They will be well hidden, if the Americans hear or see anything they will shoot you as well as Pierre and half of his men and if any of them fire back, which they will, we will have a major international incident on our hands. We might as well just let them shoot the president and blame it on the marines!'

'Firstly, if Pierre can get me and some of his men within fifty metres of the lake, I should be able to hear the slightest rustle they make or word they say and home in on them.'

'Then what?' Pierre was getting tense.

'I whisper to them, I think I can take control of them.'

'You mean like you just did to the three of us?' Yve asked.

'Similar, obviously no hand gestures.' I could see Pierre was concerned and I paused while he thought through what he wanted to ask.

'Josh, just now you stopped the three of us in our tracks with just a gesture of your hand and while I couldn't speak or even move toward you, I think I could have just taken my gun out and shot you, that's what I felt like doing but it was me that stopped myself, not you. Also, what about my men? You could prevent them from shooting as well, if that's what you ordered the two terrorists to do.'

I had already considered Pierre's concerns about disabling him and his commandos but the fact that, despite my control, he could still have shot me was "news indeed". I'd thought they would be unable to do a thing when I made them stop. 'That's very interesting Pierre, I will have to make sure I am very precise when talking to them, as for your men I think they will be safe as long as they do not speak Basque.' I thought Pierre was going to spit on the carpet at the very suggestion that one his men would understand such a heathen tongue. The ambassador, of course, quickly picked up on that little titbit.

'And when did you learn Basque, Josh?'

'After Rachel briefed us on the background of the group members, I pulled an all-nighter.'

'That's not even two days.' There was shock in Yve's voice, and the other two also looked a little dumbfounded, but the ambassador didn't look at all surprised. While I believed he genuinely liked me, he may have even felt something close to filial love, I could see him totting up the balance sheet, thinking of how he could make use of such an unusual asset. Two months ago, I would have been shocked, offended even, but now I realised it was just the way it was. I could have tried to stay off the radar, but there was something in me that was drawn to intrigue and the minute I accepted that train ticket from Marseille to Paris I was hooked in more ways than one. And as young as I was, I still knew a potential ally or enemy when I saw one. Most of all I didn't want my family involved with anything that could put them at risk, uncle Philip was perfect, though I didn't realise then how high the price would be.

Pierre looked at me quizzically for a few moments. 'So, your plan is to locate them like some kind of giant bat then talk them into giving up, without ever firing a shot?'

'Oui.'

'Well, I was going to try and pick them up with the infra-red imaging sight on my rifle, but if they're any good they will be bivouacked under a thermal cover, they may also have suicide vests on, which they will set off if we get close, so we will have no other choice but to shoot to kill.'

The ambassador turned his gaze away from me for the first time since he entered the room. 'Pierre, I have managed to get a little intel on the shooters, and I am afraid it's not good. Jean is a crack shot, trained in the Legion and definitely knows how to stay hidden until the last second. Akil prefers explosives, so chances are they are both wired up as they know whether they succeed or fail they will be shot or worse.'

Pierre was thinking it through, the pros and cons, benefits versus risk, then he spoke. 'I can't say this is giving me a warm feeling right now. We have a traitor, who will probably be inside the building, able to pull strings and turn everything against us if they get an inkling of what we are up to. Outside we have a sniper and a suicide bomber with god knows how much Semtex strapped to him, ready to die for the cause and wanting to take as many of us with him as he can. While we are stuck in the middle, with French troops on one side and trigger-happy marines on the other side. Only a few trusted French officers will know we are there and why, we could all end up looking like battered colanders at a car boot sale. What about the marines, do you plan on telling them anything?'

'Luckily, I know the American OIC, we did a few ops together, and I've set a meeting up with him early tomorrow morning, but until then everything stays between us and our own President.'

'In that case sir, it's your call or should I say order? If Josh can crawl for up to half a kilometre so quietly that only he can hear himself moving, I can keep him safe. You just need to make sure the French and the Americans don't start trading shots with us stuck in the middle.'

'I can do that. Josh, do you still want to do this?'

'It's the only way.' Shortly after that I went back to the apartment, I needed to see Michelle. I knew logically that it could be the last time I would ever see her, but for some reason I was convinced I would be coming back alive at least, but I also think I knew that I wouldn't be the same person, gifts or no gifts, afterwards. The old Josh, the person that Michelle fell in love with, needed to be with her for one more night and hope that she could still love whoever came out the other side of this shit show that we all had a part in, even if we didn't audition for it.

    Michelle and I lay naked on our sides in bed together, staring into each other's eyes. When I'd got back to the apartment, I was shaking and she held me without any questions while the trembling gradually subsided. Then she undressed me and led me to the bed, once I was settled, she undressed and got in next to me, we talked about many things but mainly about us, we were still getting to know each other and everything she told me, no matter how trivial, was fascinating to me. Eventually, I told her that I was going on a mission with Pierre and his men tomorrow night. Nothing more. She knew it would be dangerous, the state I was in when I came back told her all she needed to know. She did not try to stop me or probe me for details. Instead, she kissed me then held me through the night, while I slept safe in her arms. We did not make love and when I woke, she still slept. I slipped out of the bed and put some croissants in the oven to warm through and made some coffee, when it was ready I put the pastries, coffee and some little plastic jam pots, we purloined from the hotel in Corsica on a tray and took them back to bed. This was a first, we had both agreed after our first night together that eating in bed was barbaric, who wants to sleep on sheets full of crumbs. Michelle said nothing though, and we lay there breaking off small chunks of croissant and feeding each other. When we finished Michelle took the tray and turned her back toward me, she leaned over to place it on the floor. It was then I spotted the large flake of pastry stuck to her bottom, I quickly put my mouth over it and licked it up. When she turned around, she still had the plate in her hand, she lay on her back and tipped all of the crumbs along her body, she then swirled her finger in some raspberry jam left at the side of the plate and smeared it on both her breasts. She looked at me with those mischievous green eyes, smiled and simply said 'bon appétit mon amour.'

I stayed home with Michelle as instructed by Pierre, he came to collect me at six, it was cold, dark and raining. I was not looking forward to crawling through wet grass, especially after Yve told me they graze cattle on it during the spring and summer and to watch out for the cowpats. Surprisingly Pierre came up to the apartment, I had expected him to just text to tell me he was waiting downstairs and to move my ass. He turned down my offer of coffee and told me to leave mine. 'The minute you lie on that wet grass you're going to want to piss, and it could be a long night out there.' Then he went over to Michelle and lifted her up in his massive arms to cuddle her, I thought she might break but she just squealed and kicked her legs as he planted a kiss on the top of her head. I suddenly realised that over just a few months the three of us and Yve had somehow become good friends. What I said to the ambassador about Akil and Jean knowing more than the others was true, but it was when I realised the risks of Pierre getting caught in the crossfire of American and French troops or getting blown to bits that I'd known it was my turn to at least try and protect him.

By seven we were face down in a mixture of grass and some other shrubs that seemed to have teeth whenever you rubbed against them. I had no fear of them smelling us coming, I had already crawled through at least two cowpats and something else I couldn't identify but it smelt like the huge industrial bins at the back of the apartment building on a hot day. Pierre had dressed me in Kevlar from head to toe and painted my face a swirling mix of green, brown and black pigment. Pierre was confident that the two Basques would have been hunkered down at least an hour before we arrived, the dinner was scheduled to start at eight, but the ambassador said nothing would happen before half-past, when the president would be formally received by the French president at the far end of the room, well clear of all the windows. Philippe had added himself to the guest list and would be armed, just in case our traitor turned out to be a fanatic rather than just another mercenary.

We were still a hundred metres from the chateau itself, the lights of the dining room guiding us, hopefully closer to our target. There were sixteen of us including Pierre and myself and we were edging forward in a chevron formation with him at the centre leading and my head level with his waist. I tried to get him to let me go ahead so I could hear better, but he wasn't having it, despite his stubbornness I managed to pick up a slight vibration in my chest as we paused for a few seconds for everyone to take a breath. It was amazing the way the moment he stopped all of his men came to a halt in almost the same instant without any kind of signal or warning. Before Pierre could set off again, I put a hand on his shoulder to alert him that I'd picked up something, of course it might just be a badger or a fox going to ground as they sensed our approach, but it was the only thing, apart from the roosting birds in the trees that I'd detected, so I needed to check.

As we held our position, Pierre just looked back toward me and I nodded my head slightly, hoping he wasn't getting his hopes up just yet. I couldn't hear a thing, but then I hadn't heard anything a minute ago, I'd felt it. I didn't dare look at him as I removed the Kevlar helmet and tilted my head, placing my ear to the earth and hoping there wasn't a cowpat just there. In an effort to placate Pierre, I rested the helmet on my head as best I could. At first, I felt a faint thumping, then I could hear it more distinctly, it was a low bass resonance with what seemed like a slight echo to it. I was starting to think animal rather than human when the sound or rather sounds became more distinct. It was a heartbeat, two heart beats in fact, it wasn't an echo at all, I had found them. Then, a bit like my premonition I could see the blurred shapes of two men about sixty metres ahead, just on the edge of the lake, but this time it wasn't a vision, they were pulsing, and it was then I realised that I had been quietly tapping the ground with the fingers of my left hand. I was, as Pierre joked, like a bat but using low rather than high frequencies, but still it was some kind of echolocation or sonar.

My original plan had been to start by whispering so as not to alarm them, but I had still been worried that they would get spooked and reflexively start to shoot. The vibration on the ground gave me what I hoped was a better idea. I kept the steady rhythmic tapping up while I turned my head slightly so that my mouth was just touching the ground, still hoping that I wouldn't get a mouthful of cow shit. I started to gently hum, praying my instincts were good. I watched them using my human sonar, I could see them starting to relax, their shoulders drooping down. Then Jean actually laid his rifle down on its side and released his grip from the trigger guard. I sensed that Akil was putting up more resistance, so I started to speak into the ground. I ordered the two of them to disarm and crawl towards me -

'Akil eta Jean; entzun nazazu, orain nire agindupean zaude. Jaitsi zaizteztela nahi dut, zure armak eta lehergaiak salbatu. Ez zara saiatuko inor mintzen edo hiltzen. Ulertzen duzu?'

'Bai ulertzen dut.'

'Bai, kapitaina.'

'Orain nire ahotsera arakatzea nahi dut, lurretik gertu egon. Ez jarri zure posizioa arriskuan jarri.'

I tracked them as they slowly crawled toward our position, no one said a word, I nodded to Pierre who in turn looked around his men and immediately they started to look a little less concerned, though still with their weapons ready to fire. After about twenty minutes of very slow crawling the heads of the two Basques started to emerge through the grass. As instructed, they lay in front of Pierre, side by side and face down, their hands were positioned behind their backs, palms up. Robert, Pierre's lieutenant, manoeuvred himself around and managed to zip-tie their wrists behind their backs, then he put one tie on each of their ankles before linking the two of them together with a third to give them just enough slack to hobble along when we got further away from the house.

We managed to crab walk with four of Pierre's men dragging Jean and Akin backwards while holding them underneath the arms, their heels scuffing and bouncing along the uneven ground. Once through the French outer circle we let them stand, which allowed us to move a little quicker. We were almost back at the vehicles we had arrived in when I heard a click, instantly I shouted 'incoming' and pushed Pierre to one side, knowing exactly what the sound was. Before I could say another word, a bullet seared through my thigh and then all I could do was scream as gun fire blasted out. I was struggling to stay conscious when a cloth bag or a hood went over my head and I felt myself being lifted in the air and slung in the back of a pick-up, judging by the ridged steel base I was lying full length on and the air rushing over me as it drove off. That was the last thing I remembered before I passed out.

When I woke up, I had no idea what day it was let alone where I was. I still had the hood on but it was obvious I was laid out on a bed of some kind, with my hands secured to a metal rail or headboard. They'd not bothered to tie my legs but they had at least bandaged my thigh, for some reason they didn't want me dead, not just yet. Clearly though, they had no clue what I was cable of as they hadn't even bothered to gag me. I knew I could escape, but I also realised I needed to bide my time, I needed to find out how many people I was dealing with and where I was. I had to know if any of the others had been captured in case I needed to free them as well. Pierre and his men would put up a lot more resistance than I had, I had to believe he was still alive, I know the first bullet missed, I'd pushed him just in time and I'd felt it swish past my face, missing both of us by inches.

I didn't think I could drive, and I definitely couldn't walk more than a few metres, maybe not even that. If they had killed Pierre, I feared what I might do, and suddenly I had a sense of foreboding of what I might become, in my quest for vengeance. Just then the door slammed open, and a man spoke in fluent French, an unrefined Parisian accent, and I could tell there were two others, I could hear their heartbeats, faster than his, he was in charge. One of his underlings ripped the hood from my head, my pupils unable to constrict fast enough I winced at the bright spotlight pointing straight at me. Then I took a deep breath and waited, they would either speak to me, or hurt me to soften me up, before they asked whatever it was, they wanted to know. I waited in silence, hoping they would give more away than if I asked them questions that they were hardly likely to answer. After twenty seconds or so, the leader's impatience got the better of him.

'I think we have a little puzzle here, what do you say boys?' The two men just nodded. 'You, Josh, I think I heard Pierre call you, just after you saved his life. I really thought I had him this time, he was right in my sights, then as I squeezed the trigger ever so softly, he was gone. He took out five of my men before he hit the ground and rolled clear, I couldn't even get a second shot at him. His men finished off the rest of my crew while we snatched you, so that leaves just the three amigos. More cash for us I suppose as we still managed to take out the two Basques. Which, after all was why we there, c'est la guerre. Oh, you do look surprised.

Well, the people I work for don't like to leave anything to chance, so just in case they couldn't manage to get themselves shot or blown to bits, we were there to tidy up. Then, what a surprise when Pierre turns up in my night sight with the two of them hog-tied, and not a shot fired. Strange don't you think, though maybe not as weird as, and I am honour-bound to admit it, Pierre taking a kid, a civilian even, on one of the most important missions of his life. But there's the thing, he did take you and he almost succeeded, spectacularly so given he had both of them alive, and that's another thing Pierre likes to talk to the dead, they don't cause a fuss or answer back. So, what I want to know is, why you were there, why are you so important Josh?'

I tried to speak, to take control of them, but my speech was slurred, and it was only then that I noticed that my right wrist was connected to an IV drip hanging from the ceiling. Probably some kind of painkiller for the wound in my thigh, whatever it was, it was affecting my speech but strangely my mind remained clear, and my cognitive capacity seemed undiminished. It was like some lesser version of locked in syndrome. But that didn't matter, Pierre was alive.

He was speaking again. 'Jack, I think our boy is a little high, pull the cannula. Sorry Josh, you're going to be in some pain while we figure all this out. We'll be back in an hour, you should have the use of your tongue back by then, so be ready to talk or be prepared to die, very slowly and extremely painfully. That bullet hole is nothing to what I can do to you.'

With that he pressed down over the bandage directly on the wound, my head and back jerked clear of the bed and I screamed louder than I had ever done before, even the time I was seven and fell from a tree, breaking my collar bone. That was nothing to the burning pain that seemed to rip through my entire being. When my body returned to the mattress, I noticed a strange look on their three faces. They seemed to be in some sort of discomfort, pain even, Jack held his hand to his right ear and as they left, they all moved a little slowly, their gaits seemed odd and when Jack took his hand away I could see a trickle of blood weeping from his ear down the side of his face. He wiped it away with his hand but said nothing to the other two, too macho to believe a little boy's cry could harm him, that would be their undoing.

I started to drift off to sleep when they left but then the pain started to kick in, now I was getting worried that I might be too exhausted to defend myself or better still attack them. Though there was very little physical effort on my part, controlling people verbally was draining and I didn't know how I was going to summon the energy I would need to deal with all three of them at once. As the pain increased, I clenched my fists tight and started to talk to myself, at first, I just called myself names for being weak, but then I started to give myself orders. It was like I was outside looking in - "Ignore the pain, you need to survive for Pierre and Yve, for your family for Michelle!" Suddenly I could see them all, it was like they were willing me on, and the pain started to subside. It didn't go all together, I instinctively knew I needed to keep a little to fuel my anger, to help me strike out. I was slightly concerned that I was beginning to take pleasure in that feeling of residual pain and what I might do to them. Right now, I needed to focus, to do something constructive. The rope around my wrists was tied about a foot above my head, ignoring the sudden increase in pain level I pushed my body upward with my good leg at the same time as heaving on the rope. I could now stretch my hands up and feel the knot and began to work on loosening it, the process was slow and painful but whenever I thought about giving up, I would hear myself urging me on and then see all the people I loved. It must have taken at least half-an-hour to work the rope free of the bed frame and when I brought my arms over my head and in front of me, I could see they had not bothered to tie my wrists together very securely. It took a few minutes to work my hands completely free, but I knew I was in no condition to launch any kind of attack, physical or verbal, on the three of them as soon as they walked in, I would need a few minutes at least to build up to it. In the meantime, I didn't want one of them over-reacting and knocking me out or shooting me, I thought Jack might be up for that given his little experience before. So, I tied the rope back on the bedstead and looped it around my wrists so it looked like I was still trussed up but could actually free myself in a second. It wouldn't pass close inspection, but they would have expected me to just pass out after they left so they wouldn't be concerned about an escape attempt.

    Jack came through the door first, he grinned evilly, and I could tell he was looking forward to torturing me. Next came the leader and then the second henchman brought up the rear. Rather optimistically, I reasoned that it was good to have them together, that way I could kill them all at the same time. Well now, that was something new, I'd never thought about killing anyone before, not sure where that came from but something inside told me that it would more than likely work out that way. What would my parents think, and Michelle? Again, I didn't know why, but I thought Charlotte would be good with it and just think they got what they deserved.

'Now then Josh my boy I've got a few questions for you, and I want some truthful answers, or Jack is going to introduce you to a whole world of pain. For some reason he seems to have taken a particular dislike to you and is really hoping that you get all heroic and stay quiet, apart from the screaming that is.'

As he spoke, I watched Jack, he was like an attack dog straining on an invisible chain, waiting to be unleashed. He should have terrified me, instead I felt like I was feeding off his rage, getting stronger instead of growing weaker. The sound of the leader's voice, his name was Saul I had heard the other one whisper to him from behind, also seemed to be energising me.

'Josh you really are in luck now, it seems that young Max here has taken a bit of a shine to you, so you might get to enjoy a little pleasure as well as a lot of pain.' Saul was clearly as sadistic in temperament as Jack, but I could just feel it fuelling me up, I was really starting to buzz. They'd made a big mistake, now I knew all their names, now I would have power over them. Now I would kill them.

'Ok Josh, to start with, tell me what part you played in tonight's little tragedy and why Pierre was so desperate to try and protect you.'

I smiled at that thought, I could tell by the look on Saul's face he wasn't expecting me to look pleased and it confused him slightly. It was time to strike. 'Saul!' He was surprised that I knew his name and all three paused briefly. 'Jack and Max, don't move, do not touch any of your weapons and stay exactly where you are. I could see them leaning, straining to get free of the invisible hold on them. Jack was clearly incandescent with rage, and I could feel him straining against the mental restraints I'd put in place. He was so mad he managed to break free slightly and started to slowly move forward as though he was swimming against a riptide. I thought of screaming but knew I couldn't, the scream earlier came from a place of pain and fear. I was no longer afraid I was angry, I was vengeful. Jack was getting closer, somehow, I knew if he could touch me, he could break free completely and really hurt me. I released my hands from the rope, I just knew what to do, what I had to do to survive. I put my arms out in front of me, Jack was less than a metre away. I held my palms together and pointed them straight at him, then I moved them apart and brought them back together with as much force as I could creating a deafening clap. Saul and Max rocked backwards, I think it was only the hold I had on them that stopped them from falling over. Jack, however, hit the floor like a meteor crashing to earth, you could feel the heat off him and you could smell his hair which had been turned to black dust, he was dead, very dead, and I felt nothing. No, worse than that, I was pleased.

I looked over to the other two, my arms still outstretched in that strange clapping-shooting position. Saul looked like he might puke at any minute and Max had wet himself. 'That is why I was there tonight. Now Saul, old man, you had better do some talking. Firstly, is there anyone else in this building?'

'No, it's just us three, I mean two, now. There was a medic who patched you up, but he left, luckily the bullet was small calibre and only went through muscle.'

'Does the doctor know anything about your missions?'

'Nothing, he asks no questions, and we pay him in cash.'

'Who do you work for?'

'We have no idea. Instructions come by computer and the money is paid into a numbered account. It's all on my laptop downstairs.'

He told me the password, all the account numbers and details were in the Notes App, apparently my phone was also on the ground floor.

'Tell me Saul, what did you plan to do to me after I talked?'

He tried to resist but I concentrated a little more and he folded within three seconds.

'Max would have raped you until your arse was raw and bleeding, when he was done, Jack would have beaten your pretty face to a pulp before killing you as slowly and painfully as possible.'

'Well, I was going to make it quick like Jack, but I think I need to revise that.' They looked horrified as I aimed between the two of them and moved my hands apart and then clapped them back together but with much less force, physically and mentally, than I'd exerted on Jack. Still, they both went down to their knees clutching their chest, I think they were having some kind of mini heart attack. I had planned to drag it out and really make them suffer but I managed to pull the reins in a little on my rage. However, I also knew there could be no loose ends, no more Kurt's floating in the ether. If this ever got out, I would be dead or enslaved within a year. I concentrated, pulled my arms wide apart and brought them together with even more force than I used on Jack, and they died without uttering a sound of any kind. At least there was no smell of burning with these two, but there was no time to dwell on what I'd done, I had to get out.

The wound on my leg had opened up with the exertion of the force I had used and blood was seeping through the bandage. I talked myself into ignoring it and checked the pockets of the three dead men, they all had mobiles, but the screens were cracked, and the batteries drained completely. Slowly I made my way down the stairs one at a time hanging desperately on to the banister to support my weight. In the front room I found Saul's laptop and my phone on a small table. My mobile was still functioning with plenty of charge, I lowered myself onto the sofa and dialled Pierre.

'Josh, Josh, say something!'

'Take it easy big man, though I have to say it's good to hear your voice, but we can cuddle later. Right now, I need a surgeon and someone to do some cleaning up.'

'Are you wounded? I saw you go down just after you saved my life, again. Where are you?'

'I have a gunshot wound to my right thigh, I don't think it will kill me but it's bleeding through the dressing and hurts like hell.'

'Ok, but where are you? I'm coming to get you right now and I'll have you in a military hospital before you know it.'

'Not sure where I am, I could go outside and look but I think I might pass out in the street if I do, can you trace me.'

'Yes, just stay on the line. Rachel, can you find him quickly?'

'Oui, assuming he's in Paris or close by.'

'Did you hear that, Josh?'

'Oui. Pierre, I need someone to do a little cleaning up, someone that can keep their mouth shut.'

'How many?' Pierre knew what I was talking about without further explanation. 'Three, no blood to speak of and no visible wounds.'

'Merde, I will take care of it myself.' I heard Rachel call out.

'Pierre, I've got him he's twenty minutes from here or ten given the look on your face. Don't hang up, I'll talk to him until you get there.'

'Where's Yve, I didn't hear her and I would have done?'

'She's with Michelle, pardon but we feared the worst.'

'Don't concern yourself Pierre, I can assure you this is worse than you imagined. What about the ambassador?'

'He's flying to London in an hour to see your parents.'

'Putain! Rachel needs to contact him and get my uncle to wait until I have spoken to him, and she needs to tell Michelle I am alive and will see her very soon. You better be here by the time she has done that Pierre, I am counting on you.'

'Oui.'

***

Pierre did somehow manage to arrive in ten minutes and burst through the front door with an automatic in one hand and a first aid kit in the other. He had seen far worse wounds than mine, but he still visibly flinched when he saw my thigh, the leg of my trousers had been cut away just below my groin and the bandage was now soaked in blood and starting to drip on the floor.

'I need to re-bandage your wound before I move you, it's going to hurt but I have something you can take to ease the pain.'

'Just the bandage Pierre, I have had enough drugs for one night I need to keep my wits about me for now.' Pierre didn't bother trying to persuade me, he just started cutting through the old dressing and ignored my wincing. Within seconds he had the bloody rag off, exposing a very neat hole about the same diameter as a number two pencil, that was packed with blood-soaked gauze.

'Josh I'm going to leave the packing alone and just put some more over the top, which should stop you bleeding to death while I get you to the hospital.' That was not particularly reassuring, but then that wasn't Pierre's MO really. 'What about the bodies?'

'Three in the room above this one, from what they said they were the only ones to survive the ambush on us. I think you know them, Saul, he was in charge, Jack and Max a nasty little trio.'

'I know them and if it hadn't been for you we would have all died. Saul probably couldn't stop himself from shooting at me first instead of giving the order to his men to open fire on us all.'

'How are your men?'

'A few flesh wounds, they have had a lot worse. They all doubted my decision to bring you along, not that they dared say anything, but I think you may have gained yourself a squad of commandos as your new best friends.' There was a long pause and then Pierre looked up at the ceiling. 'You had no choice Josh, it was you or them.'

I just nodded my head, he thought I might regret what I'd done but I didn't. That's what bothered me the most, that it didn't bother me at all. I thought it should have, no matter how evil they were, I'd still killed three people. The world was no doubt a better place without them, but I had never killed anything before then, not even an insect, and yet it didn't seem to matter. I broke out of my little crisis of conscience, or rather my lack of conscience, when Pierre tightened the bandage, and I felt the pressure on the wound. My father would be appalled, not that I intended telling him, and now he knew I was alive my uncle would be working out our cover story. Though he wasn't going to be able to explain away the hole in my leg. Just then I realised that Pierre was studying me, looking at my face and then down at my bandaged leg, then he spoke. 'Josh, you're lucky I don't think there is any permanent damage to your leg. I am puzzled though, the entry and exit wounds are relatively small and quite neat.'

'Saul said the bullet was a small calibre round and had gone clean through.'

'I can see that but the men we killed were all carrying combat weapons, side arms included, they would have done a lot more damage, you would have most likely bled to death before they got you here. Robert will be along any minute with a military ambulance, a doctor and a small team to keep you safe, they will guard you 24-7 at the hospital, just in case. I'll search the house once you're on your way, but I would be most surprised if the weapon that was used to shoot you is here. Saul and his team didn't carry guns that small, and they didn't aim for the leg. The two Basques had half their heads blown off from a single shot through each of their skulls. They made a big mistake in shooting Jean and Akin, they should have taken my men out first. The Basques were going nowhere and didn't represent a threat to them, but I guess Saul losing it and trying to take me out spooked them, or maybe they thought they were still wired up and waiting to set off their explosives. Whatever, it gave us a few extra seconds, which was all we needed. Sorry, I'm rambling but what I am trying to get to, is that I think whoever shot you is still out there, so we are going to make sure you stay safe and whoever pulled that trigger is our next target.'

When I woke up the light was trying to find a way in through the tightly closed blinds, someone had also placed a screen in front of the window to obscure any possible view of me to target. Michelle held my hand so tightly it was numb, she was sat in a chair asleep, her head on my good thigh. On the other side of the bed Yve sat in a similar chair, on a small table between her and the wall was her faithful HK416, she held my other hand in her lap, but she was focussed on the door and very alert. Robert must have stayed on after bringing me to the hospital, he was sat in a chair by the window but facing the door to the room, he was nursing his own weapon across his lap. It hit me then, what Pierre had said. Guys like these, even the scum I killed, don't swap a cannon for a popgun. The was definitely someone else out there who didn't like me, he'd have to join the cue and get past my door man and woman. I shivered and Michelle started to wake as Yve turned her head toward me, she smiled but then returned her gaze to the door. Michelle leaped up and threw her arms around my neck and kissed me deeply, and then she peppered my face with small kisses, even my eyelids. When she was satisfied, she'd covered every millimetre she pulled her head back and stared into my eyes, I could see tears in hers and could feel a couple running down my own cheeks.

  My parents and Charlotte arrived in the evening, just after I'd finished talking to uncle Philippe and we had agreed our story. It wasn't too far from the truth, I'd persuaded him to let me go on what was supposed to be a routine mission, listening in on some potential terrorists and providing a real-time translation service for Pierre. Someone spotted the van, and we were ambushed as one of Pierre's men got out to relieve himself. Sticking with a thread of truth, I said I had heard a noise and pushed him to the ground and got shot in the process. I knew my father didn't buy it, but he said nothing, my mother declared her little boy a hero and Charlotte just gave me a knowing wink, she was up to something, I could always tell.

I spent the rest of the week in the hospital, and I got to know every one of Pierre's squadron as they took their turn in guarding me. They promised to take me out drinking, "like a real soldier." In the end my father had me transported by air ambulance back to London, Michelle went with me, and Pierre insisted on keeping the pilot company, he sat just behind the co-pilot with the cockpit door open, so he had an uninterrupted view to the back of the plane. He never took his eye off me until I was safely back home, and Michelle and I settled into our bedroom.

I slept a lot over the next week, Michelle and my mother often sat together watching over me, I wasn't in any danger but they both found it difficult to have me out of their sight. Pierre and Charlotte sat with me when, reluctantly, Michelle and my mother agreed they needed to take a break downstairs. On about the fourth day, Charlotte managed to persuade Michelle and my mother to go out the house with her for a few hours and leave the *two boys* to chat. Pierre was hardly the chatty sort, but I had been waiting to get him on his own so I could find out what had happened after I was taken.

'Right Pierre, before they come back tell me what happened?'

'Well, the good news is that the American President is still alive, in fact no one inside the house had any idea of what was happening outside. The marines heard some shots, but it was so far away they assumed it was either the French soldiers firing at each other or some farmer out shooting rabbits. They took defensive positions anyway, but only for twenty minutes and then stood down when the all-clear was given. When nothing had happened by the dessert course, Philippe watched his chief suspect, the Minister for Culture, slipping out the service door that leads to the kitchens. It was a stupid move really, the place was locked down and completely surrounded by soldiers and secret service. Philippe followed him out, and before he could get near an exit, he marched him up some stairs at the back and tied him up in a cupboard before he went back down for his Profiteroles.'

'What about the currency gang, what happened to them?'

'We think Saul sent a message after they got you back to the house, they held you at, telling them Akil and Jean had failed in their mission, and they had tidied up. Rachel thinks the others then received an encoded text message telling them to get out and meet at a small aerodrome a few miles from Versailles in Saint-Cyr. We found all their bodies except the two Italians, Morelli and Mancini, as you predicted, regardless of whether the plot was a success or failure their job was to clean up. Two shots each to the back of the head while they were kneeling down, wrists zip-tied behind their backs.

'Morelli and Mancini?'

'Probably not even Italian, but definitely linked to organised crime and well gone by the time we got there. Philippe thinks their leaders were probably working with a political or terrorist group or even another government, it seems everyone was using someone else.'

'C'est la vie, Pierre. That's life outside, outside our family. We don't use each other, but we do need and rely on each other.'

***

It took two months for the wound to fully heal and a further three months of physio before I could walk without a stick. It wasn't until I was close to starting university that I had anything like the muscle tone and strength I'd had before I was shot. Michelle barely left my side, and it was her nearness that got me through some very dark periods. At times I struggled to see the point of life, of living at all. For weeks I would slip into some nihilistic void, but she would stick by me and eventually pull me clear. By August, almost a year since we first met we had decided to stay in London, I would go to the London School of Economics as planned and Michelle would get herself a studio and go back to painting. It was very comfortable at the family home but we both realised we needed our own space together. With help from my parents and the salary from the French government, which continued until the day I started my course, we rented a duplex apartment in a converted warehouse on the wrong side of Shoreditch. Floor to ceiling metal-framed windows looked out over an inner courtyard with identical buildings on all four sides, it was open plan apart from a bedroom and the bathroom. The second floor was a large mezzanine above the living area with smaller windows facing the road. Michelle set this up as her studio and got a part time job waitressing at a nearby French restaurant to help with the bills. She didn't really need to, the ambassador had ensured that the French Government also compensated me for my injuries in the line of duty, but she was too proud to just live off my ill-gotten gains.

The week before term started, I contacted the university and asked to switch from Modern Languages to the London School of Economics' signature degree - Philosophy, Politics and Economics or PPE as it was usually abbreviated to. I'd realised that I would learn very little from further language studies and needed something to challenge me, and perhaps get to the root of the existentialist crisis that always seemed to *tremble* just beneath even my happiest moments. I felt like and probably was, a spoilt brat, a precocious spoilt brat even.

The term was due to start in a couple of days and I had a meeting with one of the professors about my request to change degrees. He did not ask me why I wanted to change, which I thought was strange, but then he probably considered that anyone who wanted to study any other course but his, was sadly lacking. Instead, he asked me some questions about Sartre in German, which deciding to play along, I answered in French. He then questioned me on Heidegger in French, and I answered in German. Finally, he stuck with French but asked a question on the Danish philosopher Kierkegaard, I answered in Danish and at last I saw a hint of a smile. I later confirmed that he didn't speak Danish, but whatever game he was playing with me I didn't care. I started the following Monday as an undergraduate in PPE, sadly though not unexpectedly, there would continue to be more questions than answers, or maybe that was the whole point? Maybe the meaning of life was - f*ear and trembling*, maybe there just were more questions than answers! So, I decided to ask questions of *things-past* and worry less about time-present and avoid tomorrow all together.

In contrast to my fragile contentment, Michelle was slowly establishing herself as an artist, she'd had a small exhibition in Fitzrovia, just behind Oxford Street, she sold five paintings and a series of photographs. My father and the ambassador urged all their friends and contacts to go, and one corporate customer commissioned a large piece for their headquarters. All this was fantastic, and I got more satisfaction and excitement from her success than any praise from my tutors. More than that, Michelle was so happy that I couldn't help being affected by her joy, it was better than any drug. But at night, when she was sleeping, I lay awake for hours thinking of Saul, Max and Jack. I was both appalled and fascinated by what I had done. When I did sleep, I was besieged by lucid dreams, in them I would either be running away from someone trying to kill me or trying to save Michelle or one of my family from faceless men. They always ended the same way, with me falling over a cliff edge but never hitting the bottom. It was definitely a metaphor for how I was feeling.

At the end of the first academic year, I was on course for a first and I wasn't even trying. In the second year I had a paper on Nietzsche accepted for publication in a peer-reviewed journal, the professor who had interviewed me was delighted. I was, as ever, ambivalent – unconvinced that such a thing was meaningful let alone important at all.

What stopped me going into a complete downward spiral of depression was Michelle. We were more in love than ever, that was real, that was meaningful. I knew I was lucky, that I led a very privileged life, but it was Michelle that kept me sane, it was her and my family that kept me going. I still heard from Pierre and Yve every now and then and the bond between us remained strong. I knew I could call on them if ever I needed to, but we lived in two very different worlds now, and they could share little of theirs with me now that I was on the outside. Despite all the positives in my life I knew that just below the surface something was wrong but couldn't figure out what or maybe I just wasn't ready to face it.

It took me until the end of my third year to realise that being safe, even being in love, just wasn't going to be enough for me. I needed risk, I needed danger, my dreams weren't premonitions like the one in Paris, they were just wishful thinking or unconscious desire. Even the horror of killing three people and almost dying myself could not stop me wanting more, the thought of my own demise gave new vigour to my being. It was of course Michelle who was the unwitting catalyst in this particular revelation. Knowing that, regardless of my recent graduation with a first and the publication of my paper, I was still low, she decided to organise a birthday party for me. Our flat was too small, but my parents agreed that she could use their house and Michelle and my mother made all the food, including a rather large birthday cake complete with twenty-two candles. The best thing of all was that Michelle had managed to get my parents to invite Philippe as well as getting Yve, Pierre and all fourteen of his squad to come over from Paris. My parents didn't quite know what to make of all these burley males drinking champagne as though it was lemonade and taking over most of the space in the dining room, but I was lapping it up. My grandparents didn't seem to have the same reservations and went around talking animatedly to them all, nanna and grandma even got a couple of them up to dance. Charlotte was also looking very pleased with our macho guests and had locked onto Pierre the moment he arrived, her hands seemed to be doing a conducted tour of his upper body when I looked across at them a little later. Pierre kept his hands to himself, and Charlotte looked a bit miffed at his lack of response, which I found amusing, not many people could resist her when she put the charm on. I wondered if Pierre was still *on duty*, I hadn't seen him drink anything but water all night, perhaps flirtation was also prohibited.

    I noticed uncle Philippe was maintaining a low profile near the door, watching all the interactions with great interest. I watched him watching others for a while - always working! I was about to go and join him when Charlotte suddenly appeared next to me and slid her arm around mine, then led me to one of the small anti rooms. Closing the door behind us and placing her back against it, then in her usual style she went straight for the jugular.

'Michelle tells me you're restless! Brother, I love you too much to fuck about. Oh, don't look so shocked Josh, I can match Pierre's men when it comes to F'ing and blinding, and I lost my virginity when I was seventeen. Right now, we need to be straight with each other. Frankly I think you're headed for a breakdown, especially if you stick with your plan to spend another three years studying that existentialist shit you call philosophy. Sartre was the only half sane one out the lot of them and that's because he spent all his time drinking and fucking. Uncle Philippe could do with your peculiar talents again, on an on-going basis this time. It's part of your nature Bro, if you deny it then you will be doing more harm to yourself than that pea shooter did to your luscious thigh.'

'You know about what I did in Paris?'

'Of course I know, who do you think suggested to uncle that he send you that train ticket when you were in Marseilles? I also told him how your languages were progressing at warp speed and combined with your elephantine memory, as well as being unknown and so innocent looking, made you the perfect boy for the job. I didn't mention your other skills though, but I understand from him that you let that particular cat out the bag yourself.'

'How much do you know about the night I got shot Sis?'

'Well, I know the bullshit story you told our parents, which neither of them believe by the way. They just chose to let it go, bury it, I don't think they want to know the whole truth in case it's more than they can handle. I think your decision to stay in London was genius, it was definitely your get out of jail free card. Nothing is actually free though, is it? I've watched you pay the price these last three years, pretending you can live without the thrill, it's visceral, that is real *meaning,* it's doing, not talking or reading. I suppose in your case the talking has a little more verve to it though. I tried to get the whole story out of Pierre, but all I got from him was one of his American movie clichés, "It's his story to tell." I also know that all his men think you're some kind of hero for what you did that night, but they are all sworn to secrecy.'

'Do you really want to know? You may not like me if I tell you.'

'I love you brother and that's not changing, ever. I don't have to like you to love you, but I do need to know the truth to help you and I will always help you. Seriously Josh, I admit that I am a nosey bitch, but my guess is that you haven't even told Michelle the whole story and I think, in fact I know you need to talk about it. I see it in your eyes, the despair – you're lost inside yourself, you need to talk about what happened. Not to some fancy quack but to those who love you, Michelle, me, Pierre, Yve, none of us will judge you but we will always forgive you, if that's what you need.'

I realised, of course, that she was right, and after nearly three years I really did need to tell someone, and Charlotte was the perfect person to comfort me while kicking me up the arse to spur me on. But first I had a question for her. 'Ok, I'll tell you what really happened that night. Once you have told me what the deal is with the ambassador? How come you were talking to him about secret missions and trade talks?'

'Josh, didn't you know? I thought everyone knew, I'm his latest mistress!'

For once I was speechless and my jaw dropped. Then Charlotte started laughing so loudly I thought everyone would come in to see what was going on. I needn't have worried, I'd forgotten that these rooms had been sound proofed in case they were needed for a private meeting.

'Oh Josh, your face, I thought you'd swallowed your tongue Bro. Just kidding, couldn't resist it. Mind you, the truth is even less believable. I'm a spy, I've been working for *uncle* since my second year at Oxford. It's a good place for spying, did my apprenticeship there. The Sorbonne was like finishing school for secret agents, lots of different nationalities, the ambassador reckons about twenty per cent of them are or will become spies by the time they've finished their studies. Philippe taught me how to spot a spook and how to follow them, it became a game I played – spot the spy then tell uncle so he could keep an eye on them. Most of them weren't up to anything serious but the ambassador has got tags on them all.'

So, for the first time after three years, I told someone else what I had done and more importantly exactly how I did it. By the time I'd finished I felt lightheaded and was worried I might pass out. But I needn't have worried about Charlotte's reaction, she just engulfed me in her arms, put her cheek to mine and sobbed, the tears then started to flow down my cheeks, and I wasn't sure if they would ever stop.

But they did stop and then she moved her head and gently pushed me back as she held my shoulders. I was waiting for her condemnation, but of course it never came.

'Oh Josh, you poor love holding on to that alone all this time. You need to tell Michelle, she needs to know, you can't have a relationship in the long-term unless she does. She needs to understand what you're living with, or she will think she's the problem.'

'Why would she think that?'

'Because she is a woman, the woman that loves you with all her heart.'

That night we stayed at my parent's house, in what they still insisted on calling our room, regardless of the fact we hadn't lived there for three years. I told Michelle about talking to Charlotte and asked if she also wanted to know everything that happened. I warned her it would be distressing, painful even, she did not hesitate, she just pulled my head down and rested it on her breasts, then she spoke.

'Talk. Tell me everything, don't dare try to spare me any detail.' Michelle sniffled a bit as I began to tell her what happened, when I told her what Saul had said they were going to do to me she sobbed and held me tighter, supporting me to go on. When I told her how I had actually killed them she gasped out loud and then, after a few seconds, she spoke. I had never heard her sound so angry, she did not shout or rant but there was steel in her voice.

'If I could bring them back and kill them again, make them suffer even more than the first time, I would, and then I'd do it again. Josh, you had no choice but you didn't just save yourself, think of how many others they would have gone on to torture and murder if you hadn't killed them. Even if they'd gone to prison they might have escaped or eventually been released. Sooner or later, they would have come looking for us. Even if they were locked up for the rest of their lives, they would talk to others about you and someone else, just as evil, would come after us. They would use me or your family to make you do what they wanted. Josh, I love you and I am proud of the way you defended yourself and the way that you protected me.'

I explained to Michelle why I couldn't just go back to university that I needed to be involved in my uncle's world, doing *nothing* and *being nothin*g wasn't an option I could live with. That the self-referential vacuousness disguised by theories and books no longer resonated with me. I was surprised when she said she thought I was right, but I could also see she was scared. In the end we agreed that I would talk to my uncle, but that we would stay in London for now and I would offer my services as an eavesdropper, gathering intelligence without putting myself in the line of fire. No more macho missions with Pierre in the middle of the night, or day for that matter. Then Michelle surprised me yet again with her next announcement.

'Josh, I'm going to ask Yve to teach me how to shoot, her and Pierre are staying in London for a while. I think you should take some lessons too, I'm sure Pierre would be very happy to train you.'

'Pierre has taught me a few things already, I didn't mind the self-defence, I struggled with the guns but if it's going to make us safer, I'm willing to try again.'

Philippe stayed at our house overnight and the next morning I tagged along with him as he left the house for the embassy. He never asked me why and we chatted as though this was something we did every day. His car was waiting outside the house and I just climbed in the back alongside him. I guessed that Charlotte had already had a word with him, so he was probably half expecting me to buttonhole him at the first opportunity. We went straight into his office and his secretary appeared a minute later with a pot of coffee. As she was about to leave Philippe asked her to push his morning appointments back an hour and told her we were not to be disturbed. The ambassador looked at me over his cup, and then put it back down on the low table between our two chairs.

'You know Josh your father is just down the corridor, if he doesn't spot you himself then someone will tell him, he has plenty of his own spies.'

Well, that was interesting, about the spies anyway, I didn't think father strayed into the dark side. I'd known he was scheduled to be in his office today, it was actually part of the reason I had chosen this particular morning to have my little one to one. If this was going to work, I needed to be honest with my father, I knew after my conversations with Charlotte and Michelle that I also needed to be able to talk to him, like I used to do before I went off on my big adventure and got it into my head that I should be able to do everything on my own. Misplaced independence was the secret of my greatest successes but also my biggest mistakes. In the last twenty-four hours I had learned that I needed all the help I could get if I was going to survive.

So, I told my uncle that I wanted to come back to work for him but that I'd learned my lesson and didn't intend to put myself in danger again. He hoped I might consider returning to Paris in the future, despite being posted in London it seemed that most of his extracurricular activity took place on French soil. It didn't surprise me though that he just so happened to be working on something in London at that point and could use my help. Having heard from Michelle, that both Pierre and Yve planned on being in town for a while, it clearly pointed to an active mission. According to my uncle there was a possible group of what he called "born again anarchists" gathering mass, with the potential to become a black hole and a threat on both sides of the Channel. Naturally, being anarchists, they had no particular leader but a French-Algerian lecturer at LSE, very convenient indeed, seemed to be the gravity drawing them all in. The group was a mixture of ages and nationalities, graduates, post grads and their guiding star Youssef Touati.

***

Youssef ate breakfast and lunch virtually every weekday at a vegetarian and vegan café on campus, a group of about a dozen students dropped by at various points and sat at his table, during the course of these meals they spoke in whispers and several different languages. Youssef was known to be fluent in Spanish and Arabic as well as French and English, he actually taught on the Modern Languages course that I'd switched out of three years earlier. The ambassador asked me if I could postpone dropping out of university and continue with my doctorate as the perfect cover for listening in on what they were up to.

While I hadn't changed my mind about the pointlessness of further academic study, it would be no hardship to continue provided I was also doing something, at least potentially, more worthwhile than staring through the festering entrails of some dead philosophers. The end would become the means and I was good with that, at least for the time being. I was certainly feeling happier than I had in quite a while, so I thought I'd better bite the bullet now and marched down the corridor to see my father. I was about a foot from his door, ready to knock, when I heard him call.

'Come in Josh, I'm on my own this morning.' He certainly wasn't surprised by my sudden appearance.

'You were expecting me, Papa?'

'I have my spies.'

I smiled, it seemed my uncle wasn't joking. 'I need to talk to you, it will take a while, do you have time?'

'I've cleared my diary for this morning and can cancel my afternoon appointments if need be.'

Now I was surprised. It took the rest of the morning to tell him about my sorry tale from Marseille to Paris. He was patient, he hardly interrupted apart from clarifying that he had actually heard what he thought he had when it came to my abilities. But he seemed less interested in them per se than in my mental health, I could tell he was devastated at the psychological impact and felt guilty that he had not been there for me. In the end I hoped I had made him realise that I had just not been ready to accept his help and that was my fault not his. He understood why I wanted to work for

Philippe, but he was concerned, it was possibly the lesser of two evils but it was still crazy. But mad men do strange things!

I learnt something else about my father that day, he did indeed have spies at his beck and call. Well before Charlotte and I were born he was actually my uncle's commanding officer, and I could see the regret on his face when he told me that he had shot and killed a dozen or more men in various encounters and given the orders for his men to kill many more. When he met my mother he decided he had done enough killing for his country and needed to focus more on living. My father became a diplomat, he laughed at himself when he said that. He couldn't let the world of secrets and intrigues go altogether though and over the years he had developed a little network of spies, most of whom were more adept with a computer than a gun. He made Philippe aware of any potential developments or threats he uncovered and then left it to him to neutralise them. The paranoia about double agents and moles at the top had never gone away since Kim Philby, and my father and uncle liked to operate in sterile conditions.

The following morning I went for breakfast at the Shaw Café, and several students came and went. They would sit at the table but never next to Youssef, a couple of them referred to him as Mudaris, Teacher in Arabic, but there was little conversation and what there was, was mostly between the students commenting on the quality of the food. I was determined not to get sucked in again, and spend all of my time listening in, I'd learned that no matter how discrete you thought you were if you stuck around too long you got noticed.

I'd reluctantly agreed to meet Michelle, Pierre and Yve at eleven at a building close to the French Consulate, the basement was a firing range and there were also several training and simulation rooms, whatever they might be, on the other floors.

We had only been going a short while, but I could feel Pierre was getting impatient with me, I had got worse since the first time he tried to teach me how to shoot, I was very tentative in taking aim and so far, I had forced myself to pull the trigger just twice. Michelle was the opposite, eager and grinning as she fired the gun, after a few practice shots under Yve's close supervision she managed to empty a whole magazine into one of the targets, actually cutting it in half. She claimed to have no idea how the gun had switched from single shot mode to fully automatic, but her eyes told another story. Yve, ever vigilant, had noticed my struggles as well as Pierre's growing frustration and suggested we swap. I didn't think it would make much difference to me but I could quickly see it was working for Michelle, her shoot first then shoot them again and let someone with a halo ask the questions was right up Pierre's street.

Yve was patient but after twenty minutes I'd only managed to fire the weapon twice. I think my experiences of that night in Paris had made it even more difficult than when Pierre had me practicing before. I was taking aim for the third time but had frozen, unable to pull the trigger, Yve put her hand over my wrists and gently applied downward pressure, with relief I pointed the gun toward the ground and put the safety on. She took me away from the other two and spoke to me quietly but firmly.

'What's going on Josh? You're a quick study, you understand the theory and you know what to do so tell me, what am I missing here, what am I doing wrong? Please, I just want to help you.'

That made me smile, it sounded like a variation on the old breakup line, "it's not you, it's me." But we both knew that it was all me and I needed to front up and be open. 'This is going to sound a bit odd. It's the noise, not sure why but it triggers something inside me, no pun intended. It might be from when I got shot, all the guns going off that night when I had my hearing set to max. I guess I still haven't dealt with it, I'm sorry.'

I felt dishonest, but it was as far as I could go just now. The gun blasts were only part of it, but it was mainly because they reminded me of the noise as I clapped my hands and Jack hit the floor, already dead his heart exploding inside his chest. Yve just smiled and went to her big gym bag and pulled out a much smaller gun and what looked like a metal tube, which she screwed on the end of the barrel before checking the magazine and the safety. I realised that she'd fitted a silencer to the gun, after that it felt like we were just playing a game of *secret agents*. Thirty minutes later I was hitting the target close enough to the centre to put the smile back on everyone's face.

Michelle looked into my eyes, winked and blew me a kiss, she turned, faced the target, and without a pause she started to fire her last six shots. Each bullet hit the target in almost the same spot, so close together there was a twenty-centimetre diameter hole in the centre of the target. It seemed Pierre was not the only badass in this little company. After that we went to a room on the top floor, in contrast to the basement this room was flooded with light, and you could see half of London through the windows. Pierre, of course, immediately lowered the blinds just in case there was a sniper hanging out on the nearby church spire, but then I realised that this was why he was still alive and probably a lot of other people owed their lives to his cautionary approach to all things. The room was carpeted with crash mats and the walls were lined with various weapons from swords to Bo Staffs. It seemed that Michelle had also requested some self-defence training and much to my surprise she suggested we stay in the same pairs, for a second I was concerned she might get hurt going up against Pierre but realised straight away that she would be safer with him than anyone else. Then I saw the glint in her eye and thought that perhaps I should be more worried about him.

    Yve and I went to the other end of the room, and she showed me some basic defence moves for breaking strangle holds, parrying punches and kicks. The most useful thing she taught me that first day was how to fall without hurting myself and I got plenty of practice as she made me attack her, over and over, and each time I tried to lay a hand on her I would fly through the air landing on my back. I was winded a few times, but it all seemed to come right as I got the hang of rolling into and out of Yve's throws. Before long I was managing to come up onto my feet with my arms and hands raised in the defensive position Yve had taught me. It was while I was stood waiting in that position that I heard a very loud groan and when I looked over Pierre was on his knees clutching his groin, snot dripping from his nose. Michelle looked at the two of us and smiled before saying just one word. 'Oops!'

Yve immediately burst out laughing while I tried my best to hold it in but in the end the laughter spilled out, twice as loud for being tamped down briefly. While Pierre recovered Michelle joined Yve and me.

'Yve, have you shown Josh that special technique for getting out of close situations yet.'

'Not yet.' Yve looked over at Pierre who was still on his knees. 'Perhaps now would be a good time.'

'Oh great, I might learn something too.' I knew they were up to mischief and that I was their specially selected victim. I also knew by now, that when the two of them got together it was futile to resist, as they said in the Bond movies.

'Ok Josh, I am just going to finish you off, sorry I mean finish off, with some different ways to break an opponent's hold. First put your hands around my throat, not too tight yet as I still have to talk. Remember you can reduce the pressure on your trachea by tensing the muscles in your neck. Press a little harder, can you feel them.'

Michelle was smiling when I glanced at her, they were definitely playing me and while I didn't know the rules, I was happy to be taken for a ride by these two. I tightened my fingers slightly around Yves neck and I felt her muscles push back and to my surprise she was still able to talk.

'At this point your instincts want you to pull back and away from your assailant but that is also what they're expecting, and they will be braced and ready. You need to do something they don't expect, so move forward instead.'

Yve took a step forward so that our bodies were touching, she was looking straight into my eyes and I could feel a trickle of perspiration meander slowly down my cheek. Then I was completely surprised when a soft hand slid up and under my sweatshirt to rest on my stomach just above the waistband to my joggers. This was dangerous territory, my pants had slipped during the training and were riding dangerously low, and I could feel what I hoped was Michelle's little finger tangling up in the hair that had escaped the confines of my pants. At that moment, utterly distracted, lost even, Yve kissed me on the lips and her tongue slid briefly inside my mouth. As she pulled away, I realised I had already released my hold on her and that her right knee was poised just beneath my nut-sack. Thankfully, unlike Michelle, she did not complete the move and unlike Pierre I remained standing if a little shaky. Then the two of them walked out the door, giggling loudly as they swayed their hips. When Pierre was able to stand, he just looked at me and shrugged then he looked back at the door before he spoke.

'You realise Josh, we have at least four weeks of this, twice a week for a month. I'm not sure we are going to survive.'

'Les chances sont contre nous mon ami!'

'There is only one thing for it!'

'And what's that?' I was half expecting him to suggest we join the Legion, it might have been a more sensible option than what he came up with.

'Tonight, we go the pub with Robert and all the boys'

So, they were all still in town, that was interesting. The prospect of a drunken night with a bunch of squaddies, not quite so appealing though. My only hope was to get back to the café and pray I heard something interesting enough to justify a late meeting with the ambassador. But what I heard was far from anything I expected.

It was nearly two when I got there and I wondered if they would all be gone but, as I ordered something called an Ayurvedic five-elements coffee and a falafel and beetroot wrap, I saw Youssef at the head of the table writing notes in an A4 hardback book. There was an older man in his mid-forties, I would guess, and a couple of very scrawny undergrads who looked like they saved their laundry up to take home to their mums at the weekend. At that moment Youssef looked up from his notes and caught my eye. I resisted the urge to turn my head away quickly, he smiled and returned to his book. I wasn't about to panic, I didn't think that there was any way, based on what just happened, that he would miraculously know what I was up to. He was just being disarmingly polite, when faced with a rude stranger staring at him or perhaps he fancied me. That would certainly complicate things. Whatever the backstory was, I had been noticed and would be noticed even more on subsequent visits. This wasn't what I had in mind when I'd hoped to have a reason to brief Philippe.

After that I ate my wrap and tentatively sipped the coffee, if I did come back, I would definitely be ordering a latte next time. Then, I heard his voice. I hadn't really heard him speak before, but I knew it was Youssef, it was baritone, deeply rich and sweet with a sharp fruitiness when he altered the pitch at the end of a sentence to ask a question. It made me think of the dark, unintentionally vegan, chocolate torte with raspberries on top and a swirl of cream at one side of the plate that my mother made on special occasions.

'Hello, it's Josh, isn't it? Joshua Renoir?'

No point in trying to deny that. 'Yeah, that's me, have we met? I think I would have remembered if we had.'

'Sorry, no we haven't met before. I'm Youssef Touati, I teach Modern Languages and three years ago I was supposed to be your personal tutor until you jilted me at the last minute. I remember your face from the application documents.'

'Wow! I thought I had good memory, that's amazing'

'Not really, you were by far the best applicant we had for the course that year, or since then actually. I had to fight to get you on my tutor group, if I remember correctly you were already speaking four or five different languages fluently back then.'

I was sure he knew exactly how many languages I spoke *back then* and which ones they were. I recognised we were playing a game, the rules to be determined, the objective – to find out as much as possible about the other person whilst giving as little information about yourself as possible. I suddenly realised I was having fun, the kind of fun I liked best - subterfuge and subversion. Time to play!

'Three or four I think.'

'Have you added any new ones whilst you've been studying? I can't imagine politics or economics was much of a challenge for you and philosophy is so dull, how did you keep yourself busy? Your brain firing on all twelve cylinders?'

He was good with the flattery, not so flowery that it made you sneeze, so I thought I'd give him a bone and watch where he buried it. 'I picked up a bit of Arabic during my travels but since I started here, I've been absorbed in the books, the lectures not so much.' I wanted him to think I was ripe for conversion to whatever ideology he was pedalling. He took the bait, but I had already decided to reply in English to add another layer of obfuscation, rather like when I was interviewed by another professor three years earlier.

That seemed to trigger something inside my brain, and just like that first mission in Paris I was inside his head and hearing his words in English.

'Philosophy is a reductive exercise, don't you think? The world is too complex to be understood by logic?'

'We are circumscribed by many things, material and immaterial. Politics and religion have changed the world many times and yet they hold us back, though they cannot stem the tide.'

'You should join our little company soon, you would be most welcome.' I looked over and noticed the table was empty, the door had not opened since Youssef came over. It seemed as though he had waited until the others had gone. He saw me checking out the table and clearly decided it was time to part company, but not without a promise for a rematch. 'I'm sure we will talk again soon, Josh.'

Then he was gone! Well, it didn't seem like my cover was blown but I was compromised, possibly in more ways than one. If I kept eating at the café it would be difficult to keep my distance from Youssef and his followers, which for my own safety and sanity was the last thing I needed. First, I would talk to Michelle, I'd told Philippe from the outset that I would share anything that was not top secret with her and absolutely everything with my father. I'd learned that my head was a dangerous place to be alone in. Michelle agreed that Youssef coming to talk to me was nothing to worry about yet, but that it could make things difficult, and she forbade me to meet any of them outside of the café. She also picked up on him seeming to wait until everyone else was gone.

'I'm not sure what it means but I don't believe it was chance, it definitely means something, what are the possibilities? Youssef is madly in love with you, well most people are so that's a strong probability, but just so you know I don't share outside the family. Second, he wants to recruit you to the group, but why talk to you alone? He could have invited you to their table earlier to meet a few of the others. Thirdly, and my money is on this one for what it's worth, he has something to say that he doesn't want anyone else in the group to hear.'

'I'm with you, I noticed he looked toward the door before he spoke to me in Arabic, I think he was checking in case someone from the group was about to come in.'

'So, what's the plan mon bel homme?'

'Well, I think I should track Philippe down and brief him?'

'You wouldn't be trying to get out of your "boys night out" would you?'

'Maybe.'

'Pierre will be très en colère contre toi. Just be warned, if you come back early, Yve and I have already planned a soirée entre filles, Netflix et chill. You're welcome to join us, we have popcorn, pistachio ice cream and a bottle of Amaretto, but no talking while the movie is playing.'

I decided that I needed to have a serious talk with Michelle soon and find out where this relationship with Yve was going, the flirting and innuendos were getting more intense as time went on. What about Pierre? I knew he had no romantic interest in Yve, no matter how much he respected her abilities, but there had been a few clues recently that he had found someone special. He was keeping quiet though, not that I blame him, Yve and Michelle would insist on vetting her to see if she was good enough for him and if she was, they would immediately steal her for the feminine side. Now that I had broken free of my miasma, I was far more open to what was going on around me, rather than shutting everything out to avoid mental overload I was enjoying the everyday intrigues and sparring matches between the four of us. Charlotte too when she was able to join our little clan.

Alas the "ambassador had flown to Paris on urgent business and would not be available until the morning" I was duly informed by someone called Monica who sounded like she ate razor blades for breakfast. It looked like I was going to the pub after all. It wasn't as bad as I feared, they didn't like the beer and we ended up at a wine bar drinking Pinot Noir and listening to a woman with bright blue hair playing smooth jazz on the sax. Pierre insisted on seeing me safely back to the flat and brought Robert and three others for company, nothing was going to happen to me on his watch it seemed. I found Michelle fast asleep on top of the bed clothed in just her pants and lying next to her was Yve in one of my t-shirts that had ridden up to flash most of her juicy ass, I tried not to look and failed. There was a person-sized gap between the two of them and I optimistically imagined they'd contrived to leave it open for me to join them. But my courage failed me, and I slept on the sofa. I woke up at eight with Michelle straddled naked across my groin grinding against my cock beneath my boxers. I looked around, there was no sign of Yve, Michelle smiled at me when she spoke.

'You naughty boy!'

I wasn't sure if she was talking about my erection or that I'd failed to join the two of them. I went with option one and started to push back against her, which elicited the most sinful moan I'd ever heard.

It was eleven o'clock before I got to see the ambassador, Yve and Pierre joined us a few minutes later. After I told them about Youssef, Pierre started his usual worried pacing, which was thankfully more sedate than his angry stomping. He and Yve both started to speak at the same time, but Philippe put his hand up to stop them in their tracks, then he looked at me for a few seconds before he spoke.

'Right, the mission is suspended from this moment. Josh, I am not taking any more chances with your safety and neither are you. You are not to visit the café or in any way observe, listen or make contact with Youssef or any other members of the group. Pierre and Yve, you need to watch out for Josh until we confirm there is no risk. Is that understood?' The three of us nodded and he stared at me until I spoke, 'oui ambassador.' Then he looked at Pierre and Yve who were stood side by side. 'Yes sir!' Clearly this was an order and they were in no doubt who was in charge.

'We will review the situation in two weeks, or immediately if new information presents itself. Pierre and Yve, I understand you are training Josh and Michelle in basic combat and defence skills?' Pierre answered without hesitation. 'Oui!'

'Good, use this hiatus to step it up, and have Alphonse give Josh some basic bomb making and defusing lessons but make sure he doesn't get carried away and start playing with the real thing.' Yve and Pierre looked very confused by this last instruction, they nodded anyway and the three of us went to leave. But Philippe hadn't quite finished with me.

'Josh, can you hold on for a few minutes I need a word about a family matter?' The other two left, saying they would wait for me downstairs, when the door closed I waited quietly for uncle Philippe to speak.

'Your father is in his office alone at the moment so I think you should go and bring him up to date. Also, because of our common interest the two of us are collaborating more closely than we have done in many years, and I have to say I am enjoying that aspect greatly. That said, your father has been doing his own digging and has managed to identify virtually all of the diners at the "last supper" as he likes to call them, apparently there are thirteen in all. I think he has a few things on them that he wants to share with you.'

'I thought you said the operation was over?'

'Nothing is ever over in this business Josh. I actually said it was suspended or should I say Pierre's, Yve's and your role is on ice for the time being, your father's agents will continue to ferret away and monitor what goes on outside the confines of the café.

By the way, pay attention in the bomb class. Alphonse is a little anal, which is no bad thing when you defuse bombs for a living, but I have this theory that, shall we say, your percussive talents may prove interesting, maybe even useful.'

I made my way down to my father's office and paused outside it for a second to read the gold lettering on the frosted glass of the door: Paul Renoir, Deputy Chief of Mission. It reminded me of the scene in the Maltese Falcon at the beginning where Bogart/Sam Spade coldly has his very recently murdered partner's name wiped from the door. As usual my father called me in before I could knock, acknowledging our new relationship he asked me to sit as we aborted the almost-hug at the last second. I brought him up to speed and I could see he was pleased that I was *sharing,* and that Philippe was keeping to our bargain regarding my safety.

'Josh, what you say about Youssef is interesting, it ties in with what my agents have been able to glean so far. He appears to have started his little club by accident, it's well known that he doesn't think much of many of his fellow academics, he considers most of them to be lazy and intellectually under-par. He took to eating in the Shaw Café it seems to avoid them whenever he wasn't teaching. Then with his brighter students he started asking them to meet him there for tutorials rather than his office. The net effect is that he hardly sees any of the other staff, he has become alienated from them, and he is increasingly conspicuous by his absence. This is not the behaviour of a secret conspirator, he makes no effort at all to blend in.'

'What about the others?'

'Nothing much, most of them have taken part in the odd protest march but nothing violent. Two of them were arrested in some of the recent Paris riots, but they let them go, they had no weapons and were described as idealists. Sorry, other than my instincts that still tell me that something's afoot, I've got very little.'

'What about an older man, in his forties? He was there yesterday but I didn't see him the day before, he looked out of place. Youssef came over to me after he had left, and my instinct tells me that was deliberate.'

'That's news to me, Youssef is barely forty and he's the oldest member of the group by ten years. Can you describe him?' I could see that he immediately realised it was a silly question and he shrugged then smiled at me. 'Pardon, of course you can!'

'Better still, I'll go back to the apartment and work with Michelle. I'll have his picture to you by five o'clock.'

By the ambivalent look on his face, I could tell my father was concerned about involving Michelle, but he didn't say anything. I was worried too but we had agreed to share whenever possible so we could support each other. Neither of us felt we could live without the other, which meant there was no point in trying to exclude her, that would just lead to secrets between us and make us more vulnerable. The agreement was, if it was something that she could not reveal without seriously harming others or breaching national security, then I wouldn't tell her. That way if someone ever captured her, she could tell them everything she knew. It was rather naïve, a convenience for us both, I knew that should one of us be taken we would be traded if we were lucky and executed if we were not. Either way we would be tortured first.

The following day the four of us met up at the training rooms, Yve and Michelle had been shopping together and arrived ten minutes after Pierre and I did. We were laid out on the mats doing some stretches when they came in, they were wearing tracksuits but discarded them as soon as the door closed. They were both wearing black spandex crop tops and tiny shorts, in the coolness of the air-con their nipples noticeably raised the material, I rolled over to face down on the mat and pushed my nose and mouth into it to suppress the involuntary groan I released. I wasn't looking but I knew that Michelle was grinning, and Yve was doing her best not to laugh. Pierre seemed to be unaffected, but I wondered how long he could manage that for, I'd give him ten minutes max.

    We were reversing the order today and starting with the physical stuff before going down to the range. Pierre had told us that this would give us some practice at shooting when we were tired, and our muscles were on the point of twitching and cramping with the lactic acid. I just thought he was being sadistic and wondered what I'd done to offend him as he started making us do laps around the gym, even the sight of Yve and Michelle in those shorts two metres in front of me wasn't making it any easier. After twenty minutes Pierre let us stop and drink some water then we paired up as before and I was dreading the close contact with Yve, my own shorts were Lycra and left little to the imagination. Luckily, or maybe not, Yve decided to take it up a gear and handed me a wooden staff.

    'Right Josh, this is a Jo Staff and is about 1.2 metres long compared to the Bo Staff which is 1.8 but what it lacks in size it makes up for in speed and manoeuvrability. They can be made up of two pieces, which makes them easier to carry and conceal and also means you can hold one in each hand if you are fighting in a confined space. The techniques are completely different, so we are going to focus on the full-size staff, which is easier than using two but it does hurt more when I land a blow.'

    I noted the grin on her face and the fact she'd said "when" I hit you and not "if", on the other side of the room Michelle was doing her best to kick Pierre in the side of the head, she'd got up to his shoulders, which I thought was impressive, but she clearly wasn't happy with it. A second later Pierre had her leg by the ankle and had pulled it up to his shoulder, so the Achilles rested on his collar bone, her other foot was barely touching the ground, it looked painful, and she was shaking slightly. I instinctively went to move toward her but Yve caught my arm and pulled me down a bit so she could whisper in my ear.

'Wait, he won't hurt her or let her injure herself. Just watch, your little pussy is actually a tigress.'

If it hadn't been for my concern for Michelle, the way Yve hissed the sibilants against my flesh would have made my cock explode out my shorts. Then I saw that determined look on Michelle's face, she took a deep breath and flexed on her toes a few times before flattening the sole to the ground, effectively stretching her a further six centimetres. Pierre, smiled at her and waited, Michelle closed her eyes, and I could see her chest rise and fall as she inhaled deeply, in through her nose and out through her mouth. After about a minute, she opened her eyes and nodded at Pierre who raised his hands, he placed one over her instep and the other one palm upward against her calf. Now he looked into her eyes and nodded, there was a slight pause then she pushed herself forward as Pierre pushed her leg upwards. Michelle's heel was now level with Pierre's temple and her toes extended beyond his head, she was in a standing splits her legs flat against his body.

I turned back to Yve who was grinning from ear to ear as she just mouthed the word "wow!" Then it was my turn, for the first twenty minutes Yve taught me the techniques and had me practice manoeuvring around a dummy and striking it in various places, it seemed the footwork was as important as the staff and took more practice to get right. Unlike the gun I learned quickly and was comfortable with it, I also liked that it wasn't necessarily lethal. Satisfied with my progress Yve got me to spar with her, she took it easy on me for a while, stopping her blows just short of my body and I managed to get a few taps in on her. After we stopped for a drink she handed me a padded jacket, it reminded me of wicket keeper's gloves, and a helmet with a face guard, once she was also kitted out we started to circle each other. The first blow felt like a hammer hitting my head, the sound of the stick on the helmet resounded around the gym and the inside of my skull. Then I noticed that Michelle and Pierre were sat down on a bench watching the show. The next shot she landed was to my chest but as I improved, I managed to parry most of her sweeping horizontal and vertical strikes, until she took me completely by surprise when she just jabbed her staff end first between my flailing arms. I thought the staff would have had very little power used that way, but she actually knocked me off my feet. We carried on for another five minutes and I managed to work my way around to the back of her and I just laid the staff against her shoulder blade before she spun away. Then I heard Pierre clapping and whistling, Yve just took off her helmet and bowed to me and I did the same back.

  Pierre came straight over to me once the niceties were completed. 'Well done Josh, those last few minutes were brilliant, shame you got your ass kicked for the first fifteen though.'

When he'd finished laughing at his own joke he took a long look at me. 'Seriously, I mean it, you did incredibly well. I guess Yve didn't tell you that she has been training with the Jo and Bo Staff for twelve years, she is the best I've ever seen, and I have never seen anyone get behind her and land a blow the way you did. But before you get too big headed, we still have shooting practice, and a stick won't do you any good if someone puts a bullet in your skull.'

When we entered the range, Yve was stood by my side, close enough that I felt her tense before she immediately stepped in front of me and started to reach for her gun. The range was booked for us, no one else should have been there but like Yve I immediately sensed we had company. Unlike Yve, I knew straight away who it was, and I put my hand on hers before she raised her weapon.

'It's ok there's no threat, well she won't harm us at least, it's my sister. That's not strictly true either but I'm pretty sure she won't shoot us unless we criticise her hair.' I felt rather than saw Yve and Michelle smile. Pierre didn't seem at all surprised, but we were all opened mouthed when he stepped forward and kissed Charlotte on the lips as she embraced him. Then he turned to the three of us.

'Well, I take it there is no need for introductions but what you don't know is that Charlotte is the newest member of the squad and now you can all stop speculating about my love life as well. The CO, I mean the ambassador, who as you all know is a great believer in filial loyalty, has also asked Charlotte to become part of our inner circle or as Michelle prefers to call it, The Family.' I decided to wait until I got Charlotte on her own before I grilled her about how her and Pierre got together. I'd seen that she liked him the night of my birthday party, at our parent's house, but Pierre was being Pierre and didn't seem interested. I had also noticed Charlotte smile when Pierre emphasised the L word.

Pierre was right, as usual, it was a lot harder to hit the target when you have been going flat out for an hour. I managed to get three rounds in the bull and three in the wall to the left of the target, I tried to tell Yve the gun was pulling but she wasn't having it. The other two dozen shots were peppered around the circle and given the way my muscles were cramping I was quite pleased until Pierre told me if I missed with the first shot, I wouldn't get another. It was then that an idea occurred to me about the Jo Staff and the way Yve had been able to knock me over by pushing the end into my chest, which was still hurting unlike most of the other blows she had landed. I'd need to test the theory another time though.

Before we went our separate ways Charlotte told us we were all invited to the big house, which was what we had taken to calling my parent's place, for dinner that night. I spotted Yve looking at Michelle, seemingly a little panicked, Michelle took her hand before she spoke.

'Don't fret my love, I guess you came with your battle dress and left your LBD behind. I've got something you can wear for this little skirmish, come to our place about six and we can put our war paint on together.'

'Je t'aime, Michelle.'

***

It was about three by the time we got back home, and I thought the sex and fidelity talk could not be put off any longer. Feeling very self-conscious I took Michelle's hand and sat down on the sofa, she got the hint and sat next to me, putting her free hand around the back of my neck and gently stroking, she knew how much that relaxed me, which helped to finally say what I'd been avoiding for weeks.

'Je t'aime, Michelle.' I chose to echo the declaration Yve had parted with us on. 'I'm usually good with words, but this is difficult. You and Yve are very close, and I like that you are friends but it's clear to see that you could be and perhaps are lovers, and I'm ok with that. You also know that Yve and I have the potential to be more than friends, and you seem to be encouraging us in that direction. Am I right or have I just fucked things up?'

'Je t'aime, Josh. It's different, I love Yve as a friend and also, I am sexually attracted to her. It's difficult to explain, but with you love and sex are inseparable, with every look or just the slightest touch I feel love and arousal coming together, it's like the two most sensual perfumes in the world blended in to the sexiest-ever cocktail, the aroma swirling in the air between us, binding us together. I love Michelle as a friend, but I admit I would like to fuck her as a woman, the feelings I have around her are quite visceral, animalistic even. So far, we've only kissed, but what kisses! They made me wet. We agreed to wait until you were ready to talk about it, that night you came home and saw us on the bed together it was so difficult for us to stop. We left a space for you, but you slept on the sofa, we knew you needed longer, poor Yve I heard her getting herself off in the shower before she left while you snored on the canapé. I jumped on you as soon as she was out the door, but I am sure you remember that.'

'I remember that! I'm ok with you and Yve having sex, I have to admit the idea turns me on, but what if I can't handle a ménage-a-trois? Emotionally I mean, not physically.'

'Well, I like a man who's confident about his abilities! Seriously, I don't want a full-blown love affair with you both, but I wouldn't mind sharing you occasionally. Also, and this is not very equitable, but it is what it is. How do the English say it - "I want my cake and I want to eat it." Is that right?'

'Close enough, but I'm not sure I understand what you're getting at?'

'Well, I want to share you with Yve, and I want to have Yve to myself sometimes, but I don't want you and Yve to have sex without me. Is that too selfish?'

'Huis clos.'

'No Exit? Hell is other people?'

'People's relationships are fraught with conflict, so it is good to set out your terms and conditions. No one can exit and no one new, no one outside the family that is, can enter?'

'So, you don't think I'm asking too much?'

'Michelle, you can never ask for too much from me. Anyway, I think I feel safer with that arrangement and while I'm grasping the nettle here, I might as well use both hands. After today's little revelation about Charlotte and Pierre and his mention of "family" I'm curious to know how or if they fit in with your "family friendly" policy? Sarte only had three characters and thanks to the curfew during the war, the play was just one act.'

'I was surprised to see Charlotte at the range, Yve and I had guessed Pierre was seeing someone, but we had no idea it was your sister. That first time I stayed at your home we both thought she was making a play for me, but apart from a bit of flirting it never went anywhere, and then Yve came along. Charlotte though, is definitely "family", as is Pierre and up until today I thought he might be interested in you, but maybe he only sees you as a little brother. For me he is definitely a big brother, and absolutely off the menu. Do you like Pierre, like that I mean?'

'He piqued my interest briefly when we met in Marseilles, but it was just speculative curiosity, he is a brother not a lover. I sometimes see a man I think is attractive, but they look nothing like Pierre, they're always feminine and lithe not beefy or hairy like Pierre.'

'What about Youssef? I noticed how your voice changed when you told me about him talking to you in the café?'

'If I have any inclination towards men then he is definitely at the top of the list, he is very feminine, he's like a cat stalking its prey when he walks, and his voice is musical.'

'Oh Josh, I think I'm getting jealous!' At that we both fell about laughing and when we stopped suddenly, we launched ourselves together, lips colliding, clothes ripping apart and hands everywhere. I was just about washed and dressed when Yve arrived, she kissed Michelle on the lips and me on the cheek, I clearly took her by surprise when I held her shoulders and kissed her on the lips, my tongue slipping inside her mouth. When we parted, she looked over at Michelle, who had just slipped a dressing gown on after showering, knowing she was going to be playing "dress-up" as she called it, with Yve. There was a minefield of communication in the looks that passed between the two of them, that was way beyond my skills to translate. Yve broke the silence that had been gathering.

'Do we have to go to this dinner tonight?'

Unfortunately, it was clear that the meal was not optional, and the conversation would be more business than pleasure. So, I waited on the sofa while the two of them went to the bedroom to get dressed. Michelle called me to the door three times, the first occasion was to give an opinion on both their dresses, of course they looked gorgeous, but that it seems wasn't what they were going for and I was sent back to the sofa. The second time, Michelle stood at the door alone, but I could see over her shoulder, which she knew, Yve was stood on the other side of the room in front of the mirror her back toward me. She was holding up a jade green dress to herself and I had a perfect view of her back and ass, she was naked, and she had the most amazing sleek but clearly defined muscles that highlighted her shoulders and seemed to ripple down her back to her tight bottom and long, long legs. While clothes seemed to be optional, shoes were not, and she wore a pair of nosebleed heels that just accentuated every curve in her body. Michelle was wearing a magenta-coloured dress that scooped low at the front and barely existed at the back, even the naked Yve could not outshine her, I told her she was beautiful but that wasn't the look she was going for either.

The third time they called me, Michelle was dressed in black, the top part was lace, and almost see through, the skirt ended just above the knee, but then it was split to almost the hip on her left leg exposing the white flesh above her stocking. The front of Yve's white dress plunged to the navel and was barely held together by the lace threaded through four eyelets. There was a pencil skirt that stopped four inches above her knees and accentuated her curves, taking her in head to foot was almost like accelerating through a chicane at full throttle. There was no split at the front but when they turned around the back of Yve's skirt was cut up the centre and just about covered her ass. When they turned back, I had my mouth open and didn't say a word. Speechless, it seems was what they were looking for, we were ready to go.

We arrived fifteen minutes late, which I thought was pretty good in the circumstances. Michelle insisted we enter the reception room, where drinks were already being served, three abreast with me in the centre and their arms linked through mine. Charlotte had taken over the bar and was busy mixing cocktails for everyone. The others all turned toward us and stared while we looked equally agog at Charlotte and Pierre. I don't know where he got it from, but I suspected Charlotte was responsible for Pierre's Armani suit, she of course was every bit as sensational as Michelle and Yve and when she finally saw us, she made a beeline for the two of them and whisked them off in a fit of giggles. I was pleased that Pierre looked as bemused as I felt, my parents and uncle Philippe had obviously seen it all before and took no notice.

When we went into dinner it was more formal than I had expected, there were nameplates indicating where to sit, I'd only ever seen those used at the big soirées in the grand dining room. Oddly, however, the food was laid out buffet style in heated containers down the centre of the table, the meme was Chinese restaurant, the food of course was pure French. My father and mother sat at either end of the table, I sat to the right of my mother and Michelle to her left and opposite me, Yve was in the middle with Charlotte to her left and Pierre opposite her, uncle Philippe sat in the middle opposite Yve. Clearly my parents were up to speed with Charlotte's love life.

The reason for our little gathering and the absence of any staff soon became apparent. After the main course my father tapped his knife against the crystal glass making it ring out and bring everyone to attention. 'I asked you all here tonight as the ambassador has an announcement to make, it will be public in a few days, but it has ramifications for us all in one way or another. Over the last few years or so our family, without any planning, has expanded most delightfully as can be seen clearly this evening. The ties between the eight of us are not dependent on blood or any legal binding. No, they are based on love and loyalty and the changes that are about to happen will test the strength of us all, but it will be through love and loyalty that we survive. Philippe, do your worst!'

'Thank you, Paul, the right words at the right time as always. Well to business then and the reason I dragged you here. Against my will and despite all my protests I am to be promoted to Ministre de l'Europe et des Affaires étrangères.

Much to the President's disgust I do not intend to give up my little war on terrorists, indeed I hope to drag a few other allies in to the fight in my new role. Unfortunately, as I said, the President is not so enthusiastic, and I will need to maintain a little more distance from some events. I have also prevailed on Paul to take over as the London ambassador, which has been a very difficult decision for him. Pierre and Yve, I ask you to serve and protect him in the same way you have always done for me.'

I watched as they both looked at the ambassador and nodded their agreement before turning to my father for a brief moment, then the Minister resumed.

'Charlotte and Josh, I hope I will see much of my honorary niece and nephew but for now there is plenty to keep you busy here. Michelle and Madam Renoir, I know you will provide wisdom and strength to the company, I am sure you will be key to its safety and success. But I have to acknowledge, as Paul well knows, that while your connection as a family will help protect you it will also leave you more exposed, people will join the dots and then try and break you apart.'

***

Over the next three weeks my father was up to his ears in ceremony and bureaucracy while the five of us continued to train. Michelle could strip a gun down and rebuild it in the dark even faster than Pierre, she also managed to land a couple of round house kicks to his head, which made Charlotte flinch but didn't stop her cheering Michelle on.

Yve and I continued to work with the Jo Staffs, while I'd memorised the different techniques and forms within a week, it took another week for my muscles to catch up. The steps and counter steps couldn't be learned, you had to react to your opponent and predict their next move, it was the most exhausting thing I'd ever done. I'd even tried practicing with the staff split in two a few times and I'd actually managed to disarm Yve when she came at me with a knife. Though I failed to spot the kick that landed in my groin and ended up grovelling at her feet with my hands between my legs. Michelle didn't wince or show any concern for my safety, she was far too busy laughing at me.

    On the Friday we all agreed to finish early in the afternoon and meet up for drinks at our apartment. At about twelve, Yve asked me if I felt up to trying full on combat with the Jo Staff before we called it a day. I wasn't sure I was ready for that and though I knew she wouldn't do any permanent damage, I was also very aware that she could inflict a lot of pain without any lasting effect. So, I asked her if she thought I could handle it.

    'The thing is Josh, the only way to find out is to try and even when you lose you will learn more from it than you do from our sparring sessions.' So, it was agreed, she helped me dress in full protective gear and while she sorted her own kit, the other three sensing something was about to kick off started to gather around. If there had been a few more of them it would have looked like a classic playground fight without the shouting, at least to start with.

    Yve and I danced around each other, feinting here, blocking there. I tried to get behind her, like I did the first time, but she wasn't going to get caught twice. We stalked our prey, always looking into each other's eyes, never at the opponent's staff and never at our own. One glance away and the other would strike, like a cobra with one giant fang, and it would all be over. We must have been circling each other, hitting and blocking for twenty minutes, I dared not look at the clock. But even thinking about it was a fatal mistake and Yve spotted her chance. This time I saw the move, almost in slow motion, she'd turned the staff on its end, pointing straight at my chest and was propelling it with all her force toward my sternum. I knew there was no escape, so instead I pushed the breath in my lungs forward against my chest as though I was creating some kind of airbag, at the same time I braced one leg firmly behind the other and struck with my own staff. To Yve's and everyone else's surprise, I didn't go down, instead the staff bounced back a few centimetres and vibrated frenetically. When Yve looked down, she saw that my staff rested on her throat, she smiled took two steps back and bowed from the waist and I did the same. Pierre declared us both dead, but I'd never felt more alive.

Charlotte and Pierre left about ten, claiming they were exhausted but we all knew it would be some time before they slept. That left the three of us, and after the fight earlier, the level of erotic charge in the room was off the scale. Michelle just stood in the middle of the floor and stripped her clothes off, she looked at each of us, licked her lips and said just two words. 'Your turn.' We didn't need to be told twice and as soon as we undressed Michelle took each of us by the hand and walked into the bedroom. Michelle at last made good on her promise to let Yve suck my cock while she watched. The sex was amazing and somehow also comforting, and in the morning, I woke sandwiched between the two of them. There was no awkwardness between the three of us and Yve left just after breakfast. Michelle and I spent an hour cuddling on the sofa before I reluctantly headed for the university library unsure what exactly I was supposed to be doing there.

The new ambassador, aka dad, had told us that his "de vrais espions" had so far failed to uncover anything or even identify the mysterious quarante ans, and the mission remained suspended. Father or was it the ambassador told me to get on with my studies in the meantime and Michelle told me I was too much of a distraction to be hanging around the apartment while she was trying to work. I thought I could at least make a start on the literature search for my thesis and now it was no longer my raison d'être, I felt better about the whole thing and was breezing through journal article abstracts and noting any that seemed at all relevant. I'd been at it for three days and was starting to get a little bored, especially knowing how much more of this ritual academic slog lay in front of me. Then I sensed him walking up behind me, I didn't turn, I didn't feel threatened, I knew exactly who it was. He wasn't trying to sneak up, his footsteps were naturally light, and I imagined him as a cat softly curling around my leg. Without turning around, I spoke to him, hoping to unsettle him a little by my awareness of his presence.

'Youssef, I thought you preferred the café?'

'Is being able to see through the back of your head another one of your many talents?'

He was by then standing next to me and I looked up as I spoke, determined to be as enigmatic as possible, I said just one word. 'Almonds.'

'Almonds? Sorry you have me there.'

'Crème pour les mains à l'amande.'

'Pardon?'

'You use an almond hand cream, L'Occitane I think, I noticed it at the café when you came over.'

'I feel like I'm in an episode of Sherlock and clearly there is no point in pretending I was just passing by and happened to notice you. I wanted to ask you something, a favour really?'

'If I can help, I will. What do you need?'

'Not here, there is a study room free at the back, save your references and notes and join me there in five minutes.'

I just nodded and then mentally berated myself for breaking the rules, again. I closed my Mac, everything would still be there when I opened it again, then I texted Michelle, Pierre, Yve and Charlotte on our WhatsApp group so they knew I was putting my head in the lion's mouth and where to find the body. I knew Youssef wasn't a threat, not to my safety anyway, but no harm in maintaining protocol while disobeying orders. Michelle texted me back first, equally unconcerned about my safety it seemed.

'Oo là là, behave xxx'

Then Charlotte's text came through. 'I've got this everyone, I'm downstairs checking a few things out. Josh, don't go in until I get there then I'll wait outside while you meet with him.' She must have been moving while she texted, within thirty seconds she was stood next to me just outside the door to the room, which had an opaque glass panel in, through which you could just make out Youssef. It was enough for Charlotte to agree it was safe for me to go in while she sat at a desk a few metres from the door. Inside, Youssef had moved the two chairs away from the desk and placed them opposite each other. He was sat on one but stood when I entered and came over, his arm outstretched. I shook his hand, his skin was soft, and the scent of almonds rose with the friction of our flesh.

'Josh, you don't know me at all and what is worse is that you're a student, though clearly wise beyond your years. Sorry, now I'm talking in clichés. I'll try and get to the point, I don't want to take up your time but some background is necessary.

'Youssef, I'm not in any rush, take as much time as you need.'

'The students at the café, they come and go, I don't keep any records and I'm terrible at remembering names. I was really surprised when I saw you and instantly remembered your full name, I couldn't forget your face, not even from that little passport mugshot they made you send in. But then, I suppose you do make an impression. Anyway, a lot of the staff and many of the other students think the group is some anarchist hotbed, waiting to hijack the next student protest and turn it into a full-scale riot. That's not what it's about, or at least it wasn't, the aim was to challenge traditional ways of thinking, to look beyond the accepted texts and methods. To ask questions we don't know the answers to and maybe realise there are no answers. It's hardly new, Socrates was doing the same thing four hundred years before the birth of Christ.

'Yes, and he was forced to drink hemlock and carry out his own execution. Be careful Youssef, I'm not sure things have changed that much in the last two millennia.'

'The thing is I'm being put under pressure to turn the group into what the rumours have always claimed – a terrorist cell funded and primed by people who only want to kill those that don't agree with them. Socrates would certainly appreciate the irony in that.'

'What sort of pressure are we talking about Youssef, do they have something on you, or have they threatened to harm you?'

'That I could deal with, no it's much worse. They have my mother and twelve-year-old sister in Algeria. They are holding the two of them in God knows what conditions and my mother is diabetic, she won't last long.'

'Why me and not the police?'

'I'm sorry to ask you this, but I know your father is the French ambassador in London. If he has any contacts in Algeria or any influence he can exert? It's my only hope of getting them out alive, even if I cooperate with them, I'm not naïve enough to think they will ever let them go free. My sister is young and charming, it might already be too late.'

'Ok I will talk to him, but I'm going to need more. When did it start, how were you contacted and anything else you know, anything at all?'

'It started a month before the end of the summer term this year. A man approached me just as I was getting ready to leave the café to teach an afternoon seminar. He said he'd heard about the group and sympathised with our ideals, he offered to fund our activities, provide us with our own meeting place, a private space where we could develop our ideas. I said I'd think about it, I had no intention of agreeing but he scared me and I didn't want to anger him. The next week, two new students started attending, they said very little but watched everyone and took notes. I tried to draw them out but they seemed well drilled, and only said what they needed to keep up the pretence. After a few weeks, I was sure they were there to watch us, probably take people's names and anything of interest they might say, anything that might mark them as susceptible to radicalisation. Then a few days before this term started, I received a picture in the post of my mother and sister and written in red marker across the front it just said – "DO WHAT WE SAY." Then the man who spoke to me before came in a day later, long enough for me to confirm that they were both missing. The Algerian police did not seem very interested, it was obvious they didn't approve of me working in another country and leaving my family unprotected. The man sat at the table and waited until everyone else but the two new students had left. It didn't take long, I think he spooked them as much as he did me. He gave me instructions, it boiled down to a slow brainwashing of the students toward violence and a gathering of personal information about them so they could be targeted better outside of the group. The two students would be keeping an eye on me and if I wanted to see my family again, I would need to impress them.'

'The man who was sat by you on the day you spoke to me and the last two students at the table was that them? Do you have any names?'

'Fictional only, I'm sure, the man calls himself Mr Smith, the blonde lad goes by the name of John Jones and his companion is Brian Banjo. But there is something else I can tell you that might just help. I was looking through some old jazz records outside a shop in Covent Garden yesterday, trying to distract myself, when I looked up and saw Mr Smith go into a new apartment building, not new exactly it used to be offices, but it had been empty for years, before they converted it. He had a key card, so he probably lives there.'

'Is that enough?'

'Do you have the picture they sent you? I need to borrow it and I need your mother and sister's address in Algeria.'

'You're welcome to the picture, I can't bear to look at it, I'll write the address on the back.'

'Do you think you can really help?'

'Yes.' was all I said, then I left. I texted Michelle and told her I was going to the embassy and would be late home, while Charlotte told the other two to meet us there. We met with the ambassador in a bug proof room, he was determined that nothing about this operation would go beyond the *family* unless he wanted it to. When I briefed everyone, the ambassador glanced at the door and satisfied we were still secure he spoke.

'I have some active agents in Algeria, I'll set them on finding Youssef's mother and sister. Pierre, prep your squad for an urgent extraction, expect messy but prepare for brutal. It's important that only the two women come out of there alive, I don't want anyone left who can link this back to any of you.'

I was starting to build a different picture of my father, he was clinical and detached when he needed to be. Ready to kill if he perceived a threat to any of us. I remembered when he used to read us stories at bedtime, he did a fierce impression of a lion roaring, I wet myself the first time he did it but I didn't tell him and Charlotte got me clean pyjamas. Now his teeth were bared and ready.

'We need to assume they are following Youssef, not Jones and Banjo they'd be too easy for him to spot. Whoever it is, my men haven't clocked them, which means they're good and it could be that we've been noticed. That's not very likely but we need to assume the worst until we know different, no one goes anywhere alone. Yve, set some surveillance up on Mr Smith's apartment building, keep it distant until we know he's definitely staying there and who else is coming and going. Charlotte, you watch Josh's back especially when Youssef approaches him, which he will if only to find out what's going on, you can't blame him, but it puts Josh at risk. Besides, we need to be contactable if he has anything new to tell us. The library should be safe enough, if they're watching they'll be monitoring the exit, far too easy to be spotted inside. I know it sounds OTT but I'm taking no chances.'

Charlotte hesitated slightly before she spoke, she knew she was on sensitive territory. 'Are you planning on running Youssef as a double agent?'

'I don't think he is cut out for it, besides once we rescue his mother and sister, they will know he has help and will make every effort to kill him.'

'So, we take Smith et al out as well?' Asked Charlotte.

'I'd like Josh to have a little chat with Smith first, I doubt the rest know anything of consequence. But right now, we know nothing about them – who's funding them, whether they are government backed or freelancers and most importantly, what are they really up to? I don't believe this is just some little project to create a terrorist conveyor belt. We have at least two cells coordinating across two continents, that's complex and expensive, there is most definitely something afoot.'

***

Youssef approached me at my regular seat in the library, Charlotte was five metres away hiding behind a bookshelf, having removed an armful of texts from one of the shelves so she could look through the "hole" she'd created straight at me. It had been two days, I'd give him full marks for patience.

'Youssef, you've changed your hand cream, I think that one is Shear Butter, isn't it?'

'Yes, I thought you might like it.' As he sat opposite me on the other side of the desk he pointed briefly to the right side of his chest. It was warm in the library, too hot for the blazer he was wearing, and I was pretty sure he was telling me he was wearing a wire. Things were definitely hotting up, and I realised the game we were playing was getting very dangerous.

'Yes darling, it's lovely I must buy some myself.'

'Did you manage to get any tickets for that show you thought I might enjoy?'

'Not yet lovely, my friend at the agency said they are sold out, but he'll get back to me as soon as he gets some returns, probably another couple of days.

'That will be super, I look forward to it. Better let you get on with your work for now, give me a call when you're free for a drink.'

Five minutes after Youssef left, Charlotte ambled over toward my desk, there was no one else in that section of the library but she mouthed her words, knowing I would be able to read her lips. "What the F was that about? It sounded like you two were auditioning for the gay leads in some Am-Dram production."

'Youssef was wearing a wire, he pointed to it when he joined me, that was for the benefit of whoever was listening and hopefully Youssef understood we were working on finding his family.'

'Things might be moving faster than we expected, I have just heard from Pierre he is mobilising the men, they fly out tonight. Are you ready to go back to the flat? I've told Pierre to collect me from there, I want to spend a few hours with him before he goes.'

'It's serious between the two of you, isn't it?'

'Pierre only does serious, but I'm good with that.'

'He smiles and laughs a lot more, now you're around. Come on let's get back and make his day.'

'Hold up, you're not the only one with Spidey powers and mine are telling me that the main door is being watched and we are going to be followed.'

'Is that like a premonition?'

'Sorry to disappoint you but it's just spy logic. If they're making Youssef wear a wire, then they are going to be interested in anyone he speaks to and if whoever is watching has seen you two together before they will be more than a little suspicious. There's a staff exit at the back, let's take that and we can be at the underground in minutes.'

'What if they're watching that?'

'Luckily it opens on to a busy main street rather than a back alley, we should be able to get to the station safely enough. But if they're concerned enough to watch a private staff entrance just in case, then we have a serious problem and we definitely can't lead them back to your apartment. If I see anything even slightly off, I will call in the calvary.'

'The calvary?'

'AKA daddy the baddy! He has agents in the area, and he always has a back-up plan. I'll call Pierre and Robert as well, but they may be further away. In fact, no point in playing the hero, dad will only chew my ear off, I'll call him now and make sure we've got reinforcements in place.'

Charlotte must have had a hot line or something to my father as he picked-up on the second ring. As he instructed, we made our way slowly down to the ground floor using the stairs not the lift, then waited near the door for five minutes, before we got a text – "proceed with caution, shadows in place."

'Shadows?'

'It's what dad calls his best agents, we probably won't spot them hence the name but if anyone tries anything they will make themselves known!'

Pierre and Charlotte didn't get much time together in the end. Michelle and I agreed with my father's suggestion-order to move back home, and Pierre and Charlotte got the job of escorting us across town, he even called in Robert to help. I think Pierre had been spooked by the sudden escalation in activity and *threat level*, as he called it.

The next day Michelle and I mooched about the house in the morning, Charlotte had gone off to the embassy when we told her we were staying in all day. She didn't need to be there, but she wanted to be close to dad, knowing he would be the first to hear anything about Pierre. She knew nothing would happen during daylight, and Algiers time was the same as England, but she went anyway. In the afternoon we watched old movies, not Casablanca that was a bit too close for comfort. That night we all sat around restless and fidgety, Michelle and I went to bed early but couldn't sleep. At two o'clock I heard the switch and saw the lights come on through the narrow gap at the bottom of the bedroom door. Michelle and I jumped out of bed and flung the door open, my father was there, mobile phone pinned to his ear listening, not saying a word. Then Charlotte emerged from her room further down the landing, I could hear Pierre even though he was speaking as quietly as he could to dad, he was ok. I looked across at Charlotte, nodded my head and smiled, Michelle tugged at my hand. 'He's ok, he's on his way back.'

We both rushed to Charlotte who was crying with relief and sandwiched her between us, while the ambassador finished the official call before looking at the three of us.

'Pierre is fine, no injuries at all, a couple of his men have minor lacerations but no permanent damage.'

'What about Youssef's mother and sister?' I asked.

'Both safe and on the way back with Pierre. They had been well treated as they were still deemed useful.'

'What happened to the kidnappers?' I wanted to make sure all the loose ends had been tied up before I could feel satisfied.

'Six in total, two outside the house they were keeping them in and four inside. All dead, though Pierre thinks the techie may have got a message out before they got him. They have his laptop, but it will take a while to get past the encryption on it. Everything else they burned to the ground with incendiaries in the hope it will muddy the waters. They should be back before lunchtime today.'

Just then mum appeared. 'No one is going to sleep now, so I have made tea and toast downstairs.' We all sat around drinking our tea and slathering extra butter on our toast, apart from dad who'd gone back to his secure office and was busy doing whatever secret stuff he needed to do. Charlotte, was cuddled up to mum, still crying, while Michelle and I just held hands and hoped it would soon be all over.

At eight, Charlotte and father went off to the embassy, Michelle was doing some sketches for an idea she'd been mulling over for a few months now and I was at a bit of a loose end. There was a gym in the basement, just a treadmill, some fancy exercise bike linked to the internet so you could torture yourself with other sweaty bodies around the world and some yoga mats. I cleared a space in the middle of the floor and took the Jo Staff from its case, stripping down to my boxers I started to practice the katas that Yve had drilled into me, they came easily, and the feeling of movement and the stretching of muscle and sinew started to relax me. I thought back to the fight we had the last time we trained together, I could see Yve in front of me as though she were actually in the room and we started to step and dance, parry and strike just as we did before. When it came toward the final blows, I played them and rewound them in my mind then I tried something different, but it didn't work, and I saw myself flat on my back and in quite a bit of pain. So, I rewound and started the sequence again, this time a fraction of a second before her stick connected, I turned side on to her and as Yve's staff grazed my back, I spun forward turning one-eighty degrees to face her, I was now level with her shoulder, my arms raised and my staff against her throat.

  Just as I was feeling pleased with my imaginary victory, I sunk to my knees in pain and a bright light seared my vision, I was having another premonition. In front of me Yve was tied to a chair in just her underwear, her hair was plastered to her head with sweat and blood, her eye was cut and bruised, her lip split and more blood was dripping down her chin and on to her chest. The only other thing I could see was one of those giant clock faces that people hang on their walls, the ubiquitous symbol of takeaway lifestyle. The clock showed the time as eleven-thirty, the room was sunlit so it was still morning, assuming it was today. Though there was no clue as to where the room was, I still knew it was the building Smith was staying in, the one Yve had under surveillance. I pulled my clothes on in seconds and ran back up the stairs, splitting the staff in two as I went and sliding it back into its sleeve. I screamed for Michelle and she came rushing toward me.

'Josh, what's wrong what's happened?'

'They've got Yve, they're holding her.'

'Whose got her?'

'Smith, they're at his apartment, I had a vision.'

'Call your father, he can get someone to help her.'

'I can't wait, they are torturing her right now, she won't tell them the time of the next bus, they are going to kill her! You call dad and Charlotte, tell them to get me some back up and a lot of body bags.'

There was a private car park at the back of the building, Charlotte had an old Vespa parked there and I grabbed the key from the table as I ran out the house. Despite nearly running over several old ladies and taking every bus lane possible it still took me fifteen minutes to get through the traffic. Luckily, I'd paid attention in the briefings and knew which flat Smith lived in, he was on the sixth floor but first I needed to get in the building. I pushed a couple of buttons until someone on the third floor answered me, I focused on my voice, uncertain if it would work through the intercom. Whoever Jane was, I would be forever grateful to her, she released the lock without hesitation. I started to run up the stairs, when I got to the right floor I glanced at my watch, it was eleven-fifty. I needed to get in there now, I also needed to distract them from Yve, the door was solid oak with robust locks and levers, I wasn't going to be able to kick it in. I looked around the corridor, there was no one around, I took a couple of steps back and started to hum quietly but getting louder with every second. I was looking straight at the door, and I saw the light from the spy hole disappear, someone was watching me. I brought my arms and hands together in a deafening clap, howling as I pointed toward the door, which blew off its hinges and halfway down the hall. Whoever was underneath it was probably dead, and no danger to anyone. As I stepped through the doorway, I took out my staff and held half in each hand, I couldn't risk hurting Yve with my voice and they were bound to shoot me or both of us before I could compel them, I didn't know their real names or exactly how many of them were there. The one half under the door wasn't Smith and nor was the one with the gun that came flying out of the door straight ahead, which must have been the main room where Yve was being held. Probably panicked by the *explosion* he made two mistakes, firstly he didn't shoot me as soon as he opened the door and secondly, he took a step closer toward me, he was within range. I broke his right wrist with the first blow, which sent his gun skating along the ground, the second staff hit the side of his head and I heard his skull crack as he went down. Alive for now. I walked through the open door, which gave me some cover before I stepped to one side. It was a stupid move, but I was too angry to care, I could feel my rage building like thunder gathering in the clouds. Smith kicked the door closed and stood there with his gun pointing straight at me and well out of range of my staffs, even if they were joined together. It didn't matter though, I could see Yve was already dead, slumped in the chair I had seen in my premonition, still held in place by the ropes and there was the clock, it was twelve-thirteen and somebody else was about to die.

'Well, if it's not the ambassador's boy. I suspected you had something to do with Youssef's family escaping, no matter, you will come in handy for bartering my way out of this mess. Impressive entry by the way, C4? Not quite sure what's going on with the sticks though, but you can put them on the ground now, be quick, your just as useful with a bullet in your leg.'

I stretched my arms out and let the staffs fall to the ground, before clapping my hands together. I didn't make a sound this time, I didn't need to, my rage channelled out of me like a supersonic wave. He dropped the gun as the blood spurted from his nose, the capillaries in his eyes split turning the whites to crimson, he was on his knees now and blood was spilling from his ears. The terror in his face was pathetic, finally he coughed, and blood and bile frothed from his mouth as he fell face down.

I woke up two days later in a private hospital bed, with my mother and Michelle on one side and Charlotte and Pierre on the other. Michelle was sobbing despite her delight at my waking up, Pierre also managed to raise a smile at my return to consciousness. My mother kissed me so many times I thought she was trying to wash my face, Charlotte managed to squeeze my hand before she started to cry as well.

Pierre told me that he had arrived just before the police who then cordoned the building off with the two of us still inside. Everybody else was evacuating the block and surrounding streets having been told there was a potential gas leak, regardless of the two bomb disposal vehicles parked outside. My father then turned up with a private ambulance driven by Robert, he was met outside the building by a real doctor who he led through the cordon waving his diplomatic credentials. MI5 arrived while the doctor was checking me over, he decided I was safe to move and my father convinced MI5 to let him organise my transfer to hospital, with a promise that they could question me as soon as I was well enough to talk. In the end my father reluctantly gave them enough information about Smith's operation for them to back off and focus on trying to pick up the rest of the group. Pierre reckoned there must have been at least another four just to mount the surveillance they'd been carrying out, not to mention being able to capture Yve. They found the two guys she was working with dead in the back of their van, Pierre was convinced that one of them must have slipped up and Smith's men would have killed them and waited in the van with the two bodies, ready for Yve to check in with her team, she didn't stand a chance.

    I knew then that I would never truly get over losing Yve in that brutal way, I would never be the same. I thought of leaving it all behind, Michelle would be safer without me, but I knew that was just cowardice. I could walk away and tell myself she'd be safe, but it would just be a slow death for the both of us. I was impressed with myself when I actually managed to talk to her about it, then we cried and held each other all night and when the sun came up, we were both resolute, we would live together and if necessary, we would die together. But I was glad she wasn't with me right now, in this miserable concrete box.

***

After a few weeks and realising *time* wasn't the answer I needed, I returned to work at the embassy and for a while I was satisfied with translating documents, but after a month I was getting bored and frustrated. I'd given up on my PhD, not that I had really started, I was more interested in vengeance than vivas, but I couldn't kill Smith again. At least Youssef had managed to give his men the slip, but I decided not to meet with him again, he would just be a painful reminder of what happened to Yve. I was disappointed in myself, I couldn't help thinking that they should have got Youssef instead of Yve. My uncle, helpful as ever, arranged for him and his family to settle in France and he got a post teaching at a provincial university, he agreed to stick to the curriculum in future. Socrates was dead, and so was any idealism I may have once had.

My father sensed my restlessness, and I knew he was concerned I would spiral into depression, it seemed to hang like a spectre in the air, waiting for weakness, waiting for its moment. He suggested I have a few weeks off and take Michelle to Paris to see her family. I didn't think it would help me much, but a change of any kind was welcome, and Michelle would enjoy seeing her parents in the flesh instead of on FaceTime. We chose to stay with her family rather than a hotel, Philippe had offered us the flat, but I knew Michelle wanted to be as close to her parents as possible in the time we had. I actually enjoyed it too, I'd always got on with her father and her mother treated me like her own son. I really enjoyed the lack of formality, everything was so much more relaxed than at my home, with its constant parade of visitors and ever-present threats.

At the beginning of our second week, I arranged to have lunch with my uncle, he had invited me even before we crossed the channel, but I admit I enjoyed making him wait, it was petty, but I needed that small bit of control over my life. It reminded me of the time he delighted in knowing it was Michelle's day off from her father's cafe when I didn't. Michelle decided to stay at home, despite her fondness for Philippe, to make the most of every hour with her folks. It wasn't the distance between Paris and London that bothered Michelle, it was the ever-present threat to our lives and the thought of never seeing her parents again that made her cling on to them while she had the chance.

I half expected Philippe to offer me some dubious job, he rarely missed an opportunity to exploit an asset, but if that was why he invited me then he was playing me like a fish. If you listened to his conversation, you would have thought he was my real uncle, everything was about the family, how they were doing, their health, their holiday plans… blah…blah! Bored with the game, if that's what it was, I decided to play my rather uninspiring opening gambit.

'Minister,' he looked at me over his glasses at the use of his formal title, 'I need to get out of London for a while, I need an opportunity to stretch my talents, maybe even develop new ones?'

'Have you spoken to your parents and Michelle?'

'Not yet, but I am sure that it will come as no surprise to Michelle, and I believe my father also knows that something needs to change, though I don't expect him to be happy about it. Either way, there is no point in worrying them if there are no prospects for me to diversify.'

'You know Pierre and his squad are staying in London for the foreseeable future, what had you in mind?'

'Them being in London is part of the attraction, I want to work alone. Yes, I know I will have to link with others, that I will have someone to answer to other than you. I just don't want to be part of a team, not for a long while, maybe never.'

'Josh, I haven't asked you to keep secrets from your father before but if I am to go any further then that is part of the deal. You can't tell him or Michelle or anyone else about what I'm going to ask you, whether you accept my offer or not. I can tell you now that your father would not approve, in fact he would be outraged at the whole idea even if it didn't involve you. Do you want to hear what I've got to say?'

'So, if I'm not interested, I just have to keep my mouth shut and walk away?'

'Yes, but that's the easy option, if you are interested then you still have to keep your mouth shut, only the two of us will know and you have already experienced how difficult it is to carry those kind of burdens alone.'

'It sounds like you're about to offer me a poisoned chalice, and like Socrates I prefer to choose my own destiny despite the opposition of others. Pour the hemlock and I'll think about the toast!'

'Firstly, a question for you. I've seen the destruction you can wield when angry, what I want to know is, can you control it? Can you be more subtle, make it look like someone had a heart attack or a stroke as opposed to swallowing a grenade?'

I thought about it for a minute or two and the minister held his tongue and maybe even his breath. 'I think I could learn, I've managed to dial it back a bit when the anger has started to dissipate, and I feel less threatened.'

'Could you just compel them to commit suicide?'

'I've not tried, so I can't say for certain, but my instincts say no. When I try and make people do something, they resist even if it's something trivial. The stronger the motivation the more they resist, I think the will to live would be too strong to overcome. Though I might be able to get them to kill someone else.'

'Josh, what I want is someone who can kill and make it look like natural causes. There are a number of people over the years that we have captured only to have to barter to get some of our own back. I'm sure you remember Kurt, he was one I traded, and he is one of ten or more that have come back to haunt me. While most think themselves lucky and recede into the shadows, others see it as a second career, an opportunity to kill and maim unchecked.'

'And you would like me to discretely put an end to some of them, is Kurt on that list?'

'Near the top but the order of service depends on their availability or should I say vulnerability. Is that a problem?'

'More of an incentive. I will need to give it some thought and practice, which could be a bit tricky. I don't actually have to kill them to see if it works, I can stop short, probably, but it is practice and it may not go to plan!'

'The thug under the door you blew off in Covent Garden, though he seemed dead at the time managed to survive surprisingly unscathed once he woke from the coma you put him in. It turned out that he's a French citizen and the British kindly let me have him on account. I've got him locked up outside of Lille but he's not very communicative, would you like to see if you can get him to talk?'

'I would, he will be a good test of how I can or can't control my own emotions. I suspect I may lose it, you may need some cleaners, is that ok?'

'We don't think he knows anything, so it won't be any great loss. The interrogation cells there are more like wet rooms, so a bit of cleaning won't be a problem.'

'Tomorrow?'

'I will collect you myself at nine-thirty in the morning.'

I told Michelle I was going to interrogate a prisoner, and who he was but not much else. I expected protest and warnings and was surprised at her question.

'Did you ask or did Philippe ask you?'

'I asked him, does it make a difference?'

'I think so, you need to be the one in control even if you don't always like what you have to do, make sure you do it on your own terms.'

'Are you ok with this? It's not a nice job.'

'They are not nice people, if you get the chance kill the bastard for me. Just don't put yourself at risk. I won't lose you out there or in here.' As she said the last three words she tapped her index finger against my head.

Philippe collected me as planned, the car was large and grey and matched the clouds scudding across the sky. There was a driver and a bodyguard up front and just the two of us in the rear. As we drove along the motorway I noticed a similar vehicle a few cars back, my uncle spotted me watching.

'It's ok he's with us, according to state security I should have motorcycle outriders as well, but it attracts far too much attention for what we are up to.'

Inside the compound we were taken to the observation and recording room attached to the interrogation cell. The prisoner was already seated and handcuffed to the table, his feet chained to the floor. The minister sent the tech guy out the room so that it was just the two of us. I switched off the sound and video recording, Philippe could still see what was going on through the mirror and had a set of headphones to listen in. The guard outside the cell door was clearly intrigued by the irregular activity but said nothing, he knew better than to ask questions. Inside I drew up a chair on the other side of the table, I said nothing, I just looked at him. I needed to be sure I wanted to do this, it wasn't going to make me happy, nor would it make me a better person. Quite the opposite I thought.

'I don't suppose you remember me?' He didn't even blink. 'I was the one who blew the door off and knocked you out.' He said nothing. 'I was too late to save the girl.' This time he grinned widely. Now I was sure. I spoke in a much deeper voice, he was resisting but the beatings he'd already had left him drained, still defiant but too weak to resist. He gave up the locations of a couple of safe houses in France and another across the border in Brussels, they'd been grooming students, operating across Europe for over a year and had been building up a network for one massive, coordinated assault across a number of capitals. They were linked to organised crime and most of their funding came from drugs, sex trafficking and guns. I'd assumed he was the guard and Smith was the leader, but it was the other way around, he was in charge of the networks and groups in Brussels and Amsterdam as well as Paris. He'd kept his mouth shut, because he knew the minute we gave up and put him in a general prison, even a maximum-security unit, his comrades would get him out.

Daniel Bakker, apparently his real name, was born in Amsterdam, turned out to be a much bigger fish than we thought. I considered going back to Philippe to see if he wanted me to continue, given the potential use he might make of Daniel. Then I thought of the likely consequences of him escaping, I'd already got everything out of him that he knew. Alive, he was of no more use but still dangerous, dead he was still useless but safe. Then I thought of what Michelle had said, to stay in control to do things on my own terms and, most importantly, kill the bastard. That moment I heard her say the words in my head, almost like she was actually with me and I felt a spark, like static electricity building within me. It was like a subwoofer in my chest, accenting a beat too low for others to hear - thunder. I looked at Daniel and mimicked the grin he'd given me when I said I'd been too late to save Yve. Then I began to tap the index and middle finger of my right hand gently on the table, in time to that low resonating beat in my chest. On the fifth tap I watched him wince and I smiled again, then I tapped harder – 6, 7, 8 – he started to flinch each time my fingers came closer to the table. I could see the fear growing on his face, this wasn't something he was expecting, slowly he was confronting his own mortality, I tapped a little harder – 9, 10, 11, 12, then he broke.

'What the fuck are you doing to me?'

'Ever wondered what a heart attack feels like? Or a stroke?'

I double tapped the table and I saw him stare into space, drool sliding down his chin, his left arm limp. I was in control, it wasn't enough to kill him or even render him unconscious. I would decide when he could die. I started tapping the table again, a little harder this time – 13, 14, 15, 16 – he was crying out on every beat. I thought of Yve, of that night the three of us made love, of course it was more than sex, who was I trying to fool. I tapped my two fingers on the table, I was tempted to make his chest explode but I didn't, this was an experiment after all. I held my fingers down and pressed them against the table – 'die you evil bastard.' Obligingly he did just that. A couple of days later, Philippe invited me to his offices for coffee, I thought he looked rather smug as he spoke.

'According to the autopsy Daniel Bakker died of natural causes, a heart attack that unfortunately also triggered a stroke. There were some remarks about bruising, but it concluded that this had occurred at least 48 hours before and was not linked to his death.'

'So, are we good to go?'

'Not quite, I have to square your return to Paris with your father and I am not looking forward to that conversation.'

'Can't you just order him, you're his superior, aren't you?'

'Well, that wouldn't be very diplomatic, would it? More importantly, no one, not me, not even the President can make your father do or agree to something if he refuses. You also need to be careful of your words Josh. Technically I'm your father's boss, but that's because he lets me, and I am yet to meet his superior. He is a far better man than I ever wish to be.'

'I'm beginning to see a side of my father I've never been privy to before, it's impressive, admirable even, but quite inconvenient.'

'Have you spoken to Michelle about coming back to Paris?'

'Yes, she thinks we need to get away from London for a while at least, maybe permanently.'

'What have you told her about your job?'

'That I will have to travel, that it will be dangerous, and I will probably have to kill someone every now and then.'

'You pulled your punches then. What did she say?'

'I quote, "It's good to kill bad people but try not to get blood on your shirt." I think the last bit might have been a metaphor, but I didn't want to ask.'

'I'll speak to your father in an hour, I have a call booked.'

'FaceTime?'

'Not a chance, it will be hard enough just talking to him I don't want him staring me in the eyes the way he does, it's like being caught in a searchlight and hearing the click of the safety being released.' I really was enjoying Philippe's discomfort, a bit too much maybe or maybe not. 'We still have one problem to resolve Josh.'

'What's that?'

'The people I want you to take care of won't be chained to a table in a cell, they will be out in the wild. Have you thought about how you can get close enough to them without putting yourself at risk?'

'I've thought of very little else. I decided it would be better if I could keep my distance, so I've been working on something. Do you have a bigger room we could use, the longer the better but it would need to be private?'

'There's the board room on the top floor or the range in the basement.'

'Basement would be safer, we are going to need a glass and some water as well.'

'There's a water cooler just outside the door to the range. I'll get someone to make sure the place is empty, it usually is at this time, shooting on an empty stomach is not good. Will plastic cups be ok, or shall I bring a glass with me?'

'Plastic will be fine.'

I filled the cup two-thirds with water and took it inside the range. The back wall was fifty metres from the firing line, the targets were on pulley wires and could be brought closer, but I left them were they where, and walked fifteen metres toward them and set the cup down on the floor before returning to Philippe. I took Yve's old Jo Staff out of its bag and joined the two halves together, mine had been lost or taken when I had ended up unconscious in Smith's apartment. The whole idea of using the staff this way had started that first time Yve knocked me over with her speciality end-on-end strike. I could feel the emotions surfacing and resonating within me, provided I could control them they would be the perfect fuel for this little demo. I held the staff out horizontally, pointing it at the cup, as though I was sighting it. Then I lowered my hand and firmly grasping one end I tapped the other end against the floor, quietly at first but gradually getting louder. Then the minister stared, his jaw dropping slightly, as the water in the cup started to splash up and out as though someone was dropping stones into it. I kept that going for about thirty seconds, long enough to prove I could control it. Then I started to increase the tempo and the water formed what looked like a mini geyser, rising up about twenty centimetres before tumbling back down. It was time for the finale, I tapped the staff down hard and kept it pressed against the ground, the cup exploded sending water everywhere. Plastic was definitely a better idea than glass, I'd never taken it that far before.

'Sorry minister, I think I might need to dial that down a bit. Let me get some more water and have another try. This time I placed the cup the full 50 metres away and instead of banging the staff against the floor, I just rested the tip on the ground and began tapping the top with my thumb. Nothing seemed to be happening, so intuitively I started to hum as I tapped, it looked like the water might be rippling but it was difficult to tell at that distance. Philippe picked up some binoculars used for getting a closer look at the shots on the targets.

'The waters definitely rippling, I think it may be too far away to do any damage though.'

I increased the tempo of my tapping and as I continued to hum an even stranger thing happened, it felt like I was connected to the water inside the cup. I tapped a little faster and now, despite the distance, I could see the cup as though I was standing next to it. I thought I could actually hear the molecules accelerating and colliding with each other, I tried to draw the water closer to me, I imagined millions of fine droplets streaming forward. Then the water broke free, the cup looked like it had melted and there was just a crumpled congealed mess on the floor. I stopped tapping and humming immediately, I had this image of the puddle of water on the floor suddenly flowing directly to me. I didn't want to find out if that was possible, at least not with Philippe watching.

'Josh, that's amazing but do you think it will work on a person?'

'I don't see why not, it's the same principle as I used with Bakker. The main problem is that it doesn't work through walls, so it would be good if you could get them to attend a party or some other large event, I could keep my distance and they would be dead before anyone could shout, is there a doctor in the house?'

'That imposes quite a lot of limitations, especially considering these people usually stay away from public spaces and crowds.'

'The thing is, there is nothing to help me pinpoint the glass, but I have been wondering if a man, a person with a heartbeat, would be different? I can hear Michelle's heartbeat when I'm in a different room, but sometimes I think I might hear that if she were on a different continent. The thing is I can also tell her rhythm from Charlotte's or Pierre's, even yours. If I listen carefully, I can hear you when I'm on the floor below your office in London.'

'You know that could sound really creepy?'

'Apart from Michelle, and she likes the idea of me hearing her, you're the only person I've told, and I think we should keep it that way.'

'Agreed, so what next?'

'First, I'd like to try one last experiment if you're willing to volunteer?'

'Not if you're going to give my heart a little squeeze, at my age and with my lifestyle I don't want to take any risks. It also feels a little too personal, it would be like you being inside me.'

'Remember that when you send me to kill the scum of the planet, to do it I have to go *inside* them. I doubt I'll be able to do it for very long, so make it count. All I want you to do is stay in here holding the cup of water, then when I'm outside walk up and down the range, stopping and starting, just pause for five seconds each time. Then choose a spot where you can set the cup down on the ground, turn on your heels and march in a straight line to the door and join me outside. I'm going to try and track you as you walk around and then use that to pinpoint where the cup is. Make sure you place it on the concrete floor, not a mat or a table. Are you ok with that?'

'It still sounds creepy, which is odd coming from someone who has spent most of his adult life watching and tracking others but I think I can manage that, a straight line is not too difficult for me at this time of day.'

I was too tense to respond to his attempt at lightening the moment and he never really had the timing for comedy. We went outside to the water cooler and filled a new cup, as soon as Philippe went through the door and it closed behind him, I started tuning into his heartbeat, I realised I could even hear the blood flowing through his arteries and in and out of his heart chambers. He took a diagonal line to a different gallery than we had been in before, perhaps hoping to throw me, but I had my own personal sonar picture of him, I could hear the rustle of his suit and the drip of water he spilt on the ground. After a few diversions around the gallery next door, he came back to the first one and stopped about five metres from the back wall, I remembered that target, it was in the shape of a soldier, and I imagined it standing watch over him as he set the cup down. Satisfied, Philippe turned and walked the same diagonal back toward me and I opened the door for him just before he got to it, which made him smile. I turned back to look at the wall, it was almost like there was a faint echo of where he walked and when he stopped. I traced the ghost of his last steps back to where he set the water down, I closed my eyes and visualised the cup on the floor, I imagined I could even feel a difference in temperature between the cool water and the warm stuffy air of the basement. Then I started to tap my staff against the floor very gently, I felt like a bat sending out its high-pitched squeaks to locate its prey, but mine were deep bass notes thudding through the concrete floor that connected where I stood and the floor inside that the cup rested on. And there it was, I'd already disturbed the surface, setting up a gentle ripple which was as clear to me as if I'd been holding the cup in my own hand ready to drink. Instead, I tapped the staff a dozen times softly on the ground before pressing it down. I heard the cup collapse in on itself and the water flow across the floor.

When we went in, it was exactly the same as when I'd been in the room. 'Well, that proves the wall is not an issue, I need to test it out on a live target now.'

'We have *lost* a few too many prisoners lately, how would you feel about a real mission?'

'You have someone in mind? Obviously.'

'Yes, an old acquaintance of yours actually.'

'Kurt?'

'Not yet, not for your first foray alone, let's kill a rat before we take on a rabid dog and his pack. You remember Kurt's old partner, Dietrich Gutmann?'

'I remember him.' I didn't say what I was thinking though, that I just might enjoy killing Dietrich, I thought the minister might be already unsettled enough by my little demonstration. I didn't want him thinking I was turning into some psycho and wondering if I was beyond saving or even stable enough to go on a mission. Though my own thoughts were already headed in that direction.

'He's fallen out with Kurt, which was foolish considering he protected Gutmann, but Dietrich decided to do a little business behind Kurt's back and not share the profits. I did think Kurt would have him killed himself, but he seems to be tied up with some plot along the Russian – Ukraine border at present. Dietrich is currently holed-up in Budapest, with half a dozen mercenaries to protect him. It's an old pre nineties Russian apartment block with an identical one less than fifty metres away. I think I could get you fixed up more or less opposite him, would that work? Do you speak Hungarian?'

'Not yet, but it won't take long.' I noticed Philippe's broad smile; I must have seemed like a spymaster's dream.

'As long as the buildings are not too far apart that should work, though it might be a bit more complex than exploding a cup of water. I will probably have to get a fix on him first.'

'What does that involve?'

'I will probably need to get a little closer to him, not too close, just so I can distinguish Gutmann's heart rhythm from his guards. What are his habits, does he eat out at the same place?'

'He never goes out after dark, he is driven everywhere, and he usually eats lunch at the same café most days. Always the same table, near the road where his car parks protecting his back, the driver stays in the car with the engine running in case a quick exit is required. Three men block the other sight lines to him, it's not secure but if he didn't get out at all he would probably shoot himself.'

'That sounds good, I doubt he would recognise me now, but I'll wear a bit of a disguise just to be safe. I might even be able to sit inside and get what I need.'

'Not a good idea, rule number one, don't put yourself in a place you can be cornered without back up. You remember your first job?'

How could I forget, it was in that café I fell in love with Michelle, and it was where I met Yve for the first time as she rescued me.

'Josh, I know we talked about you doing this alone, but I would never send anyone out completely without backup. I have someone already watching them, he's a sniper, a very good one. I had thought of using him to kill Gutmann and blame it on Kurt, but that would alert Kurt and we wouldn't stand a chance of getting close enough to kill him for a long time, leaving him to continue his current trail of murder and espionage.'

'So, what is the sniper going to do?'

'He can cover you at the restaurant, if any of Gutmann's men make any kind of hostile move toward you he can take them out. He's good, he could kill them all while you finish your coffee.'

'Are you sure you need me?'

'I'm sure. Crude and brutal has its place, even its own kind of beauty, especially when someone like Pierre is wielding the weapons, but this isn't that kind of job, we don't want to scare all the other fish off just to catch a minnow.'

'Ok, you talk to my father, and I'll spend the next twenty-four hours with Michelle.' Philippe suddenly looked worried as he walked away, in all the excitement he had forgotten his promise, but it turned out a little easier than he expected. I understood why when my father called me that evening, he got straight into it.

'Josh, I've spoken to Philippe. I can't say I like the thought of you moving back to Paris or working for him again, but I understand that things were difficult here. I have had to admit to myself while you've been gone, that I can't always protect you. That's clear from what happened, but what I have really struggled with is the realisation that I can't protect you from yourself, I can support you when you need me, but I can't live your life for you, and as much as I want to I can't take the blows on your behalf. I had a long talk with Charlotte, she made me realise that even if I could wrap you up in cotton wool, I couldn't fight your demons for you and that if I try, I will only push you away. So, my wonderful son, that is why I have agreed to the most stupid idea ever.'

I knew I had a lot to thank Charlotte for, if I lived long enough to see her again.

It took two days to set everything up, so I had some extra time with Michelle and more than I needed to get my head around the language. I told her what I'd done with the water, and she was ok with me practicing tracking her around the house, she even hid things to see if I could find them, and a few times we squashed some plastic beakers from when she was little. The one with the little spout was a hoot, the water shot almost two metres through the tiny hole before the lid flew off and chipped the plaster on the ceiling.

***

I flew economy to Budapest, security had a bit of an issue with my Jo Staff, but I told the man in my quietly persuasive tone that it was just a snooker cue and he let me through. The inside of the flat was ok, someone had clearly gone to the trouble of installing a new bed, some basic furniture and a fridge that was well stocked. The cooker looked primitive but at least it worked and there was a brand-new microwave still in the box. By the window that overlooked Dietrich's flat was a pair of binoculars, as they lacked the special coating, I resisted the urge to use them, remembering what Pierre had told me about the reflections from the lenses giving away your position. I could see that there was more than one person in the apartment, even without the bins, Yve had called them that. I pushed down the emotions rising and used the energy to scan the apartment, there were five people inside, four of them significantly taller and bulkier than the fifth, Dietrich and his guards. I wondered if the difference in size alone would allow me to single out my target. As I probed around, I realised it wouldn't, people it seemed were a bit more complex than a glass of water, if not always as useful. I needed to be able to tune into his heart before I could squeeze the life out him.

 I stayed in the room all night, as agreed with Philippe I did not use my phone or any of my tech, the less of an electronic footprint I left behind the better. I watched Hungarian TV for twenty minutes before concluding that it was even worse than British TV and switched it off. Then I sat in the dark for an hour looking over to the other apartment, they had closed the curtains but judging by the light flickering in the room they were sticking with the TV.

In the morning, I decided to go to the café for breakfast to check it out, it was a simple layout, inside there were fifteen tables all set for four people, a bar and a door to the toilets and the back way out. The café was actually on the junction of two roads with quite a large terrace area, the tables were four deep between the road Dietrich's car parked on and the front of the café. I was pleased to see there were lots more tables spread across the pavement toward the other road. I sat with my back to the window, diagonally opposite and as far away as possible from where Dietrich would sit, which already had a reserved sign on it. I'd put on a baseball cap with the peak pulled down as far as it would go, I wore some glasses that Philippe had given me, they were not sunglasses as he thought that might arouse their paranoia but they had a special reflective coating on that though it looked clear actually obscured my irises because they were shiny but you could still see my eyelids and surrounding flesh. I had also not shaved since the day before I met with Philippe and had the start of a decent moustache and beard. The weather was starting to get cooler so I wore a baggy Parka coat with a Kevlar vest underneath, I didn't think it would be suitable by lunchtime, but it made me feel less vulnerable and I thought I could get away with the fashion-victim look. After a coffee and some poached eggs on rye toast I went back to the flat.

At eleven I watched them all leave the room in a single file with Dietrich in the middle, there was a pause while the first two guards checked the corridor before the rest followed. It was too early for lunch, Philippe said he never arrived at the restaurant before twelve-thirty, so I waited. By twelve I ran out of patience and the nervous energy inside was building up dangerously so I set-off for the restaurant and took up my favourite seat, I ordered a coffee and some pogácsa with cheese and bacon. Their table remained empty and at twelve-forty the waiter came out and took the reserved sign away with an audible sigh. By one o'clock I was back in my room and hoping they hadn't decided to move out altogether. Eventually I gave up on pacing before I wore a hole in the already threadbare carpet and dragged the armchair from in front of the TV and placed it by the window, with my feet resting on the low window ledge I prepared for a long wait.

By two-thirty I was so on edge that I thought I actually felt the door open in the apartment opposite, just as one of Dietrich's men walked through carrying a large canvas bag, he needed both hands to heave it onto the table directly in front of the window. I watched as he unzipped the bag and peered inside, I could see wires and blocks of what looked like clay but thanks to Alphonse I knew that they were Semtex, there was enough there to blow the entire block up. Then, despite the distance and walls between us, I heard Gutmann scream at the man with the bag to, 'close the fucking curtains.' Now I had a bit of a dilemma, if Dietrich was planning an imminent attack, I would need to do something quickly and that wouldn't be subtle. I texted Philippe from the phone he had given me, it was supposed to be secure, but we also agreed to use Rachel's code and we changed the songs as a precaution. He replied within the hour, apparently Dietrich had also booked himself and his guards into a hotel in Ankara, for six days starting Sunday, when they were out doing their *shopping*, he ended the message by telling me to stick to the plan and don't rush. That gave me two, hopefully three days including today to kill him, Ankara was almost 1800 kilometres from Budapest they would have to drive virtually non-stop to do it in a day and a half. It might also just be Dietrich laying a false trail, in case anyone wanted to set up a welcome party for him.

I managed to be patient the following morning and waited for them to leave at mid-day. I noticed a slight change in protocol from the day before, this time two guards came to the door and waited in the corridor, then two men from inside and Dietrich left with the pair in the hall. That still left a couple of them to make sure the Semtex was secure. I sprinted down the stairs and walked the last fifty metres to the café, I was seated at my table a minute after Dietrich and his crew arranged themselves in their seats. I waited until their food arrived and they started eating before I looked over at them, I fixed their positions in my head and then looked down at my coffee, I found myself almost sinking into some kind of trance as I reached out to them. I located Dietrich quickly, at this distance I could easily distinguish the difference between him and his three guards, I ignored the driver in the car for now. Dietrich's heartbeat was faster and shallower than the others, there was also a slight irregularity in the rhythm, this was the heart of someone who plotted and schemed from his desk, it was the sluggish pulse of a coward but a deadly coward. His men in contrast were athletic and muscular, they breathed slowly but deeply, their hearts were strong and steady. As they talked, I picked up on their names and matched them to their unique rhythm, I had no plans to harm them, but I thought it best to be ready should things change. After twenty minutes I'd got what I needed but I stuck around in case they mentioned what they were up to, but all I heard was inane chatter about football and misogynistic bile about the women who passed by on the street. It really was a shame I couldn't just kill them as well. I could see this would be an issue for me, at the beginning I was horrified that I had killed just one person now I wasn't sure if there would ever be enough bad guys for me to kill and would I just keep going until someone stopped me, until someone killed me? I realised that Michelle and my family were my only hope that I would need their help if I was going to find a cure for my peculiar addiction.

I was sat in the armchair when the curtains opened just after six, they were just putting food out on the table the Semtex had been on. There was lots of bread piled in a basket, plates of cold meats, and olives in a large bowl. The four men sat around the table, but Dietrich remained sitting in his chair and further away from the window, he wasn't going to drop his guard just because he was hungry. One of the guards piled food on a plate and handed it to him.

I left my staff lying next to me on the floor, I couldn't figure out a way to use it, there were two floors below me and a parking basement below that. Dietrich's apartment was also on the third floor, all be it a little lower than mine as the ground sloped down as it went toward his building. I took a deep breath and started to hum, the note was so low it was barely audible, but I watched the sound wave roll toward the building opposite, knowing I was the only one who could detect it. It was spreading too far horizontally though, by the time it reached their window the force was spent. I tried again, this time I focussed on keeping it contained, I visualised a narrow corridor a few feet wide with tall walls and guided the wave along it. I felt the ripple as it passed through the glass, I thought of Dietrich, the irregularity of his heartbeat – tick-tick-tock, tick-tick toc. Got him! Suddenly it was like he was in some kind of medical scanner, I could see his heartbeat, I could see his blood pulsing almost like I had at the café. I clenched my fist as I tried to wrap the sound wave around his aorta, I thought he jerked a little but couldn't be sure and I already sensed it wasn't going to work, I needed more power, more focus. If I let my emotions swell up, let my anger rise, I knew I could reach him. I was also pretty sure I would lose control and literally rip him apart. Better to let the sniper have him, but that particular thought gave me another idea, it seemed I was still in a phase where improvisation was required. I texted Philippe – "Does your friend above have a spare sight and mounting? Can he drop it off at my door, tell him to knock and leave it outside. It's better we don't meet." He texted back within an hour – "all arranged, expect delivery soon. Good idea not to meet."

    I am sure Philippe thought I was being security conscious, well I certainly didn't want anyone else to see my face but most of all I didn't want to see the soldiers face. He would die, it was an occupational hazard, probably not this time though given he was just the backstop. I didn't want to see his face and then one day when I heard the news, see it over and over again just like I did with Yve. I still get flashbacks of Jack sometimes, in one of those rare quiet moments, but he does not keep me awake or fill my heart with dread. It was ten o'clock, I waited in darkness, the apartment was barely illuminated by the street lamps. Then I heard the slight tap at the door, I waited a few minutes before I opened it a couple of inches, there was a hessian shopping bag on the floor the handles near the opening so I could drag it inside without having to show my face. The bag had green writing printed on it, almák, below a picture of an apple. Inside was the site and a universal mounting, plus there was indeed an apple, suddenly I felt a little mean for being so rude to my almost guest. Manners wouldn't keep either of us alive though.

I took the bag to the window and looked it over, it would fit at least I thought, but I would have to wait until tomorrow to test my crazy idea. I took the telescopic sight and mounting from the bag and put them on the table. I held the mounting to my staff and fastened the clamps, they were just tight enough with a few washers improvised out of a bit of old cardboard, to hold it in place about fifteen centimetres from one end, I clicked the sight into place and looked through it and across to the other building. The curtains were drawn, and I sensed that Dietrich had gone to bed, the rhythm of his heart had slowed, and he seemed further away than earlier, his bedroom was probably on the other side of the flat.

Just before twelve the next day they did their little changeover routine, with two staying behind to guard the explosives and two new ones making up the quartet of guards to take Dietrich to lunch. I stood in front of the window but on the far side of the room, I needn't have worried the two men were playing cards with the TV going in the background. I moved a bit closer and raised my staff, pointing it straight at the back of the head of the one they had called Gregor yesterday. I peered down the telescopic sight as though it was a rifle, then I panned to the left and stopped at the next but one apartment. By the window was a small sideboard with a white lace cloth laid over it and a vase of flowers sitting on top.

    I could see clearly through the high-powered sight, it looked like a bunch of Cornflowers, and I could even make out the water line in the vase. The apartment seemed to be empty, so I focussed on the slightly murky water itself and started to hum. I started to tap very lightly at the side of the staff, nothing was happening, so I tapped a little harder, then harder again, and finally I saw the water ripple and a few large bubbles rise to the surface. It wasn't enough, I needed more but I needed to stay in control, I rested the end of the staff on my chin while I tried to think, in this position it reminded me more of a blow pipe than a rifle. That gave me another idea, my breathing and the humming had always been part of every successful attack before, and I was using them now but not so much my breath, I didn't think screaming or bellowing would work over this distance, I was sure the key was focus, a concentrated beam like a sniper's laser sight. I held the staff up to the window again but this time I placed the end about an inch inside my mouth and started to hum around it, then I began to tap. Straight away, with the very lightest pressure the water began to stir as though something was rising from the cloudy depths. I tapped a little faster and the water began to spill over on to the lace cloth, then a little harder and the vase moved slightly, just a fraction more and the glass shattered, the Cornflowers and crystal shards were flung across the room. Before I put the staff down I noticed there was a slight crack in the window, I would definitely need to dial back the power for Dietrich.

The little luncheon party returned at two and the guards that had stayed behind left but one of the others immediately closed the curtains. I held the staff to my mouth anyway and sent out a little tremor across the gap and into the room, I could identify the soldiers and there was Dietrich sat in his chair again. I was tempted to try and finish him right then, but I wanted to be sure, I didn't want him getting a few palpitations and rushing off to hospital. Most of all, I wanted to see his face when he died. I really was crossing over to the dark side but that didn't seem something I had much control over, nor was I inclined to try and develop it just then. While I sat in my own chair watching and waiting, I pondered over the two guards that left as they rotated in turn. I wondered where they went to but it didn't seem important enough to text Philippe about. I could have told him the sight was a success, but it seemed best to wait until I finished the job. From what I had been able to work out by tracking the five of them as they moved around and slept, there were two bedrooms, the living room I looked on to, plus a small kitchen and bathroom off the inner hallway. Dietrich slept in one room and two of the men slept in the other room, while the other pair stayed awake in the lounge.

Just after four o'clock the curtains opened, one of the guards was pouring coffee into mugs and there was a plate of Bahlsen biscuits, as usual, Dietrich waited for them to pass him his coffee and he took a single biscuit from the plate. This would be his last communion but there would be no soul saving confession, no last rites for the unrepentant. I wondered if I was destined to suffer the same fate, but I did not tarry, it was already late.

Now was the time, as I raised the staff to my mouth, I looked down the sight at Dietrich and started to gently tap as I watched a few ripples spread over his coffee, I used the movement to gauge the *volume* before I moved my sight to his chest and applied a little more pressure. I noticed him shift in his seat, he was feeling it but he didn't have any idea what he was feeling, he probably thought he had indigestion, he didn't understand the little message I was sending him – "your time is up…tic-tic-toc." I mapped out his heart and lungs with my magic little sonar and then I visualised a swirl of cloud that thinned in the centre and coalesced at the circumference. The cloud became a noose, and I sucked it in with my own breath as I watched the fear in his eyes, he dropped the mug and coffee spilled all over his lap. I inhaled quickly and the thread snapped shut, in my head it sounded like the crack of a whip. Dietrich's eyes went blank just before his head fell to his chest and he slid almost off his chair. One of the guards immediately looked to the window, but I had already stepped out of sight and lowered my staff. Seeing that the window was intact he shouted at one of the others who rushed to check Dietrich out, he knew he was dead, but he was looking to see if there were any wounds, any signs of malveillance externe. He looked to Gregor, who was still standing by the window, clearly not considering himself to be in any danger, and shook his head. Gregor immediately took out his phone and made a call, the other three started to pack everything up, they would be leaving very soon. I texted Philippe – "Celebrations are in order, what about the fireworks?" He replied in less than a minute – "Congratulations, see you at home I've got a Party Planner to take care of the pyrotechnics."

***

By midnight Michelle and I were lying on our sides, with every possible millimetre of flesh touching, lips locked, kissing with our eyes open and focussed entirely on each other. I felt a sense of peace that I had not known since Yve died, but I knew it was only a temporary reprieve, my demons, as Charlotte had called them, were always close by.

Philippe was happy to satisfy my curiosity about the fate of the Semtex and in so doing also where the two *spare* guards went when they left the apartment.

'Dietrich really needed eight men for the Op, but he was having to penny pinch having fallen out with Kurt. He took the risk of leaving the car unprotected while the two that usually guarded it went up to make sure the Semtex was secure at all times.'

'Couldn't they have left one of the soldiers with the car?'

'They're professional mercenaries they would never agree to one of them being alone, it would make them too vulnerable. It's easy to sneak up on a single guard and then lay in wait for Dietrich to come down. So, it wasn't in his interest either. In the hiatus we managed to get a tracker right underneath the car where no one would see it and then followed them at a safe distance until they pulled over at a truck stop, and this time they really did break protocol. All six of them went inside the café together, it seems that Dietrich's demise had rattled them quite a bit and they needed a meeting to decide their next move. The Semtex was valuable, and they'd been made suddenly redundant, it looked like they were going to stick with the plan of driving to Ankara, all be it a little earlier than expected. As far as we can tell they had a buyer in place there and wanted to collect.

While they were inside though, a couple of your father's agents that he'd loaned me managed to wire up the Semtex in the boot of their car. They followed the six of them at a distance, it was getting late and the road was empty, but the agents waited until the car was about a kilometre from the Romanian border before detonating the Semtex. The Hungarian's and Romanians are treating it as a terrorist plot gone wrong and are very pleased with themselves, despite having done nothing but I am very happy for them to claim the glory.'

'What about Kurt?'

'I would guess he will remain unconvinced by the coroner's verdict of natural causes and will suppose the mercenaries killed Dietrich then took the Semtex to sell for themselves and something went wrong along the way. He will have his hackles up for a few weeks, a month at most, but not enough for him to go to ground.'

***

At one level I seemed to have the perfect job, the longest I'd ever had to work was two weeks in Berlin, my target got spooked when he spotted his old captain on a tram and went to ground for nine days. Mostly I worked three or four days a month and I certainly got to travel a lot. But I was still obsessed by getting Kurt, I really did have a problem where he was concerned. Every assassination was like taking paracetamol for a headache, as soon as it wore off the pain was back but that little bit worse. Philippe sensed what was going on with me and as my personal drug dealer he did his best to keep me supplied. He was selective and secretive for which I was grateful, but it was still putting a strain on Michelle and I, which she bore with a smile and the occasional slap across the back of my head. I spoke less and less to my family, and I knew they were getting increasingly worried about me.

    Things came to ahead early one Friday evening, just a few hours after I'd completed a mission in Brussels without any significant complications. I was alone in a hotel room in Mons, close to the French border. I'd stripped down to get in the shower when I felt myself go lightheaded and sat down on the toilet seat. It was a vision, after the last one with Yve I dreaded another, someone always seemed to die. This vision was the most terrifying yet, I saw two men outside the new apartment Michelle, and I had recently leased. They were stood by the door trying to pick the lock, even in my fugue state I knew that wouldn't work, we had had deadbolts and reinforcing plates installed the day we got the keys. There was a long hallway from the front door, past the bathroom and bedrooms to the living room door, or Le Salon as Michelle insisted on calling it, we had also had hefty locks installed on that door. I thought that would give us enough time to get help if we needed it. The vision ended with the outside door being blown open and the sound of automatic gunfire but there was too much smoke to see anything or anyone. Michelle and I had agreed that the outside door would be locked at all times, whether I was home or not and I was confident she would stick to that. I dialled her number, I needed to make sure she was secure in the lounge not caught in the hall. When she did not pick up, I started to panic, I called Philippe and just shouted down the phone, 'Michelle needs help, now!' all he said was, 'Ok, ten minutes max.' and hung up. Then my phone rang, it was Michelle.

'Hi honey, sorry I missed your call.'

I cut in, my panic clear to hear. 'Michelle, there are two men outside the front door, lock yourself in! I've phoned Philippe he will be there in ten minutes, maybe less, I hope.'

'Josh my love, calm down I already know. I had cameras installed after you left, there is a third one halfway down the stairs on the small landing, you better warn Philippe, he's got a Heckler ready to deter anyone coming through the outside door.'

I started to text Philippe about the man on the landing from my secure phone whilst talking to Michelle on my own mobile. 'Michelle, Michelle, are you still there.'

'Still here darling but I might just have to put you on hold, it seems our callers are both rude and impatient.'

'Michelle, what are you on about? I don't understand.'

'I can see them on the camera, they're setting a charge. It looks small but I'm sure it's big enough to take the hinges off. We didn't really factor that in, did we? Here we go, I'll put you on hands free on the sofa you'll be safe there.'

Then I heard a distinctive thud followed by the sound of wood splintering, they were past our first line of defence. Where the fuck was Philippe?

'Josh cover those sensitive little ears of yours, the big bang is coming, and I need to put on my ear defenders as well.' Before I could say anything there was a tremendous boom. 'Michelle, Michelle are you ok? What the hell is happening?'

'Don't worry my love, it was just my stun grenade going off.'

'Stun grenade? You have a stun grenade?'

'Had chéri, grammar please. I set it up on a trip wire between the two bedrooms, that's why I missed your call I was literally a bit tied up at the time. Just hang on a mo, I need to tidy a couple of things up before the Gendarmes arrive. Then I heard a metallic click, like a lock being flicked open or shut and a second later two ear-splitting bursts of rapid gun fire, most definitely large calibre.

'I'm back Josh! Everything is hunky dory for now, I just need to go and hide my weapons before anyone arrives. Then I can put on my ma petite fille perdue et effrayée act, that should confuse them until Philippe arrives.'

'Michelle, are you sure you're not hurt and you're safe?'

'Never felt better! Actually, I think I may have had a petit orgasme when I shot those two little bastards. Perhaps

I'll buy myself one of those cute thigh holsters, I could wear it with just some stockings when me make love, I'd take the bullets out the gun though, I wouldn't want anything to happen to your lovely cock. Ah, I can hear Philippe's voice and I think he brought a few friends, the dick on the landing is down and looking rather forlorn. That was nearer twenty minutes than ten, by the way, but he did give me my hunky P30 and this gorgeous big juicy HK416. Oh, and that stun grenade came in handy, I think I need another one of those please!'

I stood there in stunned silence until Michelle asked me a question in a very seductive voice.

'Joshy, are you coming home tonight?'

'I am now!'

'Good, because I need to fuck you hard and then I need you to make love to me all night long. Is that ok Joshy?'

'I'm on my way, try not to kill anyone else before I get back. It sounds like you've had enough foreplay for one night.'

'Don't worry I won't start without you, just get that delicious ass here pronto. Oh, and I'll get Philippe to text you where I am staying. I think we are going to need a new apartment.'

***

After that night, we stayed with Philippe for a couple of weeks, he knew as well as I did that my assassin days were on hold for the foreseeable future, I felt I had only one mission at that point - protect Michelle. Though, I have to admit, she did a pretty good job of that without me. We decided as we no longer had a place of our own it would be a good time to go back to London. Apart from missing her family, Michelle's only regret was having to leave behind her precious HK P30 and 416, though Philippe promised to bring the P30 to London for her the next time he visited.

When we arrived at St Pancreas we took a taxi to Kensington Palace Gardens, my father had reluctantly moved out of the old house and into his official residence. Michelle and I agreed that we would stay with my parents as it was the safest place we could think of and we had both had enough excitement for a while. Mother was waiting for us, father was working, and she was excited to have us to herself, she often complained that mon père kept dragging us off with all his absurdité secrète. After hugging and kissing us both she put her arm through Michelle's and led her up the stairs and I followed as she kept going up. Eventually we reached the top of the house, which was more like a palace than a home. Mother told Michelle to close her eyes and cover them with her hands, which she surprisingly did without protest. I stood behind them, seemingly forgotten as she led Michelle through the door and a dozen steps into the room. I followed them in before moving to one side to get a bit of space and a better view. Mother peeled Michelle's fingers away from her face before telling her to open her eyes. I could see that Michelle was confused and she looked at me, I'd worked out what was going on but stayed dumb, this was mum's surprise. Michelle looked around her eyes widening, we were in the attic, but it was very grand with its faux Regency windows letting light stream in. Michelle looked back toward my mother before she spoke.

'Madam Renoir, I don't understand?'

'No more Madam, you are part of our family and I think of you as a daughter, tu dois m'appeler mère maintenant, and this is your atelier.'

Michelle squealed or screamed, not sure which, at full volume then threw herself at my mother jumping, quite literally for joy. When she'd finished the tears were still running down her cheeks. I watched as my mother put both hands up to Michelle's face and gently wiped the big salty drops away with her thumbs, I remember how she used to do that to me when I was a child and fell or hurt myself. She was right about my father's tendency to drag us off, he was like a whirlwind, and he sucked you into whatever he was doing, but without mother he wouldn't have lasted, she steadied and supported him, calmed him down when he got too distracted, allowing him to regain his focus. Now she took Michelle off, and I knew I was surplus to requirements for a few hours at least so I went in the opposite direction to explore our new abode.

We had been in London for almost a month, and I was struggling with what to do with myself. Michelle spent most days in her studio, she joined me for lunch, but I could see she was itching to get back to her creations, as she called them, and twenty minutes was about as long as she could manage before I would take pity on her and tell her to go back to her work. Though I was doing very little I still felt physically tired but realised that what I needed was exercise not a nap. I forced myself to use the gym downstairs, I would have preferred to go for a run, but I just didn't feel safe enough to leave myself that exposed. I did look forward to three-thirty everyday though, my mother insisted we both join her for tea at the appointed hour, even though she only served coffee alongside an array of patisserie. At first it seemed a rather strange idea, in Paris we would have barely finished lunch an hour before, but mother was not to be resisted and I soon began to enjoy the ritual and the company, sometimes Charlotte even managed to join the three of us. It provided me with some structure, a small anchor point in the day. On this particular occasion it was just the three of us for coffee, my mother seemed a little different, she smiled at Michelle far more than usual and would then look toward me with a facial expression that completely perplexed me. We usually dragged this interlude out for an hour, but my mother got up after twenty minutes claiming she had something to attend to. She went over to Michelle and kissed her on both cheeks, there was nothing unusual in that, but then she stroked the side of her face with the back of her hand before resting it on Michelle's stomach and smiling at her again. With that she walked briskly over to me, kissed me on the top of my head and laid her hand briefly but firmly on my shoulder and spoke.

'Good boy, good boy Josh.' Then she was gone, and Michelle was doing her best seductress smile, the one that always made me instantly hard.

'Josh, you know you can do some weird things, is your mother a witch?'

'Strange question and no doubt, I hope, you will explain, but to answer you, most definitely not. Should such things exist.'

'Josh, do you remember the night our apartment got un peu explosé and we had to stay at Philippe's?'

'You mean the night you tied me to the four-poster bed and rode me like a bucking bronco?' Now, at the corner of her mouth, she was sucking on one of her delicate fingers and I shifted on the chair to try and adjust myself to a more comfortable position.

'That would be the night we didn't have any condoms.'

'You forgot to pack them in the rush to get out of the apartment, given the two dead men on the hall floor, I think that was understandable in the circumstances.'

'And we both agreed we didn't care. Josh, I'm pregnant. Is that ok? Do you want to be a father?'

The last sentences came out of Michelle's mouth like bullets out of a machine gun, within a second I was kneeling at her feet, my ear to her belly.

'Josh, can you hear the baby?'

'Wow! Yes, I can hear its heartbeat, it's very fast. Is that ok?'

'I'll google it.' I waited while she tapped on her phone, it took seconds, but I think my own heartbeat almost doubled as I waited. 'Oui, that's normal and it can be quite erratic, according to Dr Google.'

'Je t'aime Michelle and yes I want to be a father, I didn't know that until now, I hadn't even contemplated it as something for the future but now it seems one of the few things that make sense to me, our family!'

'Je t'aime Josh, Je t'aime mon amour.'

'But what was the thing about my mother being a witch?'

'She knew, I only took the test this morning, but she knew as soon as she looked at me. I was going to wait a little while before we told our families, but it seems the cat's out the bag.'

'Maybe she is a witch, she certainly has my dad under her spell, just like you have enchanted me. Je t'aime mon amour.'

We tried to keep it low key, but the grandparents and Charlotte, Pierre and Philippe all knew. Michelle could not move without someone offering her a chair, a stool for her feet, a blanket, a cold drink, a hot drink…! I noticed that Charlotte was spending more time at home, she and Michelle had become a lot closer. It wasn't the sexual flirtation of their first meeting, they seemed to be developing a very close bond, which I found reassuring for some reason. When I asked Michelle about it, she said some of it was that they'd just naturally grown closer but that it was being spurred on by Charlotte's fascination with the baby.

'I think your sis is getting broody?'

'She wants a baby. Charlotte?'

'I think she want's at least three!'

'Does Pierre know?'

'Not yet, I think she's worried he might be getting a bit old, or he will be by the time he's ready to step back from the frontline and take a desk job.'

'Well, I've not known Charlotte to not be upfront about what she wants. What's her plan or should I say her timeline?'

'You'd better sit down for this.' I didn't want to be a centimetre away from Michelle, so I just sat cross-legged at her feet, my hands still caressing her belly.

'She's convinced that Pierre is going to propose.'

'What makes her think that?'

'Well, he's been *fishing* lately, trying to sound her out without actually saying anything much, just casual comments when they past a bridal wear shop and questions about what her favourite holiday destination would be and what would she like to do there.'

'She thinks he's testing the waters and planning the honeymoon at the same time?'

'That's about it, and then the other day she spotted him leaving your father's private office.'

'He must pop in there at least four times a week just to go over security plans for events and visiting dignitaries.'

'That's what I said, but this time he was wearing a suit and tie.'

'Now that is news, I didn't even think he owned an office suit, and I am sure he hasn't worn a tie since he was a cadet in training. So, Charlotte thinks he went to see my father to ask his permission?'

'That's her theory, what do you think?'

'She may be right, Pierre is only 37 but he is old fashioned or rather he has some traditional values. If Charlotte's responses to his comments on the wedding dresses were positive, I think he would go to father first, not to ask his permission but as a curtesy, a sign of respect. Besides, dad's his boss as well as his potential father-in-law, Pierre would feel obliged to at least give him the heads-up given how complicated it could all get. Yes, I think she's right.'

'Well, be forewarned, if he does propose and she tells me she is bound to swear me to secrecy, she will want to announce this in style.'

'So, it's ok to tell me about her wanting babies and Pierre building up to a proposal, but not the fact that he has actually proposed?'

'You can be a twit sometimes Josh! Charlotte told me I could tell you of course, and then she is hoping you will encourage Pierre to get on with it. I'd be quite happy if you gave him a big shove, I can't wait to be her maid of honour and I'd rather not look like a balloon in the photos!'

The next day, in the hope of bumping into Pierre, I asked my father if there was anything he'd like me to translate or help with in the embassy. It was the first inclination I'd shown toward going out the house let alone actually doing some work, which might have been why he looked so pleased. But then I realised it wasn't pleasure, it was relief. I'd noticed he'd looked even more stressed than usual lately, I think with Philippe gone he was having to take on too many different roles. If this was a company that had expanded, he would have restructured it by now, but it wasn't always easy to make changes to such an established bureaucracy, diplomats and civil servants don't like change unless it directly benefits them.

By ten o'clock I was sat at a computer with a headset on listening to a recording between a Greek trade delegation and a French negotiation team, there was quite a lot of agitation, asides and blatant whispers and the translators in the room were struggling, one was taking notes – see, old fashioned, they didn't trust the digital recording – and the one doing the contemporaneous oral translation couldn't keep up. I could see why my father had given me this to start with!

At eleven-thirty he sent me an email asking if I would like to join him for lunch in his office at one o'clock. That really set the alarm bells ringing, I'd never known him eat in his office. The only time I ever recall seeing any kind of food in his inner sanctum was years before he became ambassador, when I was just a child, and he gave me biscuits to eat while he held meetings. Whatever he wanted, it wasn't to tell me about Pierre's nuptials, so at twelve-fifty I walked into the outer office, which was usually guarded by two secretaries but was now seemingly abandoned. Things were getting stranger by the minute, he didn't call out to me like he usually did so I knocked on his door and walked straight in. He stood up and walked over to me and gave me a huge hug, but before I could ask him anything he put his finger to his lips. Then he went to the door I'd just come through and turned the lock before he led me through another door at the far end of the room and locked that as well. There was a conference table encircled by twelve uncomfortable looking chairs and to one side there was a low table with sandwiches and a cafetière of coffee in the middle, and two comfy armchairs either side. I could see from the acoustic lining on the walls that the room was sound proofed to the max and undoubtedly bug free, though I thought I'd check anyway. It was my turn to raise my finger to my mouth, and as he waited, I closed my eyes and just listened. All I could hear at first was my father rubbing his shoes on the carpet, fidgeting nervously, which was completely out of character. After almost a minute he settled and I could hear his breathing and his heartbeat, I was pleased that he seemed to have relaxed, and his pulse had slowed. I allowed my hearing to spread out in widening concentric circles with me at the core. I was listening for any unusual sounds, particularly high or low-pitched ones normally outside the range of human hearing. There was nothing, I opened my eyes and smiled at my father.

'All clear.'

'You can do that?'

'If the room is quiet enough, useless in most places, even a fridge running within twenty metres makes it unreliable.'

'How are you feeling? You've had a rough time lately.'

'I'd like to think I could shrug it all off, but we both know I can't, and I won't try to insult you by pretending. Let's say I'm fragile, better for coming home and the baby has really helped put things in perspective, I feel there is a point to being alive. Trite maybe, but it's what I feel, and it provides me with something real to focus on, something truly important, at a time when I would otherwise be completely adrift.'

'Thank you for being honest, I'm more fearful of reality than most but it doesn't do to close your eyes and hide behind your hands.'

'Father I can see you're stressed by far more than my psychological state and we don't need a soundproof, bug free room to talk about that. So, tell me what gives, more importantly what can I do to help.'

'I have a problem and I do need some assistance, I didn't want to ask you given what you have been through, but I don't think there is anyone else that can do it.'

'Tell me what it is and I will be honest with you and myself about my capacity.'

'I believe one of my field operatives has gone over to the other side, China to be specific. I've been watching them all closely for the last two months, after a few *coincidences* set the alarm bells ringing. This is not the first time someone has betrayed us, but we usually catch them when they communicate or meet with their contact or handler. However, while we know information is being passed across, we haven't been able to trace or observe any kind of transaction.'

'Do you think there are two of them, one covering for the other?'

'That's the only thing that makes sense. Given the material that's been leaked so far, I think that one of them is a desk officer in this building and the other is one of my field agents. There are many opportunities for them to casually meet in this place, to coordinate their activity and share information. The desk officer might have a contact on the Chinese side as well, given we are currently in protracted trade and tariff negotiations with their government there is a lot of legitimate contact between both sides, and most of it goes on in this building.'

'So ample opportunity to pass on secrets without arousing any suspicion at all. Just how many suspects are we talking about?'

'We have a direct negotiation team of five plus three legal experts, two translators and another five technical experts covering the main products under discussion; steel, batteries, telecoms, grain and coffee.'

'So, fifteen in total, that's a lot of suspects, any way of narrowing it down?'

'The five negotiators are the most likely source, they have the closest contact with the Chinese, the others either work in the background or support the meetings like the translators. It's only those five who have a plausible reason for meeting with any of the Chinese delegates alone.'

'What would you like me to do?'

'Listen from a distance, watch them from as far away as possible. I don't want to spook them but most of all I don't want you in any danger. Nothing happens outside the building, you don't follow them, you don't listen to them and you don't just happen to have lunch in the same restaurant. Though they have been known to eat here when they have morning and afternoon sessions booked and the canteen should be safe.'

'Do you want me to learn Chinese?'

'Can you?'

'I think it will be more difficult for me than European languages and it will take longer but I don't mind trying. I'll join a few on-line forums and see how it goes.'

'The meetings are officially held in-camera, the Chinese speak good English as do our people, the translators are mainly used when it gets to some of the technical language or if anything needs clarifying. Short-hand notes are taken, and the transcript is signed off by both sides at the beginning of the next meeting.'

'Does that mean there is a secretary in the room as well?'

'Pardon, oui. I have loaned them Martha my personal secretary, it seems short-hand is a dying skill and the only other person we had who could do it is off sick.'

'That's going to make our double agent wary.'

'It was either that or we get someone from an agency in and neither side would agree to that. Whoever it is expects to be watched, they think they have found a way to keep us in the dark, and while we don't know who it is we do know there is someone, which is a big mistake on their part. There is a thread hanging there somewhere and we just need to spot it and unpick it.'

'There is one thing I don't get, why are the talks being held in London rather than Paris?'

'The preliminary negotiations were held over a year ago in Paris as you would expect and the main talks were also scheduled to take place in France, but then Philippe was promoted to Foreign Affairs Minister and that caused a ripple, which threatened to escalate into a tsunami and the Chinese withdrawing. They have some history with

Philippe, unofficially he took out three of their best agents one dark night on the Korean border. Officially three Chinese tourists out for a moonlight walk stood on an old landmine. Some of Philippe's detractors in government have tried to make capital out of it as well, which didn't help. Personally, I think the Chinese were more concerned he might get directly involved in the negotiations, he is well known for his skills and hardline when it comes to brokering a deal. Now of course, I think it may well have been to make this little plot a bit easier to navigate. Whatever the real motivations, Philippe will still be the one to finally sign them off before they go for ratification.'

'I can start tomorrow, I'll talk to Michelle tonight.'

'The team are on the last two banks of seating at the north end of the floor below this one. I'll have them clear a desk for you at the other end with your back to the wall.'

'Do any of them use the gym?'

'Two of the negotiators, Francois and Claude like to spend their lunch times there, I believe they do more talking than exercise. I thought I said no contact.'

'Au contraire, I am trying to avoid it, I wanted to know if it would be safe for me to get a few stretches in and now I know it won't, I'll use the gym at home.'

***

When I got back to the house Michelle was smiling from ear to ear, she dragged me by the hand to our room, shoving me toward the bed and kicking the door shut. 'Sit!' I decided it was useless to resist and sat on the end of the bed. Michelle was wearing some kind of denim smock dress that buttoned all the way up the front, she had clearly been using it to paint in and there was a rainbow of smudges all over it. She plucked at a few buttons and the whole thing just fell from her shoulders in a pool at her feet, which she then kicked to the other side of the room. She was naked and held her belly with both hands.

'Do you think my tummy is getting bigger?' I moved her hands down by her sides and put mine in their place and gently circled them around. Her belly might have been a little more rounded than a week ago but it was difficult to tell, luckily I knew that was the wrong answer to her question. 'I think you have definitely started to ripen.' And with that I bent over and started to lick and kiss her entire stomach as I moved my hands around to gently squeeze her ass cheeks. She took my hands and arranged the two of us next to each other on the bed and I continued to lick and spread my saliva across her skin until she interrupted me by pulling on my chin.

'Josh, I thought I felt something today, not much, just a very slight movement deep inside. Do you think it was the baby, can you listen again?' I put my ear to her belly and listened passively, I did not want to risk any of my trickery harming the little thing.

'Its heartbeat is a little louder and more regular, when do we go for the scan?'

'Next week, it's a bit soon but I can't wait.'

I went to move my head upwards so I could kiss Michelle, but she put her hand on the top of my head and pushed me down past her stomach and I knew where she wanted me to lick next. It looked like we were going to be late for dinner, not that either of us cared, we were a feast for each other, and it was definitely time for the hors d'oeuvres.

The following morning, I set off for work, I had expected Michelle to be resistant to me going back to the embassy, but she actually thought it would be good for me, as long as I stuck to the rules my father had laid down. From where I sat, I could see them all at their workstations, the bank of desks closest to the wall at the other end of the room was occupied by the negotiators and product specialists. The two translators and the three lawyers, specialising in contract law, tariffs and export-import regulations, sat on the row in front. Meaning there were ten on one bank and five on the other, they could have evened the space out a bit but there seemed to be a status issue binding together the negotiators and the product specialist who clearly looked down on their colleagues. Martha stayed in the office leading to my father's room whenever she wasn't in one of the meetings, she looked relieved when she was back at her own desk, I don't think she really liked the members of the team very much. In truth they didn't seem to be much of a team at all, they were a far cry from Pierre and his men.

At twelve-thirty Francois and Claude went off to the gym and I heard Antoine and Louis discussing going to lunch together at a nearby restaurant just before they left. Apparently, they both fancied the same waitress, but she had bluntly turned them down, saying she was waiting for a film star or at the very least a footballer. Though they were both thirty-five they sounded like they were barely twenty, being away from home seemed to have reset their maturity thermostat. That left Gabriel out of the five negotiators, he stayed at his desk scrolling through his phone. The rest went down to the cafeteria on the ground floor, I'd eaten there a couple of times, and despite the French cuisine it still reminded me of school, so I decided to pass on that, for now at least. Instead, I stayed and watched Gabriel, who continued to look at his phone and I wondered if he was waiting for a message. If he was it didn't seem to come and after about fifteen minutes he put the phone face down rather too firmly on his desk. He could have been waiting for a call from a contact, but I thought it would be too risky and way too stupid to do that in the middle of the office. My money was on boyfriend or girlfriend trouble, that might also explain why he wasn't eating.

For the next couple of hours, I kept one eye on Gabriel, who checked his phone every ten minutes trying to will a message to arrive, despite the lack of any audible alert. It was Friday and it didn't look like any of the others were coming back from lunch, which was fairly normal for the end of the week. When Gabriel closed his laptop and got up to leave, I thought I'd give him fifteen minutes to clear the building and go home myself. Friday was a strange day to start a new job and bizarrely I felt like I'd done a full week's work and was more than ready for the weekend. I didn't quite manage to escape in time though, my father called just as I stood up to go. Thankfully it wasn't about work, apparently dinner that evening was to be a formal affair with the whole family present, and he wanted to make sure Michelle and I not only attended, unlike the previous night, but were on time. Clearly, he had something planned.

When I got back to the house, Michelle was missing but there was a tuxedo, bow tie and dress pants hanging on the wardrobe. I thought spiriting Michelle away to ensure I actually got dressed was a little extreme though. Dinner was at eight with canapés and cocktails at seven-thirty, it was only six o'clock, so I decided to get myself a whisky from the cabinet in the library and take it with me for a relaxing soak in the tub. When I got to the door it was ajar and I could hear Pierre pacing up and down the room rehearsing something over and over again. I decided I could live without the whisky and headed back to the bedroom. I was dressed and ready to go by seven-fifteen, there was still no sign of Michelle, so I headed back to the library to collect my brother in arms, hopefully soon to be my brother-in-law.

After a disrespectfully quick single malt we both headed to the reception salon that adjoined the dining room, inside my parents and grandparents were all assembled, to my surprise I also spotted on the periphery Robert and Rachel, arm in arm. I was starting to feel like I was in a soap opera or perhaps this was an interview for two new additions to the Family. The conversation was a little stilted, which was very out of character with any gathering of Renoirs, it was as if everyone was waiting for something. Then that something really happened, Charlotte and Michelle entered the room, and everything went completely silent. At first I thought they had forgotten to dress at all and were standing in front of everyone naked. It was quite the illusion, their dresses were nude if that's a real colour, and they contoured every curve and angle of their bodies, the diaphanous material trailed down to their ankles before spreading behind them in a series of undulating waves. I heard Pierre next to me struggling to breathe, I put my arm around his back to steady him and leaned over to whisper in his ear.

'Pierre, I hope you realise, she's done all of this for you. You don't have to worry she has just given you her answer, brother!' I think he originally planned to propose to her after dinner but seeing her looking so ravishing he couldn't contain himself. Charlotte knew she had him hooked and it was time to reel him in. She smiled at everyone in turn, as though she was a famous actress walking the red carpet for her own movie premier as she stepped toward Pierre. When she was just within touching distance, she held out her left hand, fingers slightly curved as though she was waiting for him to kiss it. Pierre took the hint and went down on one knee before her, with the tips of the fingers of one hand he delicately held her hand as he pressed his lips against her fingers. Despite his nervousness he managed to produce a stunning diamond and emerald ring from his pocket as he spoke.

'Charlotte your beauty captured my attention and adoration from the moment I first saw you, but your inner beauty has taken possession of my heart and soul. Will you consent to make me the happiest man alive and marry me?'

Charlotte was not done playing with him yet, she held up the fingers of the hand he'd kissed and started to tick them off with the other hand as she spoke.

'Now, let me see: tall - tick, handsome - tick, strong - tick, loyal – tick, tick, tick, intelligent – well not bad for a squaddie I suppose. But what about, stubborn – tick and…, oops no more! Pierre, you are the man of my dreams, I was ready to marry you the first time we kissed.'

Charlotte stretched out her hand and Pierre placed the ring on her finger, she plopped herself on his knee and kissed him until he fell backwards with her still in his arms. After that the dinner was a bit of an anti-climax but everyone was happy, even me. Pierre stayed over that night and in the morning, he sidled up to me at breakfast and quietly asked if we could have little chat alone, so we slipped into one of the small salons.

'Not changed your mind, Pierre?'

'Never!'

'Then what is it? You want some advice on military tactics within the NATO alliance perhaps?'

'Josh, please.'

'Ok, no more jokes I'm listening.'

'Charlotte wants children, lots of children!'

'But you knew that before you proposed, right?'

'Oui. But I am worried for her. Sorry, this is difficult for me to talk about, I must say it quickly - my mother and my unborn sister died in childbirth. I am terrified of something going wrong, of losing Charlotte. Do you think I'm crazy?'

'You're not crazy, I've been terrified since I found out Michelle was pregnant. I've imagined every possible thing that could go wrong. If she stretches for something in a cabinet, I have to stop myself from rushing over and getting it for her and I don't even have your experience, not that I need it, my imagination is a powerful thing.'

'But…'

'Pierre, from what little you have spoken about your childhood I don't think it was an easy one, and there was certainly no money for expensive doctors. Charlotte will have the very best specialists and facilities to care for her from conception to final contraction and beyond.'

'But…'

'Pierre we both know that there are no guarantees. You who puts your life on the line for an ideal every day, you know that better than anyone. Besides, what choice do you have? Would you have her be miserable, would you let the two of you live a life of what might have been? Neither of you would survive that.'

'But…'

'Pierre! Accept it, Charlotte is an unstoppable force, in fact that's mostly why you love her?'

'Oui!'

***

On Monday I was back at my desk early waiting for the arrival of my suspects just in case they gave a little sign, something that wasn't suspicious but just didn't quite fit or feel right. Francois and Claude, the two gym buddies, who also seemed to have regressed back to their teens, spent the first twenty minutes talking about football, apparently Chelsea won. The love rivals, Antoine and Louis struck out again on Friday and were considering trying a new restaurant today, they seemed to have a thing for waitresses. Gabriel remained taciturn but had stopped checking his phone. The rest were talking about work and preparing for the meeting with the Chinese delegation at 2pm. This also meant the gym buddies would not be able to do their usual lunch session and eat, but they agreed food took precedence over exercise. I had my Jo Staff with me as always and I'd put some workout gear in the bag just in case. I'd been neglecting it for a while, but I could still feel the pull of the staff and it would be good to go through some katas and let off a bit of steam.

Just after eleven I heard Gabriel's phone ping, and I watched as he snatched it up from his desk rather too quickly and scroll to his latest message. After he read it, he looked a little pale and headed toward the corridor, I could just make out him heading downstairs before the door swung closed. I got up slowly and walked toward the exit, he had thirty seconds on me so I wasn't optimistic of catching up with him, nor did I really want to, but if I could get a little closer that might prove useful. I needn't have worried about losing him, I paused on the landing and as the stairwell door closed behind me, shutting off the noise inside, I could hear him clearly. Gabriel had walked down to a lower level to make a call, it seemed he was not our spy, he was talking to his father about his mother. She had cancer and had just been readmitted, after taking poorly following a recent course of chemotherapy.

I returned to my desk and got on with some translating as I continued to watch the paint dry. By 12.30 they had all gone off to lunch, so I took my chance and went down to the gym. As soon as I walked in I realised it might have been a big mistake. The last time I was here, Yve and I had our final sparring match. Actually, it was much more than that, it was real! It was when I really fused with the staff, it was when all my body parts seemed to synchronise and dance to a predatory staccato rhythm. It was when Michelle and I both realised we had found a missing part to ourselves, only to lose it so quickly. For a minute I stood still, my staff ready, but not sure if I could even move, except to maybe fall on my knees and cry.

Instead, after a few very deep breaths, I started to listen to the beat of my own heart, to the blood pulsing through my veins and at last I started to circle and sweep the staff in wide arcs. Then as I began to stalk my invisible opponent, the staff at a forty-five-degree angle over my head, I felt then heard another heartbeat and the air seemed to swell around in front of me. In some way, somehow, Yve was with me. I spun one-eighty, staff striking down in a head shot, only to feel resistance and the memory of the sound of cracking oak as our staffs collided. I moved forward and my ghostly foe moved right, and I blocked the invisible blow, then I felt the pressure again, the sound and the vibration so real. As before, the match was a draw, perhaps to be fought or played out, again and again. I did not fear it, I relished my sudden communion with her spirt.

Was it real? I don't know but I felt the effect at the time and later it continued to reverberate. Afterwards my technique and speed with the staff improved greatly and every so often I would feel her presence and hear her heartbeat in those quiet moments. I talked to Michelle about it, wondering if she would mock me for my sentimental imagination, but instead she was convinced it was real, that Yve was with us in some way we didn't understand. We both thought that I needed someone else to spar with though,

Pierre was the obvious choice, but we knew he would find the association with Yve too painful. Then Michelle suggested Charlotte.

'I know she isn't anywhere near your standard but teaching her could be part of it. You might find that helps you understand more that the process of teaching her helps you reflect on your own technique. I remember talking to Yve about coaching you and she said, that while you were naturally gifted, she found she learned more about herself through working with even mediocre students than she did from just sparring.'

'I'll ask her, we could use the gym here first thing in the morning it's always empty then.'

'Well don't hang about, she's on a mission to get pregnant and once that happens Pierre won't let her cross the road without an armed guard and picking up anything heavier than a chocolate will be completely out of the question.'

I managed to catch up with Charlotte at breakfast the next morning and she was really excited by the idea, and then Charlotte being Charlotte she went off to find Michelle to drag her out shopping for work out gear. For someone who could shoot you between the eyes from a hundred metres away, she was very girlie, not that I was brave enough to say that to her face though.

***

Talking to my sister had put me a bit behind schedule and I missed the morning arrivals, everyone but Gabriel was at their workstation, he arrived an hour late and was looking very flustered. After over hearing Gabriel's call about his mother's treatment, I thought I was making some small progress, I could eliminate him at least. If I continued to rule out those outside the negotiating team that left me with just four suspects. The problem was, neither the gym buddies nor the love rivals looked to be likely spies, it was not just that they seemed to have regressed to adolescence, it was the simple fact that they never spent any time alone, apart from going to the toilet and they didn't spend longer than usual in there either. I was obviously missing the obvious, it usually seemed to be the case that when something didn't make sense to me it was because I wasn't seeing what was right in front of my nose. As I watched them all troop out to their next meeting my phone pinged and I picked it up, it was my father and he wanted to see me asap.

When I walked into his office Pierre was there, a sure sign that things were about to get physical.

'Sit down Josh, Pierre has unexpectedly come across some information that I think may relate to your job. Pierre the floor is yours.'

'Well since becoming aware that we had a potential traitor in our little network, I have been keeping an eye on them. We can't actually watch them, as they are the ones that do the watching for us, and at this point we can't trust any of them. Given the nature of this, only Robert, Rachel and Charlotte know of our suspicions. Rachel has been using AI to try and filter CCTV cameras around the city to see if we can pick up any agents where they shouldn't be.'

'And?'

'Nothing, nothing until this morning and what we have got is not much.'

Pierre clicked a few keys on a laptop and then turned it around so we could all see it. The monochrome images were very poor, grainy and out of focus, they showed a tall man, wearing a long wool overcoat despite the temperature being in the mid-teens, the view was from the back, you could see virtually nothing of his face, he was tall and starting to thin on top. The man's left arm was outstretched his fingers on the handle of the bottle green door in front of him, he pushed it open and went in, the sign hanging inside the door was turned around and you could just make out that it said closed. I looked at Pierre, but he said nothing, so I spoke.

'Pierre, that's hardly anything, what have I just watched apart from a man about to go bald entering a shop?'

'I said it wasn't much and you're going to have to take Rachel's word for this, she loaded all of the operatives' photos, heights, weights - basically anything we had on them into this fancy AI program she's been working on. Then started sifting through trillions of images coming from live CCTV within a kilometre of those premises and any known characters we have had or still have an interest in. The shop is in Hounslow, it's run by Leon Fournier, a dual national with a dubious past, he's supposed to be an antiques dealer, but we think he specialises in selling guns, nice shiny new ones.'

'And the guy going in, he could be a visiting alien, do we have a picture of him coming out so we can see his face? It could be anyone.'

'He didn't come back out the front way and there are no cameras at the back, they are conveniently vandalised every time they are replaced. According to Rachel the AI program identifies this individual as one of three agents working for us but needs more data to narrow it down. Still, it's a good start.' My father decided to join the conversation, I could sense his urgency, there was something he wanted to get to sooner rather than later.

'About a month ago, British customs impounded six German Haenel HLR 338, complete with a thousand rounds of depleted uranium ammunition. Two weeks ago, a routine inspection of the stores where the weapons were kept found that three of them, plus the ammunition, had been removed. Special Branch believed that Leon Fournier bought the guns but had no evidence, they managed to get a warrant on the pretence he was dealing in forged paintings, but they found nothing.'

'Then what?'

'Then nothing, they are understaffed and have no budget for overtime. They assumed that if he had the rifles, he'd already moved them on and closed the case.'

'So, you think the man in the overcoat bought one of the guns, what do you think he has in mind?'

'Those rifles are good for one thing only, killing from afar. They are also expensive, which means they were bought to murder some high-ranking politician or other government official. Less likely but still probable, a very wealthy businessman, almost certainly one that was dabbling in politics as well. The ammunition suggests the individual will be targeted in a building or a car rather than in the open.'

'So, what do we do? How does this fit with the guys I've been watching?' Pierre answered my first question, though he didn't fill me with confidence, possibly because he was rather lacking conviction himself.

'Rachel is trying to use the AI to cross match what we have at the shop with images from other cameras in the area. The problem is that these agents are trained to avoid cameras, they get so good that it seems like an extra sense they have.'

'Then how come we got the one outside the shop?'

'He knew the camera was there and made sure no one could get a shot of his face, he could have worn a hat or a scarf across his nose and mouth even, but he probably figured that would arouse more suspicion than it was worth. He didn't wear a watch either, agents like their watches – functional and precise, that's how they tend to think of themselves, but you wouldn't find any of them wearing a digital, Rolex or Omega and usually gold. The watch would have made it easier to identify him, all three of our suspects are right-handed and wear their watch on their left wrist, but I bet none of them have the same model. Vanity is found in strange places!'

While I was pondering this my father addressed my previous question and the more important one as far as I was concerned.

'I'm not at all sure how this links with the trade talks or if it even does. My biggest fear is that we have more than one rogue agent in the field, if that's the case I will be forced to close the whole network down, purge it clean and start again. Always supposing I could get agreement to do that, the British are not the only ones with funding problems, some members of the Sénat and Assemblée Nationale would see this as a wonderful cost cutting opportunity. We had better be nice to Rachel, she may be the next head of service controlling a network of virtual reality spies. Sorry, I don't mean to sound bitter, but we need to tie this one off and fast.'

'The rifle, the sniper, it all sounds a bit too familiar to me. Are we expecting any surprise visitors of note?'

'None, I checked with Philippe and he assured me there is nothing even in the pipeline, he has spoken with the British and Americans and they're saying the same thing.'

'What about the Chinese?'

'We can hardly ask them, if we identify a credible threat to one of theirs, we will warn their government, but we don't really have anything apart from an excess of anxiety at the moment.'

'So, we wait for Rachel. How long Pierre? How long for her to find a needle in a haystack the size of London?'

'With luck, three days. She thinks.'

'And without luck?'

'He could die of old age before we find out who he is.'

'So, while we wait, nothing changes, I still need to ferret out a pair of spies. The question is, who in my little quintet is much smarter than he looks and smarter than me so far?'

By the time I got back to my desk, the trade meeting had finished, and everyone had gone apart from a few stragglers.

***

I returned home feeling defeated but when I walked through our room door I was instantly cheered up. Stood there with big smiles on their faces were Michelle and Charlotte, both dressed in minute white spandex shorts and matching white halter tops. Charlotte spoke first.

'I've sent Pierre to have a long soak and relax, I don't want him watching my first training session in case I make a balls of it.'

'What about Michelle?'

'Michelle is there to provide moral support and first aid if you need it.'

'So why the training gear darling?' Michelle was looking noticeably coy, which I didn't quite understand until she answered.

'Well, we tried them on, and Charlotte noticed how well this outfit shows off a little development that we thought you might like to look at.'

Every part of Michelle was perfect, and I could just stare at her for hours, a few times when she'd had enough of my adoration, she knocked me out of my reverie with a flying cushion. But as my eyes trailed down from her face, across her tightly bound breasts and beyond to her stomach, that's when it hit me and it wasn't a cushion, there was definitely a slight swelling, her normally flat belly was slightly rounded, she had started to show. I closed the gap between us and dropped to my knees, I began stroking and kissing her stomach. Too quickly I felt her grab the sides of my face and pull me gently up.

'Plenty of time for that later, go and get changed I've left your new training gear on the bed with your staff.'

In the bedroom was a pair of black spandex shorts not much bigger than the ones the girls had on and nothing else. Those two were definitely up to no good and I knew I was going to be the one to suffer, even if I eventually enjoyed it. I was down to my underpants when Michelle stuck her head around the door.

'Hurry up Josh, and you need to ditch the panties the shorts need to be next to your skin to support you fully.'

I hadn't really noticed how many mirrors the gym had until then, when I trained on my own, I usually kept my eyes closed as it helped me focus and get in tune with the movement and natural rhythm of my body. Now I was having to direct Charlotte, she had done a little sparring with Pierre, but I think they had both been too much of a distraction for each other to really get into it. Surprisingly the girly silliness from upstairs had completely disappeared, she stood in front of me and listened to every word I said, then followed every move I made just as I had told her. Michelle sat to one side, I couldn't resist glancing across every now and then, I caught her once stroking her own belly and another time virtually caressing it. Charlotte managed to *accidentally* clip me on the shoulder with her staff while I was staring. I regained my concentration and apologised, she just smiled.

Charlotte made quick progress, it wasn't instinctual like it was with me when I had started, but she understood the principles and she followed instructions with ease. I could see now, why she was able to work with Pierre in a combat situation and obey orders, something I would never have thought possible. Though outside of that, Charlotte would definitely be the ranking officer, she would have her army of babies and Pierre would be willingly demoted to her lieutenant.

***

Gabriel was late again, just twenty minutes this time, but as long as the job got done and people were prepared to work through the night when needed, no one watched the clock. Apart from me that is, people have their own particular relationship with time, at all sorts of levels, but change to the normal pattern is usually significant. When I started watching them, Gabriel was always early, often spent lunchtime at his desk and was always the last to leave. Now he was regularly late, frequently popping out to take calls though he was still getting his work done, I'd checked.

The trade talks were drawing to an end, the negotiators were taking a bit of a back seat while the others worked out some of the legal details and technical snags. Gabriel should have looked more relaxed than he did, of course I didn't know what was going on at home for him, but I still thought something wasn't quite right. There wasn't much to pique my interest though and I was getting rather bored, despite my father's instructions I'd been down to the gym a few times while Francois and Claude were training. They actually did very little exercise, a few chest presses and ten minutes on the rowing machines set at low resistance. As they did upstairs, they just talked about football even though I stayed in the furthest corner from them and they would have thought their conversation private, if they bothered to lower their voices that is. The same for the love rivals, Antoine and Louis, they spent their down time talking about the waitresses and some of the female diners they'd seen, though it seemed that they hardly ever spoke to any of them, other than to order their food. It was like London had drained the French out of them, they might as well have been traders in the City.

    I'd all but given up on finding anything out when my father had refused to let Pierre and I take them somewhere quiet and interrogate them, though he did agree that if we found out who the double agent was, we could do whatever we needed. Frustrated I decided to go for a workout in the gym at lunchtime, Francois and Claude were at one of the bench presses, so I went down to the shoulder squat bar at the other end with barely a nod to them on the way. They left soon after I arrived and an hour later, I was making my way back up the stairs, but halfway up the first flight everyone seemed to be in a log jam. I heard someone nearer the front say the caretaker had knocked over a large drum of some kind of cleaning fluid and no one could get to the lift or the next flight of stairs. Not in the mood to wait around or gossip with my neighbours on the stairs who'd suddenly become hyper friendly in the enforced close contact, I went back down and headed along the corridor, it was mainly a service area with storage cupboards and locked doors with hazard signs screwed to them. But once I got to the other end the emergency stairs led back up the three floors to my office, the same staircase I'd heard Gabriel on his phone talking about his mother's chemo. One flight above me I could hear his voice again and I automatically paused, he still seemed to be talking about his mother's treatment and then the bloody obvious finally hit me, he was using code. The words and phrases more or less identical to that first time, I suspected the key would be in the differences. I took out my own phone and sat on one of the steps with my back to the wall so I could see up and down the stairs, then I pretended to text while I listened and memorised. When he finished speaking and I heard the doors on our floor close, instead of going up to my own level I walked through the open plan office on the one below. I came out above the commotion that was still going on downstairs and made my way back to my own desk to set a meeting up with Pierre and my father.

***

'Gabriel's our man, they're using a crude cypher, barely qualifies as code really. Pierre, do you remember the code we used in Paris, the one Rachel devised? It was a simple substitution, numbers corresponding to letters in two different songs. It was basic, but we only sent short simple messages, often just a few words.'

'I remember, but they're not using text and from what you said he's not reeling off numbers, he's just having an ordinary conversation about his sick mother.'

'That's what I thought the first time I heard him, but the second time reminded me of something. When we used Rachel's code, I tended to disguise anything particularly sensitive or important.'

'I don't follow.'

'Nor do I Josh.' My father looked particularly confused, which was hardly surprising given he hadn't even been involved in the Paris mission.

'Ok, I'll give you an example from one of the last jobs I did for Philippe. I was watching a group of mercenaries through their apartment window, they all went out one morning and returned in the afternoon and one of them was carrying a large holdall, which he placed on the table right in front of the window. Carelessly he opened it to check the contents without bothering to close the curtains first. They were only open a minute, but I spotted a large quantity of Semtex as well as the usual bomb making paraphernalia. It wasn't what we were there for, but I obviously needed to let Philippe know. When I coded the message, I didn't use the word Semtex or explosives, I substituted it with the word fireworks and talked about arranging a party. Philippe knew what I was on about and replied that he had the details of a very good party planner in town, and he would ask him to take care of the whole thing. By that I understood that I didn't need to worry about the explosives or try to stop them.

It's a simple double code, one part has a fixed set of rules like Rachel's number substitution and the other is improvised over the top of those rules, a bit like Jazz. You need to be somewhat in synch with each other to avoid misunderstandings. But the reply picks up on the improvisation in the story thread, which not only gives you an answer, but it also confirms that you are both marching to the same beat.'

Father looked at me as he spoke. 'So did you and Philippe work all that out in advance?'

'No, we did it on the hoof during the operation. We're both big Coltrane fans, it was natural.'

Pierre was still trying to work it through though. 'I still don't understand how that works with Gabriel and whoever is at the other end of the call?'

'I think they are doing something like the improvised story as the primary message carrier. I need time to analyse it, to compare the first conversation I heard with the second one. But what alerted me was how similar the two conversations were, even though they were weeks apart. I think a lot of the words have pre-agreed fixed meanings, more like Rachel's code but limited. So the word "mother" is probably a contact name, maybe the leader, "chemo" may be another contact or a key commodity in the negotiations. There is a lot of talk about temperature and specific measures, sometimes in Celsius and other times in Fahrenheit, which is odd in itself. Also blood pressure and several other numeric variables that doctors bandy about. I am pretty sure each of these relate to commodity values and quantities.

At the very least Gabriel is giving the other side the bottom line on our negotiating position and how low or high we are willing to go. The Chinese can see all our cards and Gabriel is dealing from the top and bottom of the deck.'

I could see the light come on in my father's eyes as he suddenly became animated.

'Yes! That all makes sense now. No wonder these talks have gone so smoothly, we usually have at least two dramatic walkouts a week during these kinds of negotiations. It's all part of the positioning, not to mention posturing, but there hasn't been a single tantrum. Paris think Gabriel is the archangel himself!'

'Before we get carried away, can we get someone to confirm or refute the sick mother story?' Pierre agreed to do that, Rachel could do it faster, but he didn't want to take her off the search for our double agent. 'Secondly, we need to follow Gabriel, without alerting him or his friends but we can't trust our agents. Any ideas?' My father smiled, the first in a while, as he spoke.

'Now we have narrowed down the suspects there are two I can trust, they have both saved my life at different times, but that's not enough manpower for full surveillance.'

'It won't take long to check on the mother then I can help follow him, It will still be thin but he doesn't seem like he's had any training, given the calls in the corridor, so we should be able to manage.'

'I agree Pierre, but we know we have a very well trained and armed rogue agent out there as well, so take no risks.'

I thought for a minute then spoke tentatively about the thing that still bothered me the most. 'I think that will tidy up our problem in the building, but I am more bothered about the agent with the rifle and how that connects to these talks?' My father pulled at the thread I'd left hanging.

'It doesn't make sense, these are career diplomats, what would be the point in shooting any of them? Even if they wanted to bump Gabriel off to tie up the loose ends, they wouldn't use a sniper rifle and armour piercing bullets, they'd slit his throat in some dark alley and make it look like a mugging.'

'Didn't you say, when you asked me to take this job, that Philippe would be coming over to sign this off before it goes to the president and the government? Would the Minister for Foreign Affairs merit depleted uranium ammunition?'

'Yes, and he certainly has enough enemies to form a firing squad never mind a single sniper. The thing is, I know the Chinese don't like him, but they are far too strategically astute to shoot him just as they are completing a favourable trade deal.'

'I agree, and I don't think the Chinese have any notion of assassinating Philippe. What if the sniper, our agent, is deceiving them as well as us. What if they are passing information from Gabriel to them as a way of gleaning how the talks are going and when Philippe is going to come to London? Does Gabriel know the Minister's travel plans?'

'As leader of our delegation Philippe would meet with him, and Gabriel would walk him through the important elements of the agreement and answer any questions before he met with both teams and gave them his approval in principle. Philippe will have sat down with some of his own trusted advisors before leaving Paris and gone through the document in detail, this is almost ceremonial, but it's considered an important part of the diplomacy. So yes, Gabriel will have Philippe's entire itinerary at least twenty-four hours before his plane takes to the air.

My father called Philippe on a secure line and brought him up to date while we listened in. The minister would not cancel his trip, he said it would play into the hands of his enemies in the government, one or two of whom were quite capable of setting this whole thing up. Philipe then identified the potential spots he would be vulnerable to sniper fire.

'Paris would be the easiest but for whatever reason they want this to happen on English soil, so I think we can rule that out. Though we do need to give some consideration as to the potential benefits of me catching a bullet in Blighty as it may give us some clues to who we are really up against. We don't have time right now though. Stepping off the airplane leaves me a sitting duck, but it might be difficult for them to get close enough with a clear sight. Getting out the car at the embassy is probably easier or through one of the windows, I assume Gabriel has already picked the room he wants to meet me in before we join the Chinese delegation, as well as the conference room for when we all come together. Ideas, thoughts anyone?' This was Pierre's area of expertise, and he was quick to take the stage.

'I agree the airport is unlikely but so is the car park here, there are no clear sight lines from outside the compound. I will check both meeting rooms as soon as we finish to assess the risks, it might give us some idea where we will find our sniper's nest. Philippe, I assume you are coming by private jet, send Gabriel the details, times of take off, landing and your expected ETA at the embassy but send someone else on that plane. I will arrange a military flight for four hours earlier, Robert will accompany you and some of my squad will transport you army-style to the embassy and I'll meet you at the back door.'

'What about Gabriel?'

'Tell him there was a last minute change, you know how it goes, don't give him anything else. Let him sweat, I will change the meeting rooms to the other side of the building. He's going to find an excuse to leave your meeting with him and probably go to his favourite corridor. Josh and I will pick him up and question him, he will talk and quickly. Then we find the second traitor.'

'That sounds good to me. I was planning on leaving at noon the day after tomorrow. I'll send Gabriel the "details' at eleven in the morning.'

***

At eleven the next morning I watched Gabriel as he sat at his workstation, I couldn't help noticing the big smile that stretched his mouth wide like some giant emoji. Philippe's travel plans had obviously landed but after his initial reaction Gabriel's countenance returned to its familiar anxious expression, he really wasn't cut out for this work, but I doubt he'd have to worry about that for too much longer. "Un espion grillé est un espion mort," was one of Pierre's cheerful little sayings. With the trap set I was thinking about leaving early for some tummy time with Michelle, but before I could switch the computer off, I had an email summoning me to a meeting in my father's office. By the time I got there, Pierre and Rachel were already drinking coffee and Pierre was even eating a biscuit, I'd couldn't recall ever seeing sugar pass his lips before, Charlotte was leaving her mark. When I smiled at him, he quickly returned the evidence to his saucer, looked at me and shrugged. I hadn't seen Rachel since Paris, but she greeted me with a warm hug and asked how Michelle was doing.

'Early days but so far she is enjoying her pregnancy and looking forward to motherhood.'

'And fatherhood?' I looked across at my own father as I replied. 'It's the reason for living, love and family.' It sounded like a toast and perhaps that's just what it was - to love and family. My father had a tear in his eye that he quickly wiped away as he got down to business.

'Rachel has some information to share with us.'

'I am, or rather my AI program is 99% certain that our rogue agent is Frantz Jäger, he's been with us for 15 years, ex Foreign Legion, speaks five different languages, including Chinese, and is an expert sniper. Digging through the files and checking with the Minister, it seems he most likely went over in the last three years. Four years ago, his brother who was also one of our agents was captured in North Korea, what he was doing there remains a mystery, we do not operate in that territory other than satellite surveillance. We tried to broker his release through the Chinese and even the Russians, as we have no direct diplomatic relations with them. The North Koreans refused to even acknowledge he existed, but after six months we did get information from a defector that the brother had been executed by firing squad. At the time Frantz made it clear that he did not think Philippe had made enough effort to get his brother back and he was convinced Philippe must have sent him over the border on a suicide mission, but after about six months Frantz seemed to get past his grief fuelled anger. He accepted that there was nothing anyone could do and according to Philippe they shook hands, and he believed it to be over.

With the information Philippe gave me about some of the fallouts within the "network" over the last decade I was able to narrow down the parameters of the search. Frantz was the only one of the original three we identified from the "antique shop" footage that had fallen out with Philippe, so I added some more of his physical details and additional file photos to the AI search around a kilometre radius of the shop that I'd set at the time he possibly collected the gun. I got a hit one hundred metres from the shop heading north, it was fuzzy but looked like a good match with the one outside the shop, and it picked up a few more facial features as well.'

I could see Pierre trying to stifle a yawn, I couldn't blame him, he just wanted an address he could go to and shoot Frantz. However, I was fascinated about how it all worked, that it worked at all, and it was definitely more reliable than my visions. Charlotte was teaching him patience though and he did well not to interrupt, I would be sure to tell her about his progress later, so he'd get his gold star. Rachel didn't even notice Pierre was on the verge of falling asleep and carried on.

'So, I ran the program again and got three more dots to join up before he turned up outside Hounslow West station, there is an estate agent's premises to one side of the main entrance, they had some new cameras put in a few weeks earlier and they picked him up. It wasn't full frontal, but I got two different profile views from a couple of cameras, his left ear, nose and eye were particularly clear despite him walking close to the back of the man in front of him. The program analysed all the partial images and matched it to Frantz's mug shot.'

Pierre couldn't hold on any longer. 'So where is he?'

'Gone to ground, no sightings since the tube station. Not reported in, not responding to messages or calls. His apartment isn't obviously vacated, but everything is tucked away and very clean, in all senses of the word, there is not a single scrap of personal information. What was interesting though, was the camera pointing straight at the front door.'

'A camera?' Pierre's question was perfunctory in tone, his interest still in decline.

'Yes, it was linked to the Wi-Fi and would have given Frantz a nice picture of our search team entering. So, he knows we're on to him, if he didn't already.'

My father broke his silence. 'He knew, this is just his dowry.'

'His dowry?' Rachel asked.

'He's now got recent photos of six operatives, to add to what he already knows about us. I doubt the Chinese knew anything about this sub plot of his and will not want to get involved now it's exposed, they're very likely to turn on him or just leave him to us. The photos give him something else to barter with, extra collateral, and there will be plenty of buyers willing to offer him sanctuary. We can't afford to let

Frantz slip away, he must be dealt with conclusively.' I was used to Philippe talking in these kinds of terms, pronouncing a death sentence without saying the actual word. I'm not sure what comfort it gave them, or whether it made them feel more civilised as though they were handing down justice in a court of law, instead of shooting him in the head on some wet cellar floor. I was curious about the words, but I was not concerned. Despite my reservations about him, Philippe was still family and Frantz was the bad guy and I'd willingly kill him and anyone else who threatened us. I still had a question I needed to ask though.

'Do you think he will call off his assassination attempt?'

My father thought for a moment before he answered. 'If, this was just business, he'd be crazy not to, but I think it's personal and vengeful. The real problem is that he's one of us, he knows Philippe and the way he operates, so he will assume we have changed our plans and set Gabriel up. Given the importance of the meeting he will assume it will go ahead and he will anticipate a change in the time and the details of Philippe's arrival. He will wager that Philippe will arrive earlier than planned rather than risk upsetting the Chinese by delaying the meeting. So where does that leave us?'

Pierre knew it was his role to answer this. 'Assuming we have a lone sniper, he can only cover a certain number of windows in the building, given we are changing the location of the meetings as well, he can't realistically hope to make a shot. Philippe is now landing at a military airfield, even less accessible to the casual sniper and he will not be exposed at any point, I've made certain of that. He is travelling here in an armoured vehicle I've borrowed from the Brits and there is no target as he enters the building. So, if Frantz turns up, he is only putting himself at risk, now that we know who it is we can brief our agents to watch for him.'

While it didn't give us a realistic chance of catching Frantz, it did keep Philippe safe and get the treaty delivered. I had one doubt though. 'Frantz will also know all that, not the detail but that we will have moved the meetings and beefed up the security. What if there are more assassins than Frantz?' Pierre started to look less certain of his plan and asked. 'What makes you think that?'

'There were three rifles stolen, while the chances are they were sold to separate customers, what if they were all bought by Frantz?' Pierre was getting agitated now.

'Where would he get two other snipers from, you're not suggesting we have three rogue agents are you?'

'It's not impossible, but very unlikely. I've been thinking, we have been working under the assumption that Gabriel's contact is working solely for the Chinese and then taking the opportunity to bump off Philippe, who he still blames for his brother's death. The more I think about it, the less convinced I am. Frantz would have had plenty of easier opportunities to kill Philippe in the last four years, and those three rifles just happen to get stolen at exactly the right time? I did a little research on the building those weapons were kept in, it wasn't Fort Knox, but the security was very good. It would have needed an insider and at least two or three others to get the gear out of there. They were kept in two steel boxes, which were taken with the guns and ammo inside, they were heavy and awkward to handle. What if

Frantz is actually working for someone else apart from the Chinese, what if killing Philippe was always the main course? What if Frantz was working with our antiques dealer and not a customer but a conspirator? The shop might have just been a safe storage place until they were ready to collect them.' There was a long silence, as the tumble weed metaphorically drifted across the room, before my father spoke.

'I will call Philippe, we can rearrange the visit.'

Pierre just looked at my father and shrugged. 'He won't listen, he thinks he's bullet proof, even though he's still got shrapnel from a 9mm inside his hip.'

I had to agree with Pierre, I knew exactly what his response would be. 'Father, you have to call him, but I can tell you he will probably start chuckling and offer to hang outside on the flagpole as bait. He will definitely see this as an opportunity and not a threat. You put your call in, Pierre and I need to walk the roof and see what we are up against and how to set our own trap. Do you want to join us Rachel?'

'Non merci! I don't like heights, even less so when there are multiple snipers itching for some target practice. I'll start scanning those areas I can access the CCTV for and I'll see what comes up on my AI maps and building plans, that might help show up our vulnerable spots and their potential vantage points.'

We made our way to the top of the embassy and out onto a balcony, from there we stepped on to a narrow gangway, we could then walk around most of the building whilst hidden from curious eyes below. There was something not quite right, I couldn't figure it out and it was niggling me. Pierre pointed to a building about fifty metres away, there was a stone parapet wall around the rooftop, small columns with thirty-centimetre gaps between them and large coping stones across the tops. It was an ideal position for a sniper, lying prone they would be completely hidden and still able to see and take aim through the gaps between the columns. There was a good view of the north end of the embassy as well as the right-hand front side. Anyone within a metre or two of the large windows would present an easy target and directly below us were the rooms originally booked for Philippe to meet Gabriel and then the Chinese. The only downside was that any sniper would be visible from the top of the adjoining building, which was a couple of stories higher and went off at right angles. It also had a parapet wall, it was made from solid brick but anyone who cared to lean over the top would be able to see the whole of the roof below.

    Pierre was looking at the other building as he spoke. 'I'll put two men up there, they will fire to maim not kill, unless they have to.' There weren't any vantage points at the front or back of the building, but at the south end there was a multi-storey office building facing us. The roof was too high and sloped backwards, you would have needed a trapeze to get an angle to shoot from up there. We had a clear view into the top floor, and it was obvious it had been vacant for some time, but just as we had an unobstructed view through the windows, anyone on the other side would be able to see into the offices and any meeting rooms below where we stood.

'There's a big storage room just below where we are standing, I can put another two men inside there first thing in the morning, before Philip even gets off his plane. They will have to shoot to kill, the lower bodies of anyone over there will be protected by the wall below the window, head and chest shots only.'

'I don't have a problem with that Pierre, I prefer my baddies dead then I know they can't come back to haunt me.' When we got back to the other two my father had managed to contact Philippe and as predicted, rather than cower in his office as all of his predecessors would have done, he wanted to bait the trap. He'd even suggested sticking with the plan he sent to Gabriel to avoid scaring them off, but my father explained about the camera in Frantz's apartment and that not doing anything would make them more suspicious. Rachel's AI didn't come up with anything more than our walk around the roof had done, but she had also sent a camera drone over the tops of the surrounding building and confirmed that at present there was nothing going on. Pierre still insisted on immediately getting two of his men up on the roof that overlooked sniper's paradise, as the two of us now referred to it.

I'd had enough for one day and was going to head home, but then I felt a shiver go down my spine and I knew there was something wrong, something we were missing and for some reason I felt threatened. It was an odd experience, and my first thought was that I needed some fresh air and the walk home would do me good, but then I changed my mind. Though very different, I thought this felt similar to my premonitions and I decided to take it seriously and asked my father if he minded if I went back with him in the car. He was pleased with the idea although a little surprised as I rarely waited for him, he tended to get stuck with something or other that made him late, much to my mother's annoyance. They both preferred it the way things were, before he was promoted to ambassador.

I was up early the next morning, but my father had left at seven, when I came down to breakfast half an hour later my mother was still complaining to Charlotte about the uncivilised hours her husband was keeping. I grabbed a croissant and a coffee and took it back to my room, Charlotte grinned at me over mum's shoulder as I sneaked back out.

On the walk to work I felt that shiver again, I looked around but couldn't see anyone, I knew I was going to regret taking this quiet shortcut. Instead of looking for threats I stood still and closed my eyes, steadying my own heartbeat I listened, turning my head slightly as I did. Twenty metres ahead was a narrow side street and there it was, a metre in from the main road, a single heartbeat, someone trying to breathe as quietly as possible, to me they sounded like a horse that had just stopped galloping. I almost missed it under all that noise, but there was a much quieter pulse, it was rapid though, like an injured bird cradled in my hand. Suddenly, I was aware of someone else coming up quickly behind me, I turned to face the new threat and he stopped short, just out of striking range not that I had the time to take my backpack off and get out my staff. The large automatic gun pointed at me was also a bit of a problem, he tilted it towards the alley as he spoke.

'We have one of your little friends of over there, she's with someone who'd like to make your acquaintance.'

My first thought was of Michelle and then Charlotte, but I knew they were both still at home, it was too late though, I could feel the wrath rising. These two would die soon and not well. First, I needed to see who they were holding, the tremulous heartbeat was now the one I focussed on as I walked toward the lane. I walked at an angle, I wasn't going to give my back to the man with the gun and risk being knocked-out with it. They weren't going to shoot me just yet, I had time to prepare but they were running out of time, the gunman was sauntering to his own funeral even as he mocked me with his lazy smile.

As I got close to the alley, I could see Frantz hiding behind Rachel with a gun pointing at her head. I needed to get him talking, not for information, I was past caring about why people did what they did. It would be good if he let slip who was pulling his strings but sooner or later, if I killed enough of them, I'd get there without their help. For now, I needed to play the game.

'So, Frantz, where is number three?'

'What are you talking about, what shit are you trying to walk this way. You're just papa's little boy on an easy ride to the top, just like the rest of your mongrel clan.'

'Yet your boss told you to bring me back, and bring me back alive, I wonder why?'

'Do I look like I give a fuck? He wants you and that bastard Dubois will get what he deserves at last.'

I could sense this wasn't going to pan out as we thought, if they were just going to shoot Philippe then Frantz wouldn't have been here, he'd have been getting ready to pull the trigger. I needed to gauge his reaction to my next gambit very carefully. If they were not going to shoot him the most likely alternative was a bomb. An image suddenly flashed through my brain, it was almost painful, it was the day the stairs were blocked when the cleaner spilled a drum of fluid. Very convenient and I now realised it didn't add up, the caretaker and his little army worked early in the morning and late in the evening when most people had gone home. They didn't cart hazardous liquids around during the middle of the day when everyone was working. They'd planted and primed the bomb in all the confusion, it was in the storeroom already, and it would have to be powerful enough to blow the whole building up. My father, Charlotte, Pierre and Philippe, it would kill them all and so many others. The rage was rising deep inside me, I was struggling to control it, but Rachel was too close to Frantz. Time to play the cards I'd been dealt.

'Frantz, there is nothing in this for you, we've got the potential sniper covered just in case, and someone has already tipped us off about the bomb in the janitor's cupboard. We've just been waiting for you to all come out of your little burrows. It seems there are traitors enough for both sides!' I could see the sweat starting to trickle down Frantz's neck, what I didn't need was for him to accidentally or callously shoot Rachel. The other guy had manoeuvred himself behind me while I was talking to Frantz, but I needed to keep looking Frantz straight in the eye while I was speaking to him, very gradually I was trying to get to the position of being able to take control of him without any possibility of him reacting and killing Rachel. But when I felt the gun barrel prod me hard in the middle of my shoulders, just above the small backpack, I realised I had to deal with the man behind me first, and while Frantz was suffering a bad case of self-doubt, I sensed an opportunity. I started to click my tongue against the roof of my mouth, it was barely audible but in my current frame of mind it carried power. The gun against my back was providing a convenient conduit from my chest to his body but I couldn't take the risk of giving him a heart attack, he might shoot me in his death throes, I needed something more controlled and less dramatic. I concentrated on the veins and arteries running from his brain, down his neck and diverging around his body, I focused on the ones to his right arm, the one holding the gun, I visualised the nerves controlling his hand, then his fingers. I stopped clicking my tongue and breathed out, humming quietly, then I clicked my finger. My arm was down by my side, Frantz didn't notice, but the sound wave spread. The man's fingers went numb, then rigid, he couldn't pull the trigger he could barely hold on to the gun, at the same time I cut the blood supply to his brain, unable to talk and shitting himself, he slid slowly to the floor. Frantz's mouth opened wide, he pointed the gun away from Rachel and straight at me, which wasn't exactly what I had planned.

'What the fuck did you do to him?' I raised my hands in the air level with my shoulders, palms pointing toward him.

'I don't have any weapons, unless you count a couple of sticks in my backpack.'

'Move away from him, slowly'

Perfect. I took a couple of steps forward and one to the side, drawing his aim further from Rachel. Suddenly I remembered something, all those years back, the night of the party when I overheard Kurt plotting to kill Philippe. Frantz was there, skulking in the background trying to keep to the shadows, he was working with Kurt and had been for years. I smiled and spoke, I had him. I had the hook I needed to reel him in and net him without a struggle, I hoped.

'I remember you now, I knew I'd seen you somewhere before, it was years ago, you were at our house the night they took Kurt.'

'Don't be fucking stupid, you were a tiny kid!' I could see that little link had shaken him just a bit, that was good. 'You stood on the other side of the room from Kurt and Dietrich, the late departed Dietrich that is. You were standing near the burgundy velvet drapes that covered the doors to the dining room, it was like you were trying to hide behind them. But you were watching the two of them. You were already working with Kurt then, weren't you Frantz?'

When he didn't answer I repeated his name louder, then louder again, something about the interrogation training they gave agents made them more difficult to crack, but I was creeping in to his brain, I could see by the tick below his left eye and a few little twitches in the arm that was still wrapped around Rachel. I needed to push a little further. 'So, Kurt wants to see me?' I had lowered my arms when we were talking, I was too far from him to be a threat or so he thought, so he took no notice as I tapped a little rhythm against the side of my leg.

'Kurt doesn't want to see you, he wants to kill you! I told him I'd take care of it myself, but no, he wants you to die slowly while he watches. But don't fret I'll make sure I take my turn on you before he finishes you off.'

That last outpouring of anger and venom was all I needed to get right inside his head, it was like the synapses in his brain all illuminated at once guiding me to the target. I spoke loudly, not quite shouting but the first word from my mouth knocked his head back and the second one froze him where he stood. 'Frantz, Frantz... dear Frantz let Rachel go and then put the gun slowly on the ground.'

I could feel him trying to resist and I tapped against my leg and hummed one of my favourite tunes, Deadmen, and slowly he uncurled his arm from around Rachel then squatted down and placed the gun on the floor.

'Rachel, go and find Pierre, tell him there is one sniper left and there is a bomb in the first-floor cleaning cupboard. No wait a second.' I clicked my fingers twice in front of Frantz's face and watched him wince in pain. 'Frantz, where is the sniper located and how is the bomb being detonated, what is the plan?'

'Sebastian is in the office building, at the south end, he will shoot Philippe if he can get him in his sight, then set the bomb off.'

'And if there is no shot?'

'He will fire into the building, wait for the panic and everyone evacuating then blow the lot up.'

Rachel seemed to be a little distracted, so I repeated what Frantz had said slowly. 'Rachel, you got that?'

'Yes, will you be ok?'

'What do you think? Now go.' Rachel looked a little dazed as she walked off, I waited a few seconds until she broke into a run and then I focused back on Frantz. 'Now you can tell me where to find Kurt?' Frantz tried to resist, it came out like a stutter. 'Again Frantz!'

'Too late… should have called in five minutes ago if we had you, then Kurt would give us the location to take you to.'

'Call him anyway and put it on speaker.' Frantz dialled the number, and we waited while it connected then it started to ring, surprisingly he picked up but he didn't speak. He knew he'd missed his chance, this time, but I couldn't resist one last prod. 'Hello Kurt, how's the treason and murder business going?' He didn't answer, I didn't expect him to, but I thought I'd try and goad him a bit more. 'I heard you divorced Dietrich and he died of a broken heart and all his little men went boom, boom, boom.'

I heard him scream 'bastard' followed by the sound of the phone smashing against something very hard. I questioned Frantz for a few minutes, but Kurt had kept him in the dark apart from what he needed to know for the operation. He didn't even know where the fancy rifles had gone, apparently his men were using their own weapons, apart from the explosives, which Kurt had supplied. Frantz had been collecting the bomb from the antique dealer when we first caught him on camera.

Pierre, turned up with four of the squad, just as I was trying to decide whether to kill Frantz or risk handing him over. I looked at my brother, I thought of Michelle and our baby, I at least needed to try and be a better person. When

Pierre had his hands in cable ties behind his back I released my *hold* on Frantz. Pierre looked at the mess on the ground, that was once a person, and sniffed the air.

'Do I want to know what happened to him?'

'He looked at what he'd become and scared himself to death. What happened to the third one and what about the bomb.'

'By the time Robert got to the door of the building Charlotte had put two in his head and two more in his chest, or should I say his back? Either way, most of his insides are splattered on the door he was about to enter.'

'What the fuck was Charlotte doing there? I left her at home this morning with my mother they were going shopping for a wedding dress.'

'She wouldn't say a word to Robert, but she just called me, you might need to sit down for this bro, so in the absence of a chair get ready to lean on the wall. Charlotte got a message, a *message* from you! She doesn't really know how to describe it, she said she heard some words in her head, they sounded just like you and they told her where to find the sniper. Josh, I asked her to repeat them, and they were exactly the same words you spoke to Rachel, who repeated them to me like she was in a trance, she even sounded like you.

As for the minor detail of a huge fucking bomb in the French Embassy, our resident bomb expert Alphonse is decommissioning it as we speak, almost everyone has very discretely been evacuated from the building and fucking Philippe is signing off with the Chinese delegation as though nothing is happening at all. Unfortunately, Gabriel could not make the signing, as he was called away urgently, apparently his mother is seriously ill.'

Pierre's slight smile gave away the true fate of our head negotiator and amateur spy.

***

I spent the next three days never more than two metres distant from Michelle, it was utter bliss. We spent hours discussing girl and boy names, we decided not to find out the sex of the baby. My mother approved, she thought it was best to be surprised, but Charlotte found it very annoying and was *most vexed*, as she wanted to buy the entire stock of blue or pink baby clothes of some boutique shop she'd discovered.

However, it seemed my good deed in letting Frantz live was not to be rewarded. I was woken one night soon after, by Michelle screaming and wailing. I was about to ask what was wrong when I saw the bed clothes, they were a dark foreboding red. We had lost our baby, Michelle was ok physically but not psychologically, neither of us were, and I wasn't sure we ever would be. While we and the whole family grieved Charlotte did her best to support Michelle, she spent hours with her, and I could tell it was helping. Pierre was there for me, but I couldn't open myself up to him or anyone else, I felt if I did, I would just fall apart completely. After three or four weeks I started to find it difficult to stay in the house of an evening with so many people around me trying to do something, when nothing could be done. I knew I should be grateful that Michelle was physically well, that we could try again as the rather too chirpy consultant said. In many ways, I was hardened to death even the thought of my own demise didn't seem to bother me much, other than knowing others would suffer while I rested in peace. The baby was different, she was ours, the embodiment of our union, our very being, and the loss threatened to fracture us into small, jagged pieces.

I started going out late at night after Michelle had gone to sleep, I told her I needed to walk, to get some air. And I did walk, I walked down seedy lanes with my gold Rolex flashing, just waiting for someone to set upon me, my staff split in two and concealed, half up each sleeve. I was surprised how they seemed to prefer to come at me from the front rather than behind. I think they liked to brandish their knife, it was rarely a gun despite all the publicity about the rise of gun crime in the city. They would try and intimidate me into just handing over my possessions, they usually hunted in pairs, sometimes more, but seldom alone. I'd withdraw the staffs so quickly they must have seemed a blur in the darkness, that would shake them up, the surprise on their faces was almost therapeutic for me and when I disarmed them, breaking a wrist or a skull in the process, it was like heroin entering my veins. If they had a gun, I was more inclined to talk them into laying it down. One night I decided to experiment with a particularly vile duo, who made it clear they were going to shoot me whether I gave them my valuables or not, so I convinced them to shoot each other. It was quite difficult to manipulate the two of them at the same time, but I think it helped that they weren't very bright.

I'd been going on these little excursions for over a month, I was taking more and more risks and getting increasingly careless. That's how I ended up in this cell, but it was a path I'd long been on, the choices I'd made, like signposts on a road. I'd gone down a one-way street and didn't have the sense or the courage to turn back.

FUTURE

I knew who was behind this, only one person would go to so much trouble to capture me when he could have had me safely shot at a distance. My encounter with Frantz told me that would never do for Kurt, he wanted, no he needed to kill me face-to-face, he was compelled to watch me suffer, to watch me die. But I was not trying to figure out how to escape or hoping Pierre would come to my rescue once more, I was beyond that. I was waiting, waiting for Kurt, waiting to kill him or to be killed by him. He clearly knew about my ability to persuade and compel people, I could probably thank Frantz for that, he was locked up but that never stopped anyone from getting information out if they had someone on the outside willing to pay, and no doubt Kurt had promised to break him free. He didn't know about my other talents, or they wouldn't have just left my staff lying on the floor. They should have gagged me, they should have broken my hands and fingers, they really should have just killed me while I was unconscious. But Kurt wanted to be the one that tortured me, he wanted to wipe the smile off the precocious little brat's face from all those years ago. I suppose we tried to solve our problems in similar ways, it was our weakness and would be the death of at least one of us.

The only puzzle remaining was why he was waiting, Pierre would have every soldier and agent under his command scouring the city for signs of me. Rachel would have already tracked me close to the lane where they took me, there would be no CCTV on the road itself, it would have been repeatedly smashed until the council gave up repairing it. The longer Kurt waited, the greater the chance Pierre would find me. Oh shit, I suddenly realised that was exactly what he wanted, Pierre and as many of his men to burst into this place, it wasn't enough for him to kill me he wanted as many of us as he could get.

The self-indifference quickly drained away, I sensed I didn't have long, I'd been waiting when I should have been killing. I joined the two halves of my staff together and started to tap it on the ground. I closed my eyes and sensed the waves spreading out to the walls beyond my cell, it was just one large open space, no furniture, just stone walls and floors. No guard, no one at all. There were some steps to the floor above, I tapped harder and faster forcing the sound waves upward. I sensed two resting heart beats, oblivious to what would soon happen, they were window dressing. I mapped out the room, two chairs and a table, a sink and a microwave, that could be of some use. I could kill the two guards but then I would just be locked in here drawing Pierre to his death. I could try and create some kind of sonic boom to blow the door off, but I thought I would probably die in the blast as well. I'd been unconscious for two days after I killed Smith, I'd well and truly overcooked it then, so blasting my way out now was not a viable option.

Suddenly I was down on my knees, my head feeling like it would blow up like popcorn on a high heat, I think I could even smell burning. I knew most of the signs though, it was another vision. I could clearly see Pierre and Charlotte, there were others as well, I think I could make out

Robert, but the rest were too blurred. They were in the room above, or they would be very soon, the two guards were quickly dispensed with. Pierre would sense it was too easy, but he would carry on any way, he would come for me, and I needed to make sure I deserved his loyalty and his love.

***

They all moved down the steps, ignoring their training – *secure your exit*. Emotions were a tricky thing. I heard the sound of boots, lots of boots coming in as Pierre and Charlotte unlocked my cell door. As I managed to stand with one hand against the wall, I heard the shots above and I knew we only had minutes, maybe seconds. When my door opened Charlotte launched herself at me, I caught her and spun her around before pushing her on the bed and as far from the door as possible.

'Thanks for saving me sis but I think I might need to return the favour. Pierre, it's a trap and we have nowhere to go and for once I need you to follow my orders.' I was rather surprised when he just nodded. 'Ok get your men as far away from the stairs as possible, put three of them in here.' Charlotte had recovered from being planted on the bed and was no longer willing to keep quiet.

'Josh, I don't need anyone to protect me.'

'Charlotte we all need someone, that's why you and Pierre are here. I don't know what's coming down those stairs, but we need some people under cover ready to shoot back when the dust settles.'

'And what are you and Pierre doing?'

'I'm going to pick off as many of the bastards as I can and Pierre is going to make sure I don't get killed, but if you want to take his place, I trust you just as much as him.'

'Stick with your plan, Pierre is a better shot than me and if I got killed, he would just shoot you anyway.'

'Nice to know where I stand. They're coming, get ready.'

I made Pierre stand a metre behind me and five of his men back against the furthest wall from the stairs. Above, eight men marched into the room and stood in two ranks of four either side of the stairwell, there was a loud shout of clear, which let me identify the leader and five seconds later a ninth man walked in. I knew straight away it was Kurt, I thought about reaching out and grasping his heart but then I heard the sound of metal clanging down the staircase. As it neared the bottom, I could see the smoke pouring out, there were two teargas canisters rolling toward us and Pierre and his men had left behind their masks. By the regular breathing I could hear upstairs, Kurt's men had not bothered to put their own gas masks on yet.

I tapped the staff hard once, holding it at a forty-five-degree angle toward the staircase, the gas immediately started to roll back and up toward Kurt's troops. Then we all heard the coughing and spluttering above and a scramble to put masks on, some dropping on the floor in the panic. I located the microwave and put pressure on the switch and heard the turntable start to gather speed. I was in uncharted territory now, but I visualised the microwave, the turntable spinning and the magnet pulsing. The glass plate inside began to gather speed and the magnet started to vibrate, then whine, then boom! I heard the screams as shards of metal and glass exploded outward, impaling faces, necks and chests. Seeing his chance, Pierre rushed forward and up two steps before he launched a grenade into the room above, he turned and shouted 'down' as he launched himself back across the room and onto the ground. We all dropped to the floor and covered our ears against the massive bang in such a confined space. For a few seconds there was an eerie silence, the smoke from upstairs rolling down but then rising back up. I checked the bodies, without even thinking. Eight still warm but no pulse, no heartbeat and a few metres away going up another set of stairs was Kurt. I knew I couldn't kill him from where I was below ground, I knew he would disappear into the ether like he always did, but I was determined to at least mark him this time.

    I kneeled on the floor and placed my palms and forearms flat against the ground as I also touched my head to the floor. I thought of Youssef praying to his god to save his sister and mother and I sent out my own perverse prayer. I felt it answered, Kurt staggered but managed to keep going but I had taken a sliver of him, I had seared a line across his heart, and I would always be able to find him. I knew now that Kurt would be enough, after him I would not need to kill again. But right now, I needed to be with Michelle, to return to my family.

    When I walked through the door my parents and Philippe were waiting, my mother was crying, and papa was close to tears as well. Before anyone could utter a word, Michelle marched forward and slapped me across the face and the noise filled the hall. All she said was 'ENOUGH' but that single word echoed around the room and through my thick skull. Then she burst into tears and put her arms around me, she kissed my lips and every part of my face, I was covered in snot and saliva, and it was wonderful. It was only now, that I truly realised just how much Michelle and my family had been going through, while I stalked the seedy streets of London in my self-indulgent quest for retribution. There was nothing we could do about the baby but mourn her loss and try to start again and I just had to finally accept that Yve was gone.

My father blamed himself for involving me in his work, but I'd only ever followed my own path and if he ever needed my help, I would always step forward just as he and my family did for me. For the time being, he refused to talk about work and banned me from coming to his office, even for lunch. Instead, he would insist on us meeting at least a kilometre or two tube stops from the embassy. But I was content to stretch canvases for Michelle or help her in any way I could.

In June there was a flurry of activity, following the success of Michelle's first small show a much larger gallery had agreed to put on an exhibition of her work and Michelle insisted on hanging the paintings herself to make sure everything was perfect. Which actually meant I was hanging the pictures and Michelle was directing my every movement.

At one point, she raised both her hands above her head, to show me exactly where she wanted a particularly large picture to hang, she stretched her arms apart and looked between them to try and gauge how much space would be left on either side of the painting. While she did this I gazed in adoration, her t-shirt had risen to just below her breasts and her leggings had slipped perilously downward exposing her whole belly, I watched her from the side as she focussed on the space in front of her. I'd seen this profile before, but the curve was more pronounced and expanded this time. When I eventually managed to look away, Michelle was staring at me with the sweetest smile on her face and she just said one word, but it was plenty.

'Oops!'

'Is there something you want to tell me, mon amour?'

'Three months, I was trying to wait in case…'

'It's going to be okay this time, I know it is. Does anyone else know?'

'You mean your mother! She knew after six weeks, she really is a witch you know.'

'She is also really good at keeping secrets.'

'In fairness though, if I hadn't had her to talk to, I think I might have gone mad. Not just about being pregnant, but about this weird life we live with all its privileges and dangers. I used to worry about you being shot or blown up, but the real threat is the one inside your head. I can't stop you being shot at, though I would gladly stand in the way of a bullet to protect you, but I can help you cope with what goes on inside that big brain, if you'll let me. Are you ready to let me in? Are you ready to be the father of our child?'

'I think so, I think I'm ready. I so want to be a father, for the two of us to have our child. I want to be worthy of you both.' Then we both started to cry.

At the usual Saturday gathering of the Renoir clan, as we sat around the dinner table, Michelle looked at me and smiled. We had agreed that she would make the announcement. Then I spotted her looking across the table to Charlotte, and they both nodded to each other and then stood at the same time. Pierre looked even more confused than me. Michelle spoke first.

'Charlotte and I would like to make a toast.' Then Charlotte joined in.

'We are both, well four of us actually, are exceedingly happy and excited to announce that Michelle…'

'And Charlotte.'

'Are pregnant!'

It seemed that Charlotte was better at keeping secrets than Michelle, judging by the way Pierre reacted, he leapt to his feet and lifted Charlotte in the air before spinning her around. Then realising what he'd done, he set her down gently and she began laughing at him.

'Pierre, I'm pregnant not ill so don't start treating me like a delicate little thing if you know what's good for you.'

Pierre made a tactical retreat, back to his chair, but the ear-to-ear smile remained fixed for the whole evening. Michelle was still standing, she was looking at my mother and mouthing something to her that I couldn't hear or make out from the side, which I knew was intentional. My mother just smiled and nodded she turned and looked for several seconds at my father without saying a word before she winked at him, something I have never seen her do in my entire life and then turned back to the rest of us. It was going to be difficult to follow the two sisters act, but now was definitely the time. With Michelle still stood up, I got to my feet and took her left hand in mine before I got down on one knee and produced a diamond ring. For once I couldn't hear anything as I spoke.

'Michelle, you've seen the worst of me and I hope that with your help and support you will soon see the best of me. Will you do me the honour of marrying me? Je t'aime Michelle.' In an echo of Charlotte's response to Pierre she grinned as she gave her reply.

'Now let me think! Handsome – tick, Brave – tick, tick, Kind – tick, tick, tick. Hmm, this list goes on a bit, but I'll skip to the end. Intelligent – tick-toc, tic-toc, you do have mixed reviews when it comes to brains, you are a genius, but you can be very stupid. Still, Je t'aime Joshua Renoir, get that ring on my finger I'm yours, I always have been, and I always will be.'

'I'll take that as a "yes" then.'

At that point no one could contain themselves any longer, they all started to clap, laugh and cry at the same time. The house truly was in *hysterics* as I rose to my feet and kissed my fiancée.

***

A few weeks later my father asked me into his study for a little chat, he wondered if I had given any thought to my future. The idea of someone my age without a clearly defined career path obviously bothered him, though I knew it was mainly out of concern for my sanity. He suggested I consider becoming a proper diplomat, no spying or killing, just a petit politicien as he called it. It was something I had already considered, but I didn't want to risk getting embroiled in some little plot and slipping into that dark place inside my head. I wasn't sure I was strong enough to resist, not yet.

I would never be clean, but I thought I could live with it. When I was in the basement just beyond my cell, with Charlotte inside, the thought of some harm coming to her utterly enraged me. Killing Kurt seemed to be the only thing that mattered, it would protect Charlotte and Pierre and so many others. When I marked him, I thought I would be unable to resist tracking him down, following his pulse like a line on Google Maps. Then, when I looked around and saw Pierre and Charlotte embracing, and everybody still alive, the compulsion began to weaken. When I saw the dead bodies littering the floor above, the urge began to fade and later when I embraced Michelle, my face still stinging, and my parents it dissipated completely, and I was filled with love not anger.

Despite my improved mood and perspective on the world, I remained a bit of a recluse and rarely ventured out the house. I wasn't afraid of someone attacking or capturing me, I was scared of what I might do if anyone was foolish enough to try. I spent most of my time trying to find things I could help Michelle with, but I think I was starting to get under her feet a bit too much. When my mother wasn't on some official duty with my father or out raising funds for who knows what charity I liked to sit with her and chat, but even when she was home, she was never off-duty, and she was always having to organise the staff for some event or another. I realised why my father never wanted to take the role of ambassador on.

One morning, Michelle came out of the bathroom dressed in smart jeans and a pale grey cashmere jumper rather than her habitual paint-stained dungarees. She looked at me sternly as I lay naked across the bed, fast becoming aroused at the sight of her all dressed up. I was hoping she would walk by me or at least turn around so I could appreciate her beautiful ass. But she was having none of it and evidently, neither was I.

'Josh, we both need to get out and check that the world still exists. I've booked tickets for a new exhibition at Tate Modern and you're coming with me, so move yourself or I will bring Charlotte in here to help me dress you.'

I knew she was trying to help me, she was worried about me staying at home all the while and she wasn't at all convinced by my protestations of happiness. She wasn't far off the truth, but it didn't matter, with the threat of her and Charlotte, I was man enough to admit defeat. I raised my hands in surrender and shuffled toward the end of the bed, my erection a thing of the past already.

'Josh you've got twenty minutes to make yourself presentable and join me downstairs for breakfast.'

I mock saluted and ran for cover behind the bathroom door. Michelle always knew what I needed, and the exhibition certainly hit the target. Ever since we met, we had discussions, or they could have been arguments, about the difference and merits of painting versus photography. The show was called Capturing the Moment and challenged the idea that there was any clear distinction between the two. Usually if I went to an exhibition, I read up about it first and arrived knowing what to expect and sadly, I realised, what to think. I was already primed to see what others directed me toward. This time I had no warning and when I got my phone out to Google the show, Michelle slapped me on the back of the hand and took it off me.

'Josh, I want you to see this for yourself and forget the critics and the publicity hype.'

I felt strangely liberated. The first room featured Freud and Bacon and their common focus on the visceral reality of the self, but Freud painted from real life while Bacon was happy to draw from photographs. On one of the plaques next to his pictures I read how he violently distorted the human body to expose the "pulsations of a person" It inevitably reminded me of how I had manipulated the more physical pulsations to rip apart so many fragile bodies and malevolent minds.

The other picture in that first room to stir my emotions was Picasso's *Femme en Pleurs* or *Weeping Woman*, the cubistically distorted image of a woman holding her dead baby. It was painted in 1937 following the bombing of the Basque town of Guernica. While I cried for our own lost daughter, I also thought of Akil and Jean, the people they had killed for an idea long past and their eagerness to die for a cause long lost. They were not Socrates.

As I wandered through the rooms, I found myself drawn as much to the plaques as the pictures, with their attempted explanations to the paintings, photographs and the crossover between the two. I spent almost fifteen minutes looking at a large, illuminated photograph, *A Sudden Gust of Wind*, of four people caught in a gale at one particular moment in time, but it was based on one hundred separate pictures and actually took more than a year to finish. Rather than fortuitously capturing a moment in time, it was completely staged. When comparing photography and painting, Wall claimed that in the photograph there is always an actual moment, the split second when the shutter opens and closes. That photography is based on the sense of instantaneousness while a painting creates the beautiful illusion of instantaneousness, as if past, present and future were simultaneously within it. Yet his picture and the whole process he followed to create it undermined any such distinction. I looked up from the text on the wall and scanned the room, half expecting to find the artist watching me and the others in the room with a wide grin on his face. I had learned that there are many more ways to see than with your eyes. As for time, I will leave that to my visions for now.

Toward the end of the exhibition, as I stood in front of the large Hockney painting, Portrait of an Artist (with two figures), bathing in his trademark vivid blue, I saw the face of someone I should have met but never did. I recognised him from the photograph his grandparents had shown me after they had given me a lift to Toulon and invited me to stay the night with them. Immediately my mouth watered at the memory of the croissants I had for breakfast, and then the two of them were there, a few metres from Tomas. I had promised to visit Tomas as they were a bit anxious about him, but I wasn't expecting such a quick return to Paris and events took over. Well, if nothing else I needed to apologise to them, not sure if they would recognise me after all this time, I tentatively began to introduce myself.

'Monsieur et Madam Beaufoy…' Before I could get another word out Madam Beaufoy shouted my name and rushed forward and pulled me into a hug, she was much stronger than she looked.

'Joshua, how wonderful to see you again.'

'I wasn't sure if you would remember me.'

'Oh Josh, no one who has met you could ever forget you, you are a special boy, I knew it from the moment we met you.'

Monsieur Beaufoy managed to lever his wife away and held out his hand for me to shake, the contact of skin with skin forged a link to the past, as though something had come full circle. The snapshot of a hopeful young man merged with the portrait of a prematurely aging youth in some strange distortion of time and place, of Sein und Zeit.

'It's good to see you sir and to finally meet Tomas.' I offered my hand to him to complete the introductions, he seemed a bit shy and hesitated before he finally took hold.

'Tomas, Monsieur and Madam Beaufoy, I must apologise. I never managed to look you up Tomas as I promised your grandparents I would.' I decided to play fast and loose with the past and the truth, 'Unfortunately I had an accident when I returned to Paris from the Cote d'Azur and was flown back to England to recover.' Madam Beaufoy, looked instantly alarmed as though the event had only just happened.

'Joshua, are you well now? Mon dieu!'

'I'm fine Madam.' Time to change the subject I thought. 'What brings you to London?'

'Tomas, he is a photographer now, he wanted to see this exhibition and we have always wanted to visit London et nous voici!'

Eventually I managed to free myself with a promise to look Tomas up when I returned to Paris. Then I managed to find Michelle back where I left her, sitting down in front of a painting by Luc Tuymans called The Shore. As I sat next to her, I noticed that she was crying, tears silently running down her cheeks not bothering to wipe them away, as if she wanted everyone to know that she was not embarrassed by her deep reaction. The picture was based on a scene in a film, A Twist of Sand, and shows a group of men on the seashore, illuminated by a light source out of shot, a search light. They are waving, thinking they are about to be rescued but are then gunned down. I did not ask Michelle what she was thinking of or what had upset her, I just held her hand and cried my own tears. I thought of the refugees of Europe and across the world, trafficked over the sea in hope and landing on a beach in despair, dehumanised in the media and a political problem to be removed from sight.

***

In the end I decided to return to my studies, it didn't fill me with excitement but the familiar routine of research and reading I thought would help me adjust, at least that's what I hoped. I also felt the need to complete it, I'd never failed to see something through to the end before. I also comforted myself with the thought that at least I could always become a lecturer and unlike Youssef I would not court trouble.

Charlotte and Michelle gave birth less than twenty-four hours apart, to two very beautiful girls. Three months later we gathered in Jane Austen style, at least the cinematic version, for our double wedding. Not quite in the right order but unlike Lydia Bennet and Mr Wickham, the whole squadron lined either side of the final ten metres of the path leading to the chapel entrance. Thirty minutes later Mr and Mrs Renoir left the church followed by Mr and Mrs Renoir, Charlotte had persuaded Pierre, that he was already one of us and that it would be inappropriate to change her name to his. Pierre raised no objections, in fact he told Charlotte he felt proud to be part of the family Renoir. As we walked along the path, which meandered between the old gravestones, toward the waiting cars, Kurt stepped out in front of me. He had a P30, just like the one Michelle kept in her bedside drawer, but it was down by his side. He looked in a bad way, his face was dirty and his clothes hung loose on him, I knew instinctively that he was no real threat to me or anyone else. I felt Pierre moving up behind me, he wasn't armed but he didn't care, his instinct to protect, to protect me was too strong. I stretched my arm out and held him back, even if Kurt intended to kill me, I could sense he had things he needed to say first. I gestured to him to move off the path toward the gravestones and he edged along sideways, unwilling to turn his back to me or the others. When we were ten metres away, I completely relaxed, I knew the others were safe, but I also didn't feel I was in any particular danger. The only one in danger here was Kurt and it looked like much of the damage was already done. I could have killed him in his weakened state with a click of my fingers,

I could trace the scar along his heart without any effort at all and with the slightest motion I could split it in half, but I sensed that Kurt was already dead. The anger and malice that, with the help of Michelle and my family I'd let go, had destroyed Kurt. He didn't know it yet, but he had come here to die not to kill. I waited for him to speak but ready to put him down, if I needed to.

'I hated you, even when you were a child, so bright and clever, everyone fawned over you. Your parents doting on you, Philippe virtually adopting you. Did you know that Philippe and I once fought together on the same side?'

I shook my head but didn't speak, whatever he had to say was better said without interruption.

'You truly were a precocious brat, but Philippe loved you, and yet I had taken a bullet for him once. I despised you then and that hatred has only grown, I can feel it like a tumour swelling inside me.'

This time I just nodded in agreement, I wasn't trying to be funny, he was right. It was a bit harsh though, to hold that against a child not even ten years old at the time. My acceptance of his judgement seemed to unnerve him a little, this wasn't going as he expected when he'd planned it all out in his head.

'I pieced together the parts from all the jobs you did, I began to understand that you were more than just a clever clogs kid with a penchant for languages. Did you know I once worked with Boris' father, you remember Boris the little dimwit who crossed swords with you at school, yes I can see you do remember him. I was working on something for his old man when he mentioned what had happened to his son years before, not that he really understood, but it was enough for me to start to unpick the thread. A thread that weaved its way through half the operations that I planned that had suddenly and mysteriously gone spectacularly wrong without any rational explanation at all.

Like that night you and Pierre dragged those two Basque fanatics away from the chateau without even a single shot. You look surprised that must be a first, you always seemed one step ahead of me. I was Saul's handler, not that he knew that, I stood to make millions out of that job and I didn't trust him to deliver. He'd outlived his usefulness, and I was going to terminate his contract. I had my beautiful point two-two single shot rifle pointed straight at his skull, you have to aim for the top half of the head with such a small bullet to make sure you kill them. It takes real skill to do that, the beauty is that his men wouldn't have had a clue what happened, no big bang or muzzle flash to give me away. But then Pierre shows up and Saul loses it and completely fucks up when you push the big lump to safety. If you had been a few minutes later I'd have bagged Saul, reloaded and got you in the head instead of missing Saul and hitting you in the leg.

When I realised that you weren't exactly normal, I thought I had you, I thought I knew how to capture you, and your little nocturnal jaunts made it so easy. But I must admit I was greedy, I wanted to kill your sister and the noble Pierre as well. So instead of shooting you straight away I used you as bait to lure them in, I left a couple of dimwits on guard, knowing Pierre would be too eager to wonder why it was so easy to get to you. I think you and your sister have dulled the big man's wits, he cares more about you than his precious squad. Ironically, I was too eager for revenge to question how you managed to kill someone as experienced and cautious as Gutmann, you sucked me in just as easily as you did Pierre. I still don't know how you killed Dietrich, I'd planned to torture that out of you before I killed you and then you took out the last eight of my men, when you should have been a sitting duck. I know Pierre threw the grenade, but it had to be you who forced the teargas back up the stairwell. Was that the microwave that blew? How did you do that?'

'Not quite sure myself, I think it was something like sound waves, I seem to be able to manipulate them, I was able to push the gas back. I suspect the microwave might have been a bit of a fluke though.'

'I knew you were a freak. So, what now, are you going to kill me? You know you want to, I could feel your rage that day, it seemed to follow me as I ran, I thought it actually touched me. It felt like I was on fire for a second and ever since I've felt a pressure in my chest, like my heart is about to burst.'

'For some reason, once I'd started killing, you were always top of my list. Maybe it was that evening when I told Philippe what you had said to Dietrich, in my twisted mind I think I traced all my bad choices and decisions back to that moment. But after the cellar the compulsion seemed to fade, things changed for me that day and I ripped up my list. I always knew that you would turn up one day, but I stopped wanting to kill you. I'd be happy if you died, but I don't want to help you end your miserable life. What about you, are you going to kill me with that gun you're clutching so tightly?'

'You could tell me to kill myself, is that how you took care of the others?'

'You can persuade most people to do almost anything, but the instinct to live is too strong unless you are already in so much despair that it seems a solution to all your ills. You're close but I don't think you are quite there yet, still angry with me rather than yourself, still committed to blaming someone else for your failings. That's how we both ended up here, in a graveyard full of old bones and lingering regrets.' It was a feeling I knew far too well.

I watched Kurt for a few moments while he warily stared at me, I knew there was something wrong, something I was missing. The gun was still in his right hand, hanging down by his side, but I realised that was just a distraction. The real threat was his left hand, he had kept it in his pocket from the second he stepped in front of me. Whatever he had in there was small, too small to be a weapon of any real use, the only thing that made sense was a remote control for a bomb, Kurt was very fond of explosives. Kurt's sudden appearance was the ultimate distraction, I had heard the movement back over at the path, Pierre had called all his men in to deal with the visible threat. While that was happening, an accomplice had no doubt planted a bomb on the now unguarded limousines. When Kurt stepped in front of me, he expected Pierre to take control and probably bundle him into the boot of one of the cars, he wanted to die but he needed to take as many of us with him as he could. He hadn't expected me to stop Pierre and lead him away without even bothering to disarm him, that had surprised him, but he must have thought his luck was in as the diversion had still worked. It was a tricky situation. If I got distracted Kurt might take his chance and shoot me. If he set the bomb off at the same time it would probably not kill the others given the distance between them and the cars, as well as the metre thick stone wall surrounding the church. I had to give him his due, he was smart and maybe that's what really started all this off between us, the day he was outsmarted by a child was something he could not accept. Just like I could never forget the name he called me. What's the expression - the truth hurts.

I looked straight into Kurt's eyes, I stared through them to the recesses of his consciousness and said one word "STOP" it reverberated through the gravestones, and I saw Kurt shimmer in the sound waves, as though he were just a mirage in the desert. The gun slipped from his hand as he rocked on his feet and his eyes glazed over.

'Kurt, slowly and carefully take out your left hand from your pocket, do not try to set the bomb off.' He did exactly as I asked him and when his hand was free, he held out his arm and opened his fingers, there was something that looked like a remote key for a car. 'Kurt, put the control on the floor and step back five paces.' I waited until he was safely out of reach of the gun and remote control, I needed to be sure there were no more surprises. 'Kurt, how many men do you have with you and are they able to detonate the bomb?'

'Just Carlos left now, I am the only one able to blow the Semtex. I wanted to be the one that blew you and your family apart. There is only the one control, couldn't risk Carlos getting twitchy if I needed to improvise.'

'How do we disarm the bomb?'

'No time for booby traps or complicated mechanisms, just cut the live feed from the battery and remove the detonator from the plastique.'

'Kurt, kneel down on the floor and put your hands on your head.'

When he was in position, I raised my hand above my head and clenched my fist, that had always been Pierre's signal to the rest of us to come straight to him, and within seconds he and Robert were standing next to me and I briefed them on the bomb and Carlos. Robert said he would handle both and went back towards the waiting guests. Pierre looked at Kurt and then at me as he spoke.

'What do we do with him?'

'Do we have a car with a good strong boot?'

'Oui, the Audi A6 has an armoured partition between the boot and the back seats and special locks, no way of opening it from the inside even if he unties himself.'

'That will do for now, I will walk him to the car, you meet me there with some zip ties.' I wasn't going to kill Kurt, but I was going to let him die, I couldn't put my family at any more risk. I could hear his heart, it sounded like it was hiccupping every third or fourth beat and it was slowing down. I doubted he'd survive being locked in the boot for more than an hour and I planned to leave him there until I'd been embarrassed by the best man's speech and danced for several hours with my bride. By the time Pierre and I had gagged and trussed Kurt up in the boot, Robert and Alphonse had defused the bombs, there were actually two, devious to the last.

We parked the Audi a few hundred metres from the reception venue, with the boot touching the trunk of a large oak just to be sure he couldn't find a way out. Kurt hadn't made a sound for the last twenty minutes of the journey and Pierre asked if we should check on him, but I could hear his faint heartbeat and I didn't think he had long to go. I probably shouldn't have been, but I was good with that. Clearly, I hadn't completely reformed but I was hopeful that with Michelle and my family around me I would continue to improve. But I would always be willing to kill or die to keep them safe, and with that thought, I decided to make sure and finally put Kurt out of his misery. I clicked my fingers once and he was dead.

About The Author:

Joseph Warner has a BA from Warwick University and an MA in Creative Writing from Manchester Metropolitan University. Joseph worked as a social worker until 2023, when he finally decided he preferred fiction to reality, and to the artifice of corporate endeavour.

Printed in Great Britain
by Amazon